Author Note

I have always loved antique cookbooks, and my grandmother owned over a hundred of them. I used to pore over old recipes and imagine the women who had baked pies, cookies, cakes and special meals for their families. From these recipes the character of Emily Barrow was born.

When she falls upon hard times Emily must cook for her own family, and she finds her escape in creating wonderful dishes. After she elopes with the Earl of Whitmore, Emily refuses to turn her back on her culinary pastime, no matter how inappropriate it might be for a countess.

I hope you enjoy Emily's tale, and try out her recipe for Ginger Biscuits—I made them for my own children this past Christmas. You can find more historical recipes and behind-the-scenes information on my website: www.michellewillingham.com. I love to hear from readers, and you may e-mail me at michelle@michellewillingham.com, or write to me at: PO Box 2242 Poquoson, VA 23662, USA.

Warm wishes.

Acknowledgements:

With thanks to Dr Deena Obrokta,
Dr Dawn Reese, and Dr T
for your invaluable consultation on amnesia
and post-traumatic stress syndrome.
Endless thanks to my fabulous editor
Joanne Grant for your amazing eye for detail
and your hard work.
I couldn't do it without you!

Dedication:

To my mother Pat, for your unfailing
support, for your belief in me,
and for watching the kids when I desperately
needed your help.
You've been behind me 100% from the very
beginning, and I'll always be grateful.

THE ACCIDENTAL COUNTESS

Michelle Willingham

 MILLS & BOON

First published in Great Britain 2009
Large Print edition 2010
Harlequin Mills & Boon Limited,
Eton House, 18-24 Paradise Road, Richmond, Surrey TW9 1SR

© Michelle Willingham 2009

ISBN: 978 0 263 21150 4

Harlequin Mills & Boon policy is to use papers that are natural, renewable and recyclable products and made from wood grown in sustainable forests. The logging and manufacturing process conform to the legal environmental regulations of the country of origin.

Printed and bound in Great Britain
by CPI Antony Rowe, Chippenham, Wiltshire

He pulled off the poultice and glared at her. 'Who are you?'

She blanched. 'You don't remember me?' The question held sardonic disbelief. 'My name is Emily.' She leaned in, her gaze penetrating. Almost as if she were waiting for him to say something.

Hazy bits of the past shifted together. Emily Barrow. My God. He hadn't seen her in nearly ten years. 'What are you doing here?'

'I live here.' With an over-bright smile, she added, 'Don't you remember your wife?'

Her revelation stunned him into silence. His wife? What was she talking about? He wasn't married.

'You must be joking.' Stephen wasn't an impulsive man. He planned every moment of every day. Getting married to a woman he hadn't seen in years wasn't at all something he would do.

She crossed her arms over her chest, drawing his gaze towards her silhouette. The soft curve of her breasts caught his eye. The top button of her gown had come loose, revealing a forbidden glimpse of skin. The fallen strand of golden hair rested against the black serge, a coil of temptation, beckoning him to touch it.

She'd never been able to tame her hair, even as a girl. He'd helped her with hairpins on more than one occasion, to help her avoid a scolding.

Now the task took on an intimacy, one more suited to a husband. Had he truly married her? Had he unbuttoned her gowns, tasting the silk of her skin...?

Michelle Willingham grew up living in places all over the world, including Germany, England and Thailand. When her parents hauled her to antiques shows in manor houses and castles, Michelle entertained herself by making up stories and pondering whether she could afford a broadsword with her allowance. She graduated *summa cum laude* from the University of Notre Dame, with a degree in English, and received her master's degree in Education from George Mason University. Currently she teaches American History and English. She lives in south-eastern Virginia with her husband and children. She still doesn't have her broadsword.

Visit her website at: www.michellewillingham.com, or e-mail her at michelle@michellewillingham.com

Previous novels by this author:

HER IRISH WARRIOR*
THE WARRIOR'S TOUCH*
HER WARRIOR KING*
HER WARRIOR SLAVE†
THE ACCIDENTAL COUNTESS

The MacEgan Brothers
†Prequel to *The MacEgan Brothers* trilogy

Also available in eBook format in Mills & Boon® Historical *Undone*:

THE VIKING'S FORBIDDEN LOVE-SLAVE

Look out for Michelle's next Victorian novel, linked to THE ACCIDENTAL COUNTESS THE ACCIDENTAL PRINCESS Available from Mills & Boon® Historical Romance in 2010

Chapter One

When selecting poultry for cooking, choose a chicken with soft yellow feet, short thick legs, and a plump breast. First, kill the chicken by wringing its neck...
—Emily Barrow's *Cook Book*

Falkirk House, England—1850

Cool hands sponged his forehead. Stephen Chesterfield fought against the darkness that threatened to pull him into oblivion once more. Pain lashed his skull, ripping through him in violent waves. His mouth felt lined with cotton wool, and his body ached with vicious pain.

'Drink,' a woman said, lifting a cup of warm tea to his mouth. It tasted bitter, but he swallowed. 'You're very lucky, you know.'

Lucky? He felt as though someone had cracked

his skull in two. He hadn't even the strength to open his eyes to see who was tending him.

'How am I lucky?' he managed to whisper. Lucky to be alive, she'd probably say.

'You're lucky I haven't got any arsenic for this tea,' she remarked. 'Or another poison, for that matter. Otherwise, you'd be dead by now.' A warm poultice dropped across his forehead, scented with herbs.

'I beg your pardon?' His knuckles clenched around the bedcovers, and he forced his eyes open. The room blurred, and he tried to grasp his surroundings. Where was he? And who was this woman?

The creature intending to murder him had the face of an angel. Her hair, the color of warm honey, was pulled back into a loose chignon. Long strands framed a face with tired amber eyes. Despite the hideous serge mourning gown, she was rather pretty, though her cheeks were thin.

She was familiar, but her name hovered on the outskirts of memory. Like a childhood acquaintance, or someone he'd known long ago.

'You broke your promise. If it weren't for you, my brother would still be alive.' Anguish lined her voice, eroding the waspish anger. Her eyes glistened, but she kept her chin up.

She blamed him for her brother's death? There

had to be a mistake. He didn't even know who *she* was, much less her brother.

He pulled off the poultice, and glared at her. 'Who are you?'

She blanched. 'You don't remember me?' The question held sardonic disbelief. 'And here I thought this day could not get any worse.' With a clatter, she set the saucer down.

He had little patience for her frustration. Damn it all, he was the one who'd been wounded. And each time he tried to reach back and seize the memories, it was as if they faded into smoke. What had happened to him?

'You didn't answer my question,' he responded. 'What is your name?'

'My name is Emily.' She leaned in, her gaze penetrating. Almost as if she were waiting for him to say something.

Hazy bits of the past shifted together. Emily Barrow. The Baron of Hollingford's daughter. My God. He hadn't seen her in nearly ten years. He stared hard at her, unable to believe it was true. Though her rigid posture proclaimed her as a modest woman of virtue, he remembered her throwing rocks at his carriage. And climbing trees to spy on him.

And kissing him when he'd been an awkward, adolescent boy.

He shook the thought away, thankful that at least some of his memories remained. 'What are you doing here?'

'I live here.' With an overbright smile, she added, 'Don't you remember your wife?'

Her revelation stunned him into silence. His wife? What was she talking about? He wasn't married.

'You must be joking.' He wasn't an impulsive man. He planned every moment of every day. Getting married to a woman he hadn't seen in years wasn't at all something he would do. Unless he'd gotten extremely deep in his cups one night, she had to be lying. And by God, if Emily Barrow thought to take advantage of him, she would be sorry for it.

'I would never joke about something like this.' She held out the cup of tea, but he dismissed it. He had no intention of drinking anything she gave him. His vision swam, and a rushing sound filled his ears.

Closing his eyes, he waited for the dizziness to pass. When the world righted itself, he studied the room. Heavy blue curtains hung across the canopied bed, while bookcases overflowing with books filled another wall. The pieces of remembrance snapped together as he recognised his bedchamber within Falkirk House, one of the country estates. For the life of him he didn't know how he'd arrived here.

'How long have I been at Falkirk?'

'Two days.'

'And before that?'

She shrugged. 'You left for London a week after our wedding. I haven't seen you since February. Why don't you tell me where you've been?'

He tried to reach for the memory, but nothing remained, not even the smallest fragment of a vision. Like a gaping hole, he'd lost a part of himself. It frustrated the hell out of him, having pieces of his life gone. He could remember most of his childhood and adolescence. He even recalled working upon a list of accounts for one of the estates in January. But after that…nothing.

'What day is it?' he asked, trying to pinpoint the last memory he had.

'The twentieth of May.'

He clenched the bedcovers. February, March, April, almost all of May…three and a half months of his life were entirely gone. He closed his eyes, trying to force himself to remember. But the harder he struggled, the worse his head ached.

'Where were you?' she asked. There was worry inside her tone, though he found it hard to believe she cared. Not after she'd threatened to poison him.

'I don't know,' he answered honestly. 'But I certainly don't remember getting married.'

'You might not remember it, but it's true.'

Something was wrong, something she wasn't telling him. There was a desperate air about her, as though she had nowhere else to go. Likely he'd caught her in the lie.

'You are welcome to leave,' he suggested. 'Obviously my return offended you.'

Tears glimmered in her eyes, and softly, she replied, 'You have no idea what I've been through. I thought I'd never see you again.'

She dipped the cool cloth back into the basin, wringing out the water. Then she set it upon his forehead, her hand grazing his cheek. The gesture was completely at odds with her sharp words.

'You're not my wife.'

She crossed her arms over her chest, drawing his gaze towards her silhouette. A bit on the thin side, but the soft curve of her breasts caught his eye. The top button of her gown had come loose, revealing a forbidden glimpse of skin.

'Yes, I am.' She lowered her arms, gathering her courage as she stared at him. But her full lips parted, her shoulders rising and falling with a quickening breath. The fallen strand of golden hair rested against the black serge.

She'd never been able to tame her hair, even as a girl. He'd helped her with hairpins on more than one occasion, to help her avoid a scolding.

Now the task took on an intimacy, one more suited to a husband. Had he truly married her? Had he unbuttoned her gowns, tasting the silk of her skin? From the way she drew back, he didn't think so.

'I want to see a doctor,' he said, changing the subject.

'Doctor Parsons examined you last night. I'm to change your bandages and keep the wound clean. He'll return tomorrow.' She lifted the lip of the tea cup to his mouth again, but he didn't drink.

The china clattered, revealing her shaking hands. Despite her bitterness, there was a look on her face that didn't quite match her words. He caught a glimpse of something more…something lost and lonely.

He forced himself not to pity her. For God's sakes, the woman had threatened to kill him.

At last, she gave up and set the cup down. 'I didn't poison this cup,' she said with reluctance. 'There wasn't any arsenic to be had.'

'Laudanum would work,' he advised. 'In large doses.' Though why he was offering suggestions, he didn't know.

'I'll remember that for next time.' Colour stained her cheeks, but she didn't smile.

'Why did I marry you?' he asked softly.

She picked up the tray containing the teapot

and cup. 'You should rest for a while. I'll be happy to answer your questions. Later, that is.'

'I want to know now. Sit down.'

She ignored him and moved towards the door. He might as well have been ordering a brick wall to sit. If the unthinkable had happened, if he really and truly had gone off and married her, one thing was certain. He had lost more than his memory.

He'd lost his mind.

Emily fled to a nearby bedchamber and set the tea tray down with shaking fingers. The Earl of Whitmore was back. And he didn't remember a single moment of their marriage.

Damn him. Hot, choking tears slid down her cheeks, despite her best efforts to keep herself together. It was like having him back from the dead. He'd been away for so long, she'd almost started to believe that he *was* dead, even though there was no body.

She'd tried so hard to forget about him. Every single day of the past few months, she'd reminded herself that she'd meant nothing to her husband.

Her hand clenched, and she wept into her palm. Only a week after their wedding, he'd returned to London. He'd gone into the arms of his mistress. While she, the naive little wife, tucked away at the country estate where she wasn't supposed to learn about her husband's indiscretions. It made her sick, just thinking about it.

Marriages were like that, she'd heard. But she hadn't wanted to believe it. Such a fool she had been. She'd been swept away by his charm. Her fairy tale had come true, with the handsome Earl offering to marry the impoverished maiden.

But it had been a dream, hadn't it? He'd used her, wedding her for reasons she didn't understand, and had all but disappeared from her life.

Now that he'd returned, her humiliation tripled. She knuckled the tears away, a chastising laugh gathering in her throat. He wasn't worth the tears. The sooner he left Falkirk, the better.

Emily forced herself to rise from the chair, suppressing the desire to smash every piece of china on the tea tray. Self-pity wouldn't get her anywhere. She was married to a stranger, to a man who hadn't kept his promises.

And if he annulled the marriage, she had nowhere to go.

The sound of a shouting child broke through her reverie. Emily gathered her skirts and rushed towards the bedchamber she'd converted into a temporary nursery. Inside, her nephew Royce sprawled upon the floor, playing with tin soldiers.

'Attack!' he yelled, dashing a row of soldiers to the floor. The tin soldiers and a book of fairy tales were the only things he had brought with him after Daniel had died. She smiled at Royce's boyish enthusiasm.

When he let out another battle cry, the shrill fussing of an infant interrupted. Royce's face turned worried. 'I didn't mean to wake her up.'

'It's all right.' Emily lifted the baby to her cheek. Her niece Victoria was barely nine months old. A soft fuzz of auburn hair covered the baby's head. Two emerging teeth poked up from Victoria's lower gums. The baby reached out to grab Emily's hair.

As she extricated Victoria's fist, Emily strengthened her resolve. Though her marriage was in shambles, she had her family. She would keep her brother's children safe, for she had sworn it upon Daniel's grave. Now she had to gather up the shreds of her marriage and decide what to do next.

'Aunt Emily?' Royce stopped playing and drew his knees up to his chest. 'Has Papa come for us yet?'

'No, sweeting. Not yet.' Like the worst sort of coward, she hadn't yet told Royce that his father was never coming back. How could she destroy her nephew's safe world of hope? Royce would learn the truth soon enough.

She pulled Royce into an embrace with her free arm, holding both children fiercely. 'I love you both. You know that.'

Royce squirmed. 'I know. Can I play?'

Emily released him. The seven-year-old waged imaginary wars against the helpless tin soldiers, shouting in triumph when one soldier defeated an enemy.

She sat down in a rocking chair, holding the baby. Victoria wailed, her eyelids drooping with exhaustion. Emily patted the baby's back, wishing she could join the child in a fit of howling. She almost didn't see the shadow of the Earl hovering at the doorway.

'What are you doing here?' She stood, clutching the baby as though Victoria were a shield. 'You're bleeding. You shouldn't be out of bed.'

His frigid gaze stared back at her. 'This is my house, I believe.' Tight lines edged his mouth, revealing unspoken pain. His dark brown hair was rumpled beneath the bandage wrapped across his temple. He leaned against the door frame, thinner than she'd last seen him, but he did not betray even a fraction of weakness. A rough stubble upon his cheeks gave him a feral appearance, not at all the polished Earl she'd expected him to be.

And suddenly, she wondered if she knew him at all. Not a trace remained of the boy she'd idolised as a girl. Gone was his lazy smile and the way he had once teased her. His eyes were a cold-hearted grey, unfeeling and callous. Even in his wounded state he threatened her.

Emily took a step back, almost knocking over the

rocking chair. 'Your head took quite a blow. You're not ready to be up and about.'

'That would be convenient for you, wouldn't it? If I were to stumble and bleed to death.'

She kept her composure at his harsh words. 'Quite. But your blood would stain the carpet. There's no reason to trouble the servants.'

'I pay the servants.'

'And your fortune would continue to do so after you are dead.'

Why, oh, why did spiteful words keep slipping from her mouth? She wasn't usually such a harpy, but arguing made it easier to conceal her fear. He could make them leave.

'I am glad to see I married such a docile model of womanhood.' His sarcasm sharpened her already bad temper. Then his gaze narrowed on the children. 'Who are they?'

Emily's defences rose up. 'Our children.'

'I believe I would have remembered, had I fathered any children.'

'They belong to my brother. You are their guardian.'

'Their guardian?'

Emily cast him a sharp look, praying she could stop him from saying more in front of the children. It would break Royce's heart to learn of his father's death. 'We will speak of Daniel later.'

'Where is their nursemaid?'

'I don't want a nurse,' Royce interrupted. 'I want Aunt Emily.'

'Royce, now, you see—' Emily tried to placate him, but he refused.

'I don't want one!' he shrieked, throwing a tin soldier on the floor.

Emily knew what was about to happen. 'Here.' She stood and thrust her niece into the Earl's arms. He took the baby, holding Victoria at arm's length as though she had a dreaded disease.

She knelt down beside Royce, trying to reason with him. 'Shh, now. There, there. We won't be getting a nurse. You needn't worry.'

'Papa will come soon,' Royce said, his face determined. 'He will take us away from here.' With a defiant scowl towards Lord Whitmore, the boy let her comfort him.

The guilty burden grew heavier. She couldn't keep Daniel's death from Royce much longer.

'Emily—' There was a note of alarm in Whitmore's voice. Immediately, she released Royce and went to the Earl. She took the baby just as Whitmore's knees buckled and he collapsed against the door frame. He bit back a moan of pain, and blood darkened the bandage around his scalp.

Quickly, she placed the baby back in the cradle, ignoring Victoria's wails of protest.

'Help!' she called out, hoping a servant would hear her. 'Someone come quickly!'

She knelt beside the Earl, supporting his weight with her arms. The flicker of a smile played at his mouth.

'So you decided not to let me die after all,' he whispered.

His eyes closed, and she muttered, 'The day isn't over yet.'

Stephen was not certain how much worse his life could get. He had a so-called wife who despised him, two unexpected children, and no memory of the past three months. This last aspect was the worst, and so he had summoned the butler Farnsworth to find the answers he needed.

He struggled to sit up in bed, though the effort made him dizzy. Farnsworth arrived at last, clearing his throat to announce his presence. The butler had a fringe of greying hair around a bald spot and his cheeks were ruddy and clean shaven.

'Tell me what happened the night I returned,' Stephen prompted.

'My lord, I fear there is little to tell. It happened two nights ago.'

'Who brought me here?'

'It was a hired coach. He didn't know who you were. His instructions were only to deliver you to the door.'

'Did he say who had arranged for my travel?'

'You did, my lord. The coachman was an irritable sort, being as it was the middle of the night, and he insisted on being paid his fee immediately.'

Obviously this chain of questions was going nowhere. 'What belongings did I have with me?'

'Nothing. Only the clothes on your back, such as they were.'

'What do you mean?'

'They were in tatters, my lord. Simply ghastly. They smelled of rotting fish, and I had them burned.'

Had he been taken aboard a ship? He might have learned more if the butler hadn't incinerated his belongings.

Stephen controlled his temper and asked softly, 'Did you check the pockets before you destroyed the garments?'

'No, my lord. I didn't think of that.'

Stephen ground his teeth and said, 'Thank you, Farnsworth. That will be all.'

The butler cleared his throat and hesitated. 'My lord, about Lady Whitmore?'

'What is it?'

'Well, sir, the staff and I were wondering…' Farnsworth coughed, delaying his statement once more. Apparently there was some other detail the butler intended to share. Either that, or he was in dire need of some medicinal tea to treat the irritating cough.

Stephen clenched his fists in the coverlet. *Get on with it.*

'Yes?'

'To put it bluntly, my lord, your wife has been making several…changes.'

'What kind of changes?'

The agitated Farnsworth fidgeted with his hands. 'I have been a loyal servant to your household for over thirty years, my lord. I would never speak ill of the Chesterfields. But I fear she may have gone too far.'

Stephen wondered if Emily had moved a vase in the front hall six inches to the left. Or perhaps she'd poisoned the cat in a fit of vengeance.

Farnsworth's paranoia seemed ridiculous under the circumstances. He couldn't recall the past three months of his life, and the butler worried that his wife had gone too far?

'What. Has. She. Done?' he gritted out.

'She's sacked Cook. And—' he lowered his voice to a whisper '—she says she won't hire another. She's planning to do all the cooking herself.'

Bloody hell. The woman really did mean to poison him.

Chapter Two

In the kitchen, a woman must keep the premises orderly and clean at all times. Husbands should also be thus managed.
—Emily Barrow's *Cook Book*

Later that night, his intense headache deepened into a dull throbbing. Sleep would not come. Eyes dry and nerves raw, Stephen pushed back the coverlet. His bare feet padded across the Aubusson rug before his knee slammed into a mahogany blanket chest at the foot of the bed. Cursing, he fumbled his way towards the fireplace.

A large mirror hung above a dressing table. He could barely make out his own features in the shadows. Lighting a candle, he studied the man staring back at him. At one time, he had a well-ordered, predictable life. Now, a haggard expression gazed back at him. An angry red scar creased a jagged line across his bare chest, a knife wound he didn't remember. The blow to his head was a recent wound, possibly from thieves or worse. Yet someone had saved his life and sent him here.

He didn't know himself any more.

The uncertainty unnerved him. Every time he searched his memory for a fragment of the past events, his mind shut down. He didn't remember his supposed marriage, or anything leading up to it. It was as though an invisible wall barricaded him from the truth.

He was about to retreat when his gaze narrowed on a black symbol edging the back of his neck. Turning, he tried to distinguish what it was. Though he could not see the entire design, he recognised it as a tattoo.

Why? When had he got it? Never in his life would he have considered such a thing. Now, the indelible ink marked yet another facet of the mysterious past.

He tried in vain to see more of the emblem, but from the awkward angle, he could not see the full pattern. Stephen stepped away from the mirror. He would find the answers he needed, regardless of the effort.

Emily held some of those answers. She was wary of him, and well she should be. Likely she had lied to him to protect the children, using him for a place to stay.

He simply couldn't believe that he'd married her, even though they had been friends as children. More than that, if he were honest with himself. Like Eve, she had tantalised him with the sweetness of a first love. Then his father had found out and had forbidden him to see her again.

How had their paths crossed after so many years? And why couldn't he remember?

A fretful noise caught his attention. Stephen paused a moment, then opened the door to the corridor. The whimpering grew softer, then stopped. Was it an animal? He frowned, wondering what else had been brought into his house without permission.

As he passed down the hallway, he heard the sound coming from a bedchamber. He opened the door and inside saw a bundled shape beneath the covers. It was too small to be Emily, and as his vision adjusted to the dark, he recognised the boy he had met earlier. What was his name? Ralph? Roger? The child's face was buried in the pillow, his small shoulders shaking.

Stephen's throat constricted, but he did not move to comfort the child. It was as though his feet were locked in place. He was not the child's father, nor his guardian, regardless of what Emily might claim. It was not his place to interfere. And it was better for the boy not to expect comfort or coddling from others.

His own father had taught him just such a lesson until he had learned how to suppress tears. The future heir could not cry or show any emotion. His father had beaten it out of him until Stephen had become a model of composure.

When the boy's sobbing eased into the heavy breathing of sleep, Stephen took a step forward. He lifted the coverlet over the child, then left as silently as he had come.

The sun had not yet risen, but the sound of rain spattering against the stone house brought Emily a sense of comfort. The scullery maid Lizbeth lit the fire, and a flickering warmth permeated the room while Emily mixed the bread dough.

She knew the servants viewed her with a mixture of curiosity and discomfort. A baron's daughter should never venture into the kitchen to work. But it was a deep need within her, to be useful. Giving orders to the household staff made her uneasy, for she had practically been a servant herself until recently.

She had done her best to keep the family together after Papa had died. Her brother Daniel's business failings were a constant source of anxiety, but Emily had learned to suppress her criticism. None of their relatives would help them, not after—

She closed her mind, not wanting to think of the devastating scandal. She had done what she had to, bartering at the marketplace after Daniel had gambled away their finances.

He'd been grieving for his wife, a man out of his head. She'd forgiven him for it, even if it meant sacrificing her own marriage prospects.

But now she was married.

Emily kneaded the bread dough, letting its rhythm sweep away her fears and troubles. The familiar yeasty smell eased her tension, and she let the mindless task grant her time to think.

Whitmore was going to get rid of her. She was torn apart, so angry with him for his infidelity and for abandoning Daniel. And yet, she needed his protection for the children. She rested her forehead upon a floured hand. Somehow, she had to make the best of this.

Silently, the scullery maid began frying sausages for the morning meal. With a plain face and a figure the size of a barrel, Lizbeth always had a cheerful smile. Emily had liked the maid from the moment she'd met her.

'You've horrified him, you know,' Lizbeth remarked as she flipped the sausage links. 'Mr High-and-Mighty.'

'The Earl?'

'No, my lady.' Lizbeth blushed. 'I mean Farnsworth, the butler. He's told the master that you sent Henri packing.'

'Good.' Emily didn't care if Stephen knew about her dismissing the cook. The ill-tempered man had been robbing the household blind over the past few months, claiming ridiculous costs for food. They were well rid of him.

'And you needn't worry about the cooking, my lady,' Lizbeth added. 'Mrs Deepford and myself will take care of it until the new cook arrives.'

'Thank you, Lizbeth.' Emily relaxed slightly. Her hasty offer to cook for the household was impossible, she knew, though she had enjoyed seeing Farnsworth's look of horror. 'I am sorry to have caused you both more work.'

'Oh, no, it's grateful we are. Henri should have been sacked long ago.'

A small part of Emily worried that she had overstepped her bounds. The Earl might not appreciate her interfering with staff members, not with her own precarious position. She needed to apologise for her cross words earlier.

'Have you heard anything else?' Emily asked Lizbeth. 'From the Earl, I mean. Has he remembered anything?'

'No, my lady. I've not heard that he has.' Lizbeth cracked an egg into a bowl.

The bell sounded, and Lizbeth jumped up. 'It's his lordship. He'll be wanting his breakfast tray.'

'I'll take it,' Emily offered. She wanted to speak

with him about the children. The heaping platter of delicious food could improve his temperament while she explained why throwing their family out into the streets would be a very bad idea.

Her stomach grumbled, but she ignored it. She had eaten a slice of toasted bread and a cup of tea, which was enough for her.

By the time she finished climbing the back staircase leading to the Earl's bedchamber, she was out of breath. The heavy tray made her arms ache, but she pressed onwards. Knocking lightly, she heard him call, 'Enter.'

The Earl was seated in a wingback chair, reading *The Times*. He wore charcoal trousers, a dark blue frock-coat, pinstriped waistcoat and a white cotton shirt. His dark cravat was tied in a simple knot without any fuss. The shadow of a beard lined his cheeks, and his intense gaze rested upon her with interest.

His hair was wet, drops of water glistening at his temples. He'd taken a bath, she realised.

A slight shiver ran through her at the thought of him sinking into a tub of water, his muscled arms resting upon the edge. She had seen for herself the hard ridges of his stomach, the reddened scar across his pectorals.

A wicked image arose, of soap sliding over those muscles, of what it would be like to touch him.

What it would be like, if he lowered his body upon hers, until she yielded to him.

Like before…

An unbearable loneliness caught her. He had kissed her on the night he'd left, as though he would never let her go. Now it was as if that man had never existed.

An invisible fist struck her in the stomach, the hurt rising. When he'd arrived back at Falkirk, her first instinct had been to rush towards him, to hold him tight and thank God that he was alive.

But he didn't know her any more. He'd broken promises and betrayed her with another woman. She couldn't let go of that.

She blinked back the emotions threatening to spill over. Whitmore didn't feel anything towards her any more, and she didn't know if he ever would again.

'Are you planning to set that down or continue staring at me?'

Her face flamed, but she managed to lower the tray. 'Your breakfast, sire.' She bobbed a false curtsy.

'I would prefer "my lord".'

Emily had meant the address as sarcasm, but clearly the Earl did not recognise it. Her temper flared. 'Will there be anything else? Shall I bow down before you and lick your boots?'

'Perhaps later.' The interest in his voice made it

sound as if he didn't mind that idea at all. She whirled and marched towards the door.

'I am not finished with you yet,' he said. She sent him a look filled with venom, but his attention remained on *The Times*. He lifted a pair of spectacles to the bridge of his nose. She had never seen them before, never knew he wore them for reading. It reminded her that this was not a man who could be easily fooled.

Proper, stiff and steadfast in his beliefs, he had become every bit the shadow of his father, the Marquess. Her nerves coiled in her stomach at the thought.

'Would you care for tea?' she asked, fighting to keep her voice steady.

He lowered the paper and regarded her. 'Is it poisoned?'

His overbearing attitude made her consider dumping the pot over his head. 'You won't know that until you are dead, now, will you?' She smiled sweetly and poured the tea into a china cup. 'Milk and sugar?'

'I drink mine black. There's less chance of you adding something to it.'

'Unless I already have,' she dared, offering him the cup. Perhaps he'd choke on it.

His expression remained neutral, and he refused to take the cup. 'You drink first.'

'I haven't poisoned it,' she insisted.

'Drink.'

The arrogant tone of his voice annoyed her, but she obeyed. The hot tea tasted of rich spices with a heady aroma. 'There. Are you satisfied now?'

'Not quite.' The Earl set the newspaper aside and gestured toward the food. 'I want you to taste everything that is on the tray.'

'I am not hungry.'

At those words, he sent her a look that said he knew she was lying. 'You look as though you haven't eaten properly in weeks. You're too thin. I won't have the servants believing I don't feed my own wife. If that's what you are.'

'I don't care what they think.'

'But I do. And if you wish to remain in this household along with the children, you will heed my wishes.'

There. The threat was out. He really could make things worse for her, forcing her and the children to leave. And then where would she be? She could not support the children, nor give them a home.

Emily's cheeks flamed, but she stabbed a sausage with a fork. She wished it were one of his more delicate parts.

She took a bite of the eggs, savouring the flavor. Oh, sweet saints above. She closed her eyes for just a second, enjoying the food. Perhaps with a bit more salt or even chopped pieces of bacon, the eggs would taste even better. Ideas for cooking recipes swarmed through her mind as she enjoyed the taste of Elysium, courtesy of His Arrogance.

The sound of a ringing bell broke through her moment. Emily opened her eyes, but the Earl gave no hint as to why he had summoned the parlour maid.

'I did not spit in your food.'

His eyes held not a trace of humour. 'I never said you did.'

She pushed the plate towards him, but the awkwardness continued, making her wonder what else he wanted. 'You may eat,' she said. 'As you can see, I am still alive.'

He made no movement towards the food. He stared at her, his gaze questioning. His eyes were the soft grey of a London morning, his mouth firm and stoic. She had thought him to be a handsome man at one time. His features were strong, as though carved from stone.

He was a statue now. A man with no feelings, who never revealed a trace of what he was thinking.

Why had she let herself fall prey to his promises? The Earl had rescued her from a crumbling, debt-ridden estate. He'd sworn that he'd find her wayward brother and pay off Daniel's debts. She had been so infatuated, she hadn't stopped to wonder why.

A knock sounded, but instead of a maid, the disapproving eyes of Farnsworth frowned down upon her. Emily sensed the butler's silent censure of her clothing and her mannerisms. She was supposed to behave like a Countess, not a servant. Emily straightened, though it would do nothing to change Farnsworth's opinion of her.

'Bring Lady Whitmore a plate of her own. And more tea,' Whitmore added.

'No, really—I don't need a thing.'

His dark glare silenced her. When the butler had departed, he folded his arms across his chest. 'We must come to terms on a few things. I give the orders, and you are to obey them.'

Did he think he was the King of England? 'Yes, your Majesty.'

He, apparently, found no amusement in her mockery. 'Furthermore, when Farnsworth brings up the tray, you are to eat every morsel of food.'

'And if I don't?'

'You wish for the children to eat, do you not?'

At his implied threat that he would refuse them food, her fury exploded. 'You wouldn't dare starve innocent children on your own ridiculous whims.'

'They aren't my children,' he pointed out. 'And if you want me to house them, clothe them and feed them, you will obey.'

Stephen saw the look of fear in her eyes and felt

a trace of guilt for making the threat. Not too much, however. From the looks of it, Emily had not eaten a full meal in far too long. If a false implication would encourage her to eat, he had no qualms about exaggerating.

Her cheekbones stood out in a face so delicate, it could have been crystal. Her eyes were large, a haunting whisky brown. A stray tendril of golden hair rested against her cheek where a smudge of flour marred her skin.

'They are your responsibility,' she said.

Farnsworth returned with the tray a few minutes later. Emily ate, her eyes blazing with murder. And yet, he could see the desperation in her carefully controlled appetite.

'I have some questions I want you to answer,' he began. 'Starting with our wedding day.'

She gave her full attention to the eggs, behaving as though she hadn't heard him. Stephen reached out and took her left hand. Upon her third finger rested the family heirloom ring. A large ruby glinted from the gold band. He rubbed his finger across the stone, her fingers cool within his palm.

'I don't remember the marriage ceremony at all. I don't even remember giving you this ring. For all I know, you stole it.'

She glared at him. 'Do you want it back?'

'Possibly.' He stared at the ring, trying to piece

the memory together. Emily struggled to pull her hand away, but he held it fast.

'Tell me about our wedding.'

'It snowed that day,' she whispered. The look upon her face was of a woman lost.

'Did we have feelings for one another?' he asked quietly.

At that, Emily choked. She covered it with a laugh, but he could see the shadow of hurt behind her eyes. 'You adored me. We married on impulse.'

'I mean the real reason, Emily.'

She studied her breakfast again. 'I don't suppose I truly know the answer. I thought you cared for me.' Pain silhouetted her words. 'I was wrong.'

'Did I compromise you?' he asked, running his thumb over the edge of her hand. Her palms were rough, like a servant's.

Emily jerked her hand away. 'No. And I'd rather not talk about it, if you don't mind.'

'Why did you marry me?' What was this sadness in her eyes? She kept up such strong defences, he couldn't see past the anger to understand it.

Emily set her plate aside, ignoring the remainder of the food. 'I had my reasons.' Upon her face he saw veiled embarrassment. She had spoken of feelings between them. Had he ever claimed to love her?

She was pretty, as she'd always been. Outspoken, with a tongue like a razor. And if she'd married him on such a sudden whim, her impulsive behaviour hadn't changed.

'I must return to London,' he said, changing the subject. He kept detailed ledgers in his study. If there were answers to be had, he would find them there. 'As soon as I am healed, you will journey with me.'

'No!' She caught herself and amended, 'That is, I'd rather not.'

The alarm in her voice alerted his suspicions. 'Why are you so afraid of London?'

'Your father won't want to see us. And the children need me here.' She fumbled with her hands as though searching for a stronger excuse.

'I will hire a nursemaid. In fact, I have already ordered Farnsworth to procure several for you to interview. I cannot believe the man has not already done so.'

'I hired a wet nurse for the baby. Anna takes care of both Victoria and Royce.'

'Royce needs a tutor, as well as a nursemaid.' When she made no reply, he switched his tactics. 'Don't you think my family will wonder why I haven't brought my wife with me?'

Her cheeks turned scarlet. Her reluctance had to mean they weren't married. He was sure of it.

But she startled him by lifting her chin. 'I don't care what they think. I won't go to London with you. Not now. Not ever.' She rose to her feet and strode from the room. The door slammed shut behind her.

She was afraid. And unless he was very much mistaken, Stephen had a grave feeling that his wife knew far more about the night he had disappeared than he'd suspected. It did not bode well for their future together.

Chapter Three

Cakes served at tea time must always be light and delectable. A hostess should smile and greet her guests with a gracious heart.
—Emily Barrow's *Cook Book*

Later that morning, Dr Parsons checked the bandages and nodded his approval. 'Your wife has done well caring for you,' he remarked. 'The wounds are clean, and your bruises are healing nicely. I should think you will be back on your feet within days.'

'I intend to go to London,' Stephen remarked. 'Three days from now, if possible.'

'My lord, I would advise against undue haste. If I may, I'd ask you to wait another week before you go.'

'I do not recall anything of the accident,' Stephen admitted. 'Nor what happened to me during the past three months.'

'Memory loss can occur with an accident.' The doctor replaced the bandage, tying it off. 'I have seen it in many patients, particularly those with traumatic incidents. Often a man's mind will over-shadow the event it does not wish to remember.'

'When will the rest of my memories return?' Stephen demanded.

'To be frank, they might not. In cases such as yours, it is difficult to say. Your head wound and contusions are recent, but I doubt if they had anything to do with your memory loss.' The doctor added, 'I suspect that you were the victim of violence several months ago, judging from the knife wound. It may be that you won't want to remember it. But I can say with all confidence, your headaches and pain should be gone within a few days more.'

Pain was the least of his concern. He was tempted to ask the doctor about the strange tattoo he'd found on the back of his neck, but decided against it. For all he knew, he had done something rash.

Like marry a woman he hadn't seen in ten years.

After Dr Parsons departed, Stephen thought about his earlier conversation with Emily. He had not questioned her caring for the children, but her claim that he was now responsible for their welfare troubled him.

He decided to speak with the boy. If he could not obtain the answers from his wife, he would get them elsewhere. He summoned Farnsworth and ordered him to fetch the boy. Minutes passed, and no one came.

He waited longer, pacing across the carpet. Someone should teach the boy discipline and how to be prompt. It was never too early to learn good manners. When five more minutes passed, he opened the door to the hallway.

'Come now.' Farnsworth leaned down, holding out a sugar biscuit as bait. A sullen-faced lad gave the butler a defiant glare, but he took a single step forward. 'It's all right. Come here, please,' the butler crooned.

'Good God, Farnsworth. The boy isn't a dog. Cease treating him like one.' Stephen's patience had reached its limit.

'My lord, he won't listen.' The butler straightened, and predictably the boy disappeared behind a door.

'I shall handle this.' Stephen strode towards the bedchamber. When he tried the door handle, it was locked.

'The key, if you please, Farnsworth.'

'My lord, I am terribly sorry. I shall have to fetch it.' The butler scrambled off, grateful to escape.

For a moment, Stephen listened outside the door

while pondering his next move. Treating the boy like a child would not work. Instead, he knocked.

'Go away!'

That was to be expected. Any proper opponent would be foolish to simply surrender. But he, of course, had the proper incentive.

'You wish to leave my house, do you not?'

A pause. The strategy was not a move the boy had anticipated. 'Yes.'

'I suggest an exchange of information. You tell me what I wish to know, and I will see to your departure.' He did not mention where, but school was a likely prospect. The boy needed an education, after all.

A longer pause.

The door clicked and opened slightly. Stephen hid his smile of victory. It would not do to upset the balance just yet. He needed answers, and he was counting upon the child's honesty to get them.

Stephen entered the room while a pair of young suspicious eyes watched him.

'Roland, is it?' he began.

'My name is Royce.' The boy sent him a hard look and crossed his arms. 'And I don't like you.'

Stephen shrugged. 'I can't say as I like you much either.'

His response seemed to meet with Royce's approval. The lines had been drawn, the enemy lines established.

'Sit down.' He gestured towards a footstool, but Royce refused. Stephan began with, 'How long have you been living here at Falkirk?'

'Since February.' The boy's attention moved to the door as though he were planning an escape.

'Your aunt brought you here?'

The boy's face softened at the mention of Emily, then grew defensive. 'She sent for us, yes.' He fidgeted, looking down at his hands. 'You're very tall,' he said suddenly.

'Do not change the subject.' Stephen resumed his interrogation. 'Why did your aunt marry me?'

Fear swept across Royce's pale, thin face. 'I don't know.'

'I think you do. You'd best tell me the truth.'

The boy's attention lowered to the floor, and he clenched his fists. 'I want my papa.'

Stephen gentled his tone. 'I was sorry to hear about your father.' He reached out to the boy, but Royce bolted for the door.

Stephen caught him before he could flee. The child's shoulders trembled, and he broke into sobs. 'I want Papa.' Tears ran down his cheeks, and Royce fought to free himself.

It was useless. He should have known better than to demand answers from a child.

'What have you done?' The door flew open, and Emily swept into the room. As soon as she saw

Royce, she bent down and gathered him into her arms. 'You've made him cry.'

Like a furious mother lioness, she released the full force of her wrath. 'He's only a boy.'

'I asked him a few questions,' Stephen admitted. He felt sheepish, for the idea had not been a good one.

Emily mustered a smile for Royce. 'Go and see Lizbeth. She has a slice of cake waiting for you.'

The promise of cake was all that was needed to send the child dashing from the room. When Royce had gone, Emily unleashed her fury. 'You are heartless. What did you say to him?'

There was true fear in her eyes, not just anger. 'I asked him a few questions.' He took a step closer, watching her tremble. 'What are you so afraid of, Emily?'

'He doesn't know his father is dead.'

'Why not?'

A deep weariness edged her expression. The rage grew calm as she gathered her composure. 'It's my fault. I couldn't bear to hurt him. He lost his mother when Victoria was born. And now his father.'

Stephen took her wrist, feeling her pulse quicken. Her hands were warm, and he smelled the light fragrance of vanilla near her nape. Like the sugar biscuits, he realised. And he found himself wanting to draw nearer. 'Hiding the truth won't make it go away.'

'And sometimes no one will believe the truth when it is spoken.' She held his scrutiny, jerking her hand away. 'Go to London. You'll find the answers you seek there.'

Her icy demeanour had returned. With her honey-gold hair tucked neatly into black netting, her face scrubbed clean, she appeared a paragon of virtue. She had changed her dress into an older gown, a dull black bombazine. Its hemline was frayed and it had been remade more than once.

He grew irritated at her martyrdom and seized both wrists. Taking her left hand, he gripped her palm so that the wedding ring pressed into her skin. 'Stop sniveling and answer my questions. What happened to your brother?'

'His creditors killed him while you were visiting your *mistress*,' she spat. 'He bled to death.'

'I don't have a mistress,' Stephen contradicted. Emily tried to break free, but he refused to let go. 'Do you truly believe I would let a man die if I had the power to stop it?'

'No,' she admitted. Even so, doubts clouded her face.

He moved closer, hoping to unravel her lies. But when his hand slipped around her waist, he saw the genuine grief in her eyes. Beneath the bombazine, the heat of her skin warmed his palm. His fingers touched one of the tiny buttons upon her gown, toying with it. 'Who told you I was with my mistress?'

'The men who brought Daniel's body to me.' She tried again to pull away, but he held her captive. Regardless of the means, he would have his answers.

'And who were they?' His hand moved up her spine, tracing the dozens of tiny buttons until he reached one at the nape of her neck. With the flick of a thumb, he revealed a bit of skin. He wanted to gauge her reaction.

'I—I don't know,' she stammered. 'I thought they were your solicitors or from your father. They were looking for you.'

Her hand clamped over his when he grazed her skin. 'Don't touch me.'

He ignored her, loosening another button. 'Why not?'

'Because you don't mean it. You don't want me. Any more than I want you.'

A sudden flash of memory took hold. Emily stood before the fireplace in his bedchamber at Falkirk, her hair hanging down. Her fingers moved to unbutton his frock-coat, and her face was flushed with desire.

He dropped his hand away from her when the fleeting vision faded. Where had it come from? Was it real? Had they been lovers? Frustration clawed at his mind when the emptiness returned.

He leaned in close, so his face nearly touched hers. 'Tell me why I married you.' With her so near, he could smell the fragrance of vanilla. Her clear eyes were confused, her cheeks pale.

She gripped her hands together so tightly her knuckles whitened. With a light shrug she met his gaze. 'You said you wanted to take care of me, to help our family. And like a fool, I wanted to believe you loved me.'

He studied her a moment. She looked so lost, so vulnerable. Behind her mask of bitterness he caught a glimpse of the girl he'd once known. She'd been his best friend, long ago. And now she was his wife.

The lost three months felt like a lifetime.

'How did it happen?' he asked. Had he courted her? Was it an impulsive move, or had he been forced into it?

'It was just after St Valentine's Day,' she remarked with a hint of irony. 'In Scotland. I have the marriage certificate, if you want to see it.'

'Perhaps later.' Documents of that nature could still be forged. He preferred to send a trusted servant to see the parish records.

He suspected that he would not get an honest answer from her, not when she was desperate to protect the children's welfare. It had to have been an arrangement between them, a bargain of sorts.

But for her, there had been more.

Emily tried to pull away, but he refused to let her escape. She was so fragile within his grasp, like a glass about to shatter.

'Were there feelings between us?' he asked. He leaned in so close he could feel her breath upon his face. If he moved his mouth to the side, it would graze her lips in a soft kiss. He waited for her to push at him, to curse him for touching her.

She gave him no answer. Instead, her body seemed to conform to his. Her hands rested upon his shoulders while he idly traced a path up her spine. The years seemed to fall away until she was once again the young girl he'd practised kissing in a stable. Only now, he held a woman in his arms. A beautiful, hot-tempered woman who made him lose his sense of reason the moment he touched her.

He didn't kiss her, though he wanted to. There were too many unanswered questions.

When he stepped backwards, Emily grasped her arms to shield herself. 'Are you going to annul our marriage?'

The fear in her eyes made him hesitate. He wanted to say yes. Instead, he answered truthfully, 'I don't know yet.'

He traced the outline of her face with his thumb. 'I am going to find out what happened to me, Emily,' he told her. 'Stay here until I return from London.'

Her broken smile bothered him. 'Where else could I go?'

* * *

'Sweet Christmas.' Christine Chesterfield, the Marchioness of Rothburne, covered her heart with her palm when she saw Stephen. He embraced his mother, and she squeezed him tightly just before her fist collided with his ear.

'I should have you horsewhipped. You frightened me to death. I thought heathens had kidnapped you and taken you off to some forsaken island in the middle of nowhere.'

Stephen rubbed his ear and managed a smile. For all he knew, his mother might have been correct concerning his whereabouts. 'I sent word before I arrived.'

'You should have contacted me long before then. You left Lord Carstairs's ball, which made Lady Carstairs extremely cross, by the by. And then you *vanished* since February. Even the servants couldn't tell me where you were.'

Lady Rothburne guided him to sit down, and poured a cup of tea. 'Now, you simply *must* tell me everything that's happened since you left.'

'There isn't much to tell,' he admitted. He did not possess enough memories to offer an honest accounting, so he gave her what truths he could. 'I've been convalescing at Falkirk House in the country.'

'You were injured?' Immediately she reached

out and patted the ear she'd boxed. 'Forgive me, Stephen. I didn't know. But you're well now?'

'Better. I have little memory of what happened. I came to London to look for the answers.'

Lady Rothburne took a deep sip of the tea, and worry lines edged her mouth. 'I don't like the thought of some ruffian doing you harm. I shall call upon Lady Thistlewaite and ask for her assistance.'

At the mention of his mother's dearest friend, Stephen suppressed a groan. Lady Thistlewaite had her sources of gossip, like most women. Her methods, however, left much to be desired. He could envision it now, a stout matron knocking upon an unsuspecting man's door with her parasol, demanding, 'Are you the barbarian who clouted Lady Rothburne's son upon the head?'

'And,' his mother continued, 'I think you should attend the Yarrington musicale next week. It will take your mind off matters.' She put on a bright smile and took his hand. 'Your father and I insist.'

At the mention of the Marquess, a gnawing irritation formed in his gut. 'Mother, I really don't think—'

'Oh, pish posh. I know exactly what you need. A lovely young woman at your side, that's what. Someone to share your troubles. And Miss Lily Hereford has missed you quite dreadfully. Why, the two of you make such a good pair. I have my heart quite set upon you marrying her. In fact—' she leaned in close as if imparting a great secret '—your father and I have already begun drawing up the guest list for your wedding. Miss Hereford would make you the perfect wife, after all. She is a woman of impeccable breeding.'

At his mother's assertion, Stephen's mouth tightened. 'Married?'

His mother laughed. 'Well, of course, Stephen. If anyone is one of society's most eligible bachelors, it's you.'

She was serious. Blood roared in his ears as his mind processed what she had said.

It seemed Emily Barrow had lied to him after all.

Chapter Four

When a cake darkens before it has fully risen, the fire may be too hot. More cakes have been ruined by an inadequate flame or by one that is too fierce. It is not necessary to stoke an inferno...

—Emily Barrow's *Cook Book*

He'd been gone for only three days, but Emily's uneasiness grew with each passing hour. Was the Earl all right? Had his wounds healed fully?

Stop it. She took a deep breath and knelt down on the soft lawn of Falkirk House beside the herb garden. *He's gone. That was what you wanted.*

But no matter how she tried to slip back into her former pattern of living, it wasn't the same. With a pair of scissors, she hacked several handfuls of fresh thyme for the roasted chicken she had planned. Despondency seemed to settle over her shoulders, like a familiar burden. Normally the gardens lifted her spirits, particularly the scent of fresh herbs. And here, the large grove of arbour vitae hid her from the house in a quiet green space.

What if the Earl never came back? Or what if he divorced her? Her throat ached with unshed tears, even as she ordered herself not to cry. He hadn't loved her when he'd offered to marry her. And now she simply had to live with those consequences.

A rough palm covered her mouth. She tried to scream, but her attacker's fingers encircled her throat.

'If you make a sound, I'll snap your neck,' he whispered. In a swift motion, he shoved her to the ground, pressing her face against the damp earth. Emily couldn't breathe, her heart seizing with fear.

'You know what happened to your brother, don't you?'

Her pulse raced at the knowledge that Daniel's enemies had found her. She tried to nod.

'I want his papers, ledgers of all his investments. Where are they?'

He released his grip upon her mouth.

'I—I don't know,' she stammered, lifting her chin to gasp for air.

He forced her back into the dirt, his fingers squeezing her neck. 'Don't lie to me.'

'Perhaps at my father's house—'

Before she could say another word, she heard Royce calling out to her. 'Aunt Emily!'

'Tell no one of this,' her enemy warned. 'Or his children will suffer for it.' A fist collided with her ear, and she bit back a cry of pain.

When she turned around, the man was gone. Royce continued calling out to her, and Emily stumbled to her feet. With trembling hands, she wiped her face clean of the dirt.

They've found us was all she could think. Daniel's enemies, perhaps even the man who had killed him.

She clenched her skirts, her gaze travelling down to the trampled herbs. Why did he want her brother's ledgers? His demands made no sense. Daniel's business investments had never been anything but failures.

They weren't safe here any longer. She could not allow Royce or Victoria to fall prey to her brother's enemies. Wild thoughts of sending the children to America or even to the Orient crossed her mind.

London. She would have to take the children to London. The Earl could protect all of them. The thought made her indignant. She hated to rely on anyone but herself. But they were less likely to be harmed if she stayed close to Whitmore.

Her bruised heart ached at the thought of being near him. His promises had all been a lie, and now she was entangled in a marriage that was never meant to be.

Worse was her reaction to his touch. Though he had done nothing more than hold her, it had evoked memories she'd tried to forget. Her body warmed at the thought. Skin to skin, his flesh joining with hers.

No. Never again. She'd learned her lesson after their wedding night. It wouldn't happen again. Resisting his advances would be easy enough if she closed her eyes and remembered every wrong he'd committed.

Emily gritted her teeth at the thought of journeying several days in a coach. Royce would think it was a grand adventure while Victoria would wail the entire trip. A sickening knot formed in her stomach. Of course, she could take the train to London, but the very idea terrified her. She didn't like moving at such speeds.

She went inside and found Royce curled up on the staircase, his mouth pursed as he struggled to read a book of fairy tales he had brought from home. When he saw her, he smiled. 'There you are. Will you read to me, Aunt Emily?'

She wanted to say, *'Of course'*, and ruffle his hair. Instead, she shook her head. 'Not now. I need to tell you something important. We're going to London.'

'To find Papa?'

She shook her head, steeling her courage. The

time had come to admit the truth. Why did she have to do this? Why did she have to tell him that another parent had died? It was bad enough when his mother had died in childbirth. To tell him that his father was gone quite simply broke her heart.

She knelt down. Royce eyed her with suspicion. 'You're going away.'

'No. That isn't what I've come to say.' She paused, trying to find the right way to tell him. There weren't any words gentle enough to say what needed to be said.

'Royce, your father is not coming back.' She took his hands in hers.

He bobbed his head. 'Yes, he is. Papa promised me. He always keeps his promises.'

'He can't keep this one, Royce.' The pain in her heart cracked and a tear escaped. 'He died, sweeting.'

Royce's face never changed. It was as though she hadn't spoken at all. He never breathed, never moved.

'No. I don't believe you.' He pulled his hands away and picked up a tin soldier that had fallen on the braided rug. Making a shooting noise, he pretended the soldier had killed an imaginary enemy.

'It's true.' She reached out to embrace him, but he jerked away.

'No. I know he'll come. He said he would.'

Emily bowed her head while Royce continued to manipulate the soldier, acting as though she hadn't spoken a word. With the tears caught deep in her throat, she squeezed his shoulder. 'We're leaving in the morning. Gather the things you want to take along.'

His demeanour changed in the fraction of a moment. 'I can't leave. Papa knows we're here. This is where I'm waiting for him.'

Emily rose to her feet. 'I am going down to the kitchen. I'll have Mrs Deepford prepare your favourite meal tonight.'

'I won't go.' His voice trembled, a note of anger rising.

She did not reply, but turned her back to leave. Something small and sharp struck her on the shoulder before it clattered to the floor. Emily saw the fallen soldier Royce had thrown, but did not bend to pick it up.

Behind her, her nephew wept softly.

The next morning, Stephen dispatched messengers to all the parishes across the Scottish border. Though his mother insisted he was unmarried, he wasn't sure whom to believe. At certain moments, erratic images flashed shadows upon his mind, of Emily in his embrace. He didn't know if they were true or not. Behind her insurmountable wall of hatred lay a woman whom he'd cared about once.

But he couldn't believe he'd married her.

The library door opened, and his father, James Chesterfield, Marquess of Rothburne, stood at the doorway. The Marquess studied Stephen without speaking a word. James wore black, as he always did, a streak of grey marring the temples of his dark hair. Tall, thin and ingrained in the belief that his blood was superior to everyone else's, his father knew precisely how to command a room with a domineering presence.

'Would you care to explain your actions?' James began without prelude.

Stephen did not rise to the bait. 'It is good to see you again also, Father.'

There was no welcome, no show of affection. Often, Stephen wondered whether his father had any feelings toward his children. They never talked. Since the death of Stephen's eldest brother William many years ago, his father had behaved as if nothing were amiss. He had never spoken of the tragedy.

The Marquess firmly believed in duty and tradition. It didn't matter that Stephen was never meant to assume the title. He was the heir now, and as such, he was expected to embrace those expectations.

'Your mother tells me you got married.'

The unspoken words were, *Without my permission.*

Stephen did not deny it, nor did he affirm his

father's accusation. 'The choice of a wife is mine, I believe. I do not require your consent.'

'You are wrong in that.' James straightened into the posture of a military general. 'Your responsibilities as my heir include choosing a suitable wife.'

'There is nothing unsuitable about Emily Barrow. She is a baron's daughter,' he reminded his father.

'And her family is ridden with scandal. You might as well have married a scullery maid. No one in polite society will receive her.'

And, of course, society's dictates were of the utmost importance. Stephen suddenly grasped a very real reason why he might have wed Emily. Marrying her was the perfect way to defy his father's wishes. James Chesterfield could not control his choice of a wife.

'Is that all?' he asked. He stared at his father, eye to eye.

'Not quite. You will see to it that no one learns of your…indiscretion, until I have investigated the means of dissolving the marriage. I hope, for your sake, that it can still be done.' Having voiced his decree, the Marquess saw no reason to remain. He departed without another word.

Stephen opened a cabinet and poured himself a brandy. As he warmed the glass in his hand, his fingers tightened around the stem. The Marquess seemed unaware that he could no longer dictate his son's choices.

He took a sip of the brandy, revelling in silent defiance. It occurred to him that it was more than past time to secure a new residence. He'd suffered long enough at Rothburne House, his future inheritance. And though he would have to live here again upon his father's passing, there was no reason to endure James Chesterfield until that day came. Tomorrow, he promised himself. He'd look into the matter tomorrow.

His life was his own, and he didn't care what his father's preferences were.

Stephen set the brandy glass down, his mind settling back to Emily Barrow. Beneath her thin, fragile exterior was a woman with an iron will, a dangerous woman who resented him. She was using him to provide for her niece and nephew. Just as he was using her to rebel against his autocratic father. The thought sobered him.

Had Emily believed he'd loved her? Why would he lie to a woman in that way? He didn't like to think of behaving in such a dishonourable manner. And yet, the answers lay just beyond his reach, strange pieces of a puzzle that would not fit together.

Until he had the answers, he could not force her out of his life.

* * *

Emily longed to find a pistol and shoot herself.

After travelling for days in a tiny coach, stopping only to eat meals or to sleep at an inn, Victoria had commenced to scream at the top of her tiny lungs. For hours. And hours. The wet nurse Anna had tried her best to calm the infant, but Victoria continued to sob.

Royce had joined in the chorus, whining that he wanted to go home, and threatening to run away to find his papa. Emily counted silently to fifty and reminded herself that London was not far now. It had begun to rain, the fat drops drumming against the coach in rhythm to the horses' hooves.

When Victoria had cried herself into exhaustion and Royce's tousled head rested in Emily's lap, the familiar sights of London surrounded her. In the night, she could see only the murky waters of the Thames gleaming against the gaslights. Familiar dark smells infiltrated the coach, dredging up a deep, horrible fear.

I cannot do this, she thought. How could she arrive upon the Marquess's doorstep, demanding to see her husband? But she had no choice. Falkirk House was no longer safe.

The coach slowed and drew to a halt. The driver opened the door for her. 'Wait here,' Emily whispered to Anna. The wet nurse nodded, cradling Victoria in her arms.

She prayed that Stephen would grant them shelter. It was long past the time for callers, and rain pounded the streets. The moonless sky brooded against the elegant stone façade of the Marquess's residence. Tall glass windows reflected flickering shadows of the night.

Emily ignored the rain and marched up to the front door. Knocking, she reminded herself that she had to behave with the haughtiness of a Countess, whether she felt like one or not.

A footman opened the door, his eyebrows raised as though she were a rat come in off the streets. Emily returned the man's curious glare with one of purpose. 'Step back from the door, if you please. I do not intend to stay out in this weather.'

He blinked a moment. 'The servants' entrance is in the back, madam.'

'I am hardly a servant.' Emily stepped forward, pushing him out of the way. 'And if my husband heard you accusing me of such, he would be most insulted.'

The footman's expression turned curious. Emily unfastened her cloak and bonnet, offering them to the man. He did not accept the dripping garments.

'Whom shall I say is here?' the footman enquired, still seeming as though he intended to throw her out.

'I am Lady Whitmore,' Emily said, sweeping past him. 'And the Earl is expecting our arrival.'

When lightning did not smite her into the polished hardwood floors, it was a good sign that perhaps her lie would be forgiven. Well, it wasn't really a lie. Stephen had asked her to come to London at first; she could simply say that she'd changed her mind. Yes, that was it.

'What is your name?' she inquired of the footman.

'I am Phillips,' the footman replied. His posture was so rigid, Emily rather thought he resembled a hat rack.

'Phillips, we have been travelling a long time. Please have our rooms prepared and ask the kitchen staff to arrange a meal for the children and myself. We should like to be served in the dining room.' Emily completed her request by crossing her arms, deliberately giving him a view of the ruby heirloom wedding ring on her left hand.

At the sight of the ring, Phillips's demeanour changed instantly. 'If you would be so kind as to wait here, I shall inform Lord Whitmore of your arrival.'

Emily set her cloak down and held the bonnet, pacing as she held back her nerves. Minutes passed by, and at last she heard the sound of footsteps. The footman returned, followed by the Marquess of Rothburne. Emily clenched her bonnet so hard, her knuckles turned white.

Tall, with grey-tipped dark hair, the Marquess regarded Emily with an irritated air. His hawkish nose looked down upon her.

'What is going on, Phillips?' Lord Rothburne demanded.

'I am here to see my husband.' Emily gripped her wedding ring so hard, the metal bit into her skin.

Lord Rothburne nodded to the footman. 'Leave us.'

Her defences rose up immediately. She could tell the Marquess planned to get rid of her. Did Stephen even know she was here? Not likely, given the smug expression of Phillips as he'd left. Panic set in, replaced by desperation. After her family's scandal, she had no friends in London, no one to turn to. She couldn't possibly let Lord Rothburne send them away.

'You are not welcome here,' he said without preamble. 'Furthermore, you are not going to touch a penny of my son's fortune.'

'I don't want his money. I don't need it.'

The Marquess glanced at Emily's faded dress with unconcealed disdain. At his attempt to intimidate her, she stiffened. She had no choice but to fight for the children. If they went home, Daniel's enemies would find them.

'I want to see the Earl,' she repeated.

Lord Rothburne folded his arms, annoyed at her

defiance. 'I do not care what you want. My son does not wish to see you again. And if you do not leave of your own accord, I shall have Phillips remove you.'

Emily was strongly tempted to call out to Whitmore, in the vain hope that her husband would somehow appear and rescue them.

With a nod from the Marquess, the footman scurried from beside the staircase and opened the front door. Outside, the rain slapped against the cobblestones. Emily had no choice but to beg. She couldn't leave, not with the children's future at stake.

'Please. Just let me see him for a moment. I won't cause any trouble.' Outside, she could hear Victoria crying again, amid the noise of the London streets.

The Marquess said nothing, his face stony with resolution. Emily stepped backwards, and the icy rain pelted her bare skin. A moment later, Phillips tossed her the cloak, and Emily caught it before the door shut firmly.

She stared up at the illuminated windows, not caring that the rain had soaked through her thin gown and hair. Her husband hadn't come. What had she expected?

Woodenly, she returned to the coach, not knowing what to do next. She donned the cloak and then her bonnet, tying the soaked ribbons into a bow.

'Are we going inside, my lady?' Anna asked, bouncing Victoria against her shoulder.

Emily reached out and stroked her niece's head while she held back the tears that threatened. 'No.'

She should have been prepared for this. Lord Rothburne had never approved of her childhood friendship with Stephen, a fact that apparently had not changed. Though Whitmore held the courtesy title of Earl and the power that went with it, the higher authority rested with his father.

'What will we do?' Anna asked.

'I don't know.' The coachman was waiting for her to make a decision, but she could not think of any alternatives.

Had her husband really wanted to send her away? Or was it the Marquess's doing? Whitmore might not know she was here.

In her mind, she conjured up the image of a handsome prince, locked in the tower. Or, in this case, the unsuspecting Earl who had left his wife and children freezing out in the cold.

Before she could stop herself, she opened the door.

'Where are you going, my lady?'

'Tell the driver to circle around the streets. Keep going, and don't stop until you see me outside again.'

The sheer force of her will-power drove her to do something rash. The rain blinded her, but she pushed through it, moving toward the servants' entrance. As she'd hoped, it was unlocked.

The kitchen staff stared at her in shock. A plump cook nearly dropped the kettle she held in her hands.

'I won't be but a moment,' Emily said to them, holding up the ruby ring. 'I'm going to collect my husband.'

Emily found the back staircase and took the steps two at a time before the startled servants could pursue her. If Stephen were here, she would find him.

Dripping wet, she steeled herself in case the Marquess appeared. He didn't. She listened carefully at each door, moving down the hall. Not knowing her whereabouts, at last she chose a door and opened it.

A snowy-haired woman in a champagne-coloured dress sat reading. She stifled a shriek at the sight of Emily. 'Emily Barrow, what on earth are you doing here?'

She recognised the Marchioness, Lady Rothburne. 'I am looking for my husband.'

Lady Rothburne gaped at her. 'Does Stephen know you are here?'

Emily shook her head, just as a footman burst in through the open door. 'My lady, I am so sorry. She came in before we could stop her.'

'It is all right,' Lady Rothburne said, dismissing the footman. 'I know Miss Barrow.'

Emily held back her sigh of relief. 'Please forgive me, Lady Rothburne, but I am in a bit of a hurry. Which room is he in, please?'

Lady Rothburne tilted her head to one side, a curious look upon her face. 'My husband doesn't know you are here, does he?'

Emily didn't want to admit the truth, so she said, 'I must see the Earl. I would not be here, if it were not urgent.'

'He is down the hall, second door on your left.' Lady Rothburne eyed Emily's sodden clothing. 'Would you care to change your dress? I believe my daughter might have a spare gown or two. Hannah is away at school, and she would not mind.'

'Thank you. But I won't be long.' Emily nodded a farewell to Lady Rothburne and peered out the door. No one was about, so she tore across the hallway. Throwing open the door, she closed it behind her. Stephen was in the midst of disrobing, his shirt fully unbuttoned and hanging off his shoulders.

Upon the back of his neck was a black tattoo, similar to her brother's. Now where had he gotten that? He hadn't had it on their wedding night.

'What are you doing here?' Stephen pulled the shirt back on, a frown upon his face. 'I thought you were going to stay at Falkirk.'

At the sight of his bare chest, she backed away. Where was his valet? Being alone with a half-dressed man was not at all wise.

He moved towards her, and Emily averted her eyes, trying not to look at his chest. Deep ridges of muscle were marred by a jagged scar several inches long. The skin had healed, but the redness remained from the knife wound.

'I changed my mind.' She offered no explanation, hoping he wouldn't enquire further. He likely wouldn't believe her, even if she told him the truth.

'You're soaking wet. Come over by the fire and dry off.' He studied her hair and Emily realised that most of the pins had come out. It lay in tangled masses, half-pinned up beneath her bonnet, half-hanging about her shoulders. She tucked a stray lock behind her ear, though it did nothing for her appearance.

'I don't have time. The children are outside,' she said. 'I would have brought them with me, except your father tossed me into the streets.'

Stephen's face tightened with anger. 'Did he?'

It infuriated him that his wife had come to London, and James had treated her poorly. 'I am glad you didn't let that stop you.'

He took a step forward and removed her bonnet, then the rest of the pins holding back her hair. Freeing the dark golden locks, he finger-combed it, stroking his thumb along her jaw. Even as bedraggled as she looked, she captured his attention.

'Stand by the hearth and warm yourself,' he murmured. 'I'll send a servant to collect the children.'

'They aren't valises,' she argued. 'And your father won't want them here.'

He didn't particularly care what James wanted, but it was late, and he had no interest in arguing. 'I'll make other arrangements, then. I just purchased a town house a few miles from here. It should do well enough, although I haven't hired a staff yet, and there aren't many furnishings.'

He palmed the back of her nape, massaging the tension. The softness of her skin intrigued him, and he let his hand slide lower.

Her hollowed face held him spellbound. Soft full lips tantalised him, and her womanly curves made him want to remove the layers between them and touch her.

'What—what are you doing?' Her skin rose with goose bumps, her voice shaky. 'Keep your hands to yourself, Whitmore.'

She was behaving like a virgin, not at all like a woman he'd married. He lowered his mouth to her shoulder, inhaling the vanilla scent of her skin.

She shivered. Her cheeks were pale, her eyes bleak. 'Don't make me remember this.'

He stopped, but held her hand, his fingers encircling the heavy gold ring. She behaved like an untouched woman, innocent and fresh. But she didn't push him away, either. Her consternation made him suspect that there had once been more between them. Reluctantly, he let her go.

Her shoulders lowered with relief. Stephen donned his shirt and waistcoat, hurrying with the buttons of his frock-coat. 'Come.'

He took her by the hand, leading her down the servants' back staircase. 'The coach is outside?'

She nodded. Stephen located his overcoat and an umbrella, following her. The freezing rain buffetted the umbrella, and she was forced to remain beside him to be shielded from the rain. He took her palm, and she studied the streets. 'There. I see it.'

Stephen signalled to the coachman and within moments he helped Emily inside the vehicle. He recognised the driver from Falkirk House and was thankful that at least his wife had enough sense to bring an escort with them. After giving the coachman directions, they were on their way.

When he sat beside Emily, the young boy scowled. 'What is *he* doing here?'

'Royce,' Emily warned.

'I am taking you to a warm bed to sleep,' Stephen remarked. 'Unless you'd rather I leave you outside in the rain?'

Royce's frown deepened, and he crossed his arms. 'I'd rather sleep anywhere than in your house.'

Stephen was not about to tolerate such insolence. Knocking against the coach's door, he ordered the driver to stop.

'What are you doing?' Emily looked horrified.

Stephen opened the door. 'Be my guest,' he invited the boy. The rain splattered against the coach door, the wind blowing it in their faces. At the sudden rush of cold, the infant began howling, her face pinched with surprise.

There was just enough fear, just enough uncertainty to keep Royce frozen in his seat. When he didn't move, Stephen shut the door.

'Understand this. I will not abide rudeness in the presence of your aunt. You will respect my authority and obey.'

The boy's face filled with fury, but he managed a nod.

'Good.' Stephen signalled for the coachman to drive on. But one matter was certain—he and the boy were now clear enemies.

Chapter Five

A good wife should never purchase inferior in-gredients. It is better to be frugal and save pennies wisely, in order to procure the very best cream and butter. Others judge a cook by her confections…

—Emily Barrow's *Cook Book*

Stephen unlocked the door of the town house. He'd only been inside on one other occasion, when he'd decided to buy the property. It had belonged to a debt-ridden widower, Lord Brougham, who was more than happy to sell it. Though it was by no means a large residence, it was located near Mayfair in an excellent part of town.

A musty odour blanketed the hallway, and the entire house needed a good airing. Stephen rested his hand on the staircase banister, while Emily ushered the children inside.

She held the infant close to her cheek, while Royce clung to her skirts. Though she held her posture perfectly straight, her eyes were dimmed with exhaustion. How had she managed the two-day journey with no one but his coachman and the wet nurse as escorts?

'There isn't a nursery,' Stephen apologised, leading them up the stairs to one of the bedchambers. 'And obviously there are no servants at the moment.' He ventured a rueful smile. 'I hadn't expected to move my belongings for another day or two. It wasn't prepared for your unexpected arrival.'

'It will do nicely.' Emily ventured a smile, the first peaceful gesture he'd seen. 'Can you help me find a place for Victoria to sleep?'

They went upstairs, and Stephen located two wingback chairs in one of the guest chambers. He pushed them together to form a bed for the baby. Victoria rubbed her eyes, fussing and arching her body.

Emily stroked the baby's back and dropped a kiss upon her niece's cheek. When Victoria would not quiet down, she reluctantly passed her over to Anna to nurse. Royce removed his shoes and dived into his own bed, burrowing under the coverlet as though trying to shut out the world. For a moment, Emily envied him, wishing that she could just as easily forget all that had happened.

Her husband was a stranger to her now, a man who felt nothing at all towards her. It was like a waking nightmare, to love someone and to be forgotten afterwards.

Would he expect her to share his bed tonight? She stiffened, wanting to avoid it for as long as possible. How could she share the most intimate act with him when he cared nothing for her?

Memories of his kiss, of the way he'd laid her down like a cherished bride, pulled at her heart. He'd made love to her, joining their bodies until she lost herself.

It was how she felt now. Lost.

He'd come riding into her life, and it had taken only days for him to rekindle the feelings she'd buried. Didn't every girl want to believe in fairy tales? He'd made one happen for her.

But it had been a lie. And the only way to shield her heart was to stay as far away from him as possible.

Whitmore held out his hand to her. She forced herself to take it, even though she didn't want to. His palm warmed hers, and he led her into the parlour, where he had lit a small fire.

The flames warmed the room, and Emily stood before the hearth, drying her clothes. Stephen sat down in a chair, watching her. His intense gaze embarrassed her.

'Why are you staring at me?' She held herself erect, gripping her arms until her fingers left marks on the skin.

'I'm wondering if we really are married.' He leaned forward to watch her. His hair still held droplets of rain, and one trickled down his cheek toward a sensual mouth. She tried not to remember the tantalising darkness of his kiss.

'Of course we are married.' She kept her eyes upon him, though his intense look made her skin flush.

He stood and walked behind her to close the door. Her damp clothes chafed against her skin, making her even more uncomfortable. Alone in the darkness with only the glowing coals upon the fire and a single candle, she felt more vulnerable than ever before.

'Do you have any other living relations?' he asked. 'If I were not your husband, who would look after you and the children?'

'My uncle. He lives in India.' Tension hovered, and with every second that passed, she grew more nervous. Why was he asking this? Was he planning to send them away?

His grey eyes turned thoughtful. 'I've sent word to the local parishes across the Scottish border. If you have lied to me—'

'I haven't.'

Despite her claims, he would not accept the truth.

She doubted if even the scrawled signature upon the marriage certificate would satisfy him.

His gaze grew heated and he lifted her hand to his cheek. The rough edge of his face needled her fingers. 'Did I share your bed?'

She fumbled for a lie, anything to keep him from touching her. 'You left me a week after our wedding. We—we never consummated the marriage.'

'Then it will be easy to get an annulment.' He lifted her palm across his lips, and she fought the protests rising.

A razor of hurt slashed at her heart. She'd given herself to him, and he'd forgotten about it. The most wonderful night of her life had meant nothing to him.

'Unless you want to share a bed with me?' His dark voice grew compelling, seductive.

Emily closed her eyes to gather her composure. She hated the way her body came alive, the way she wanted his embrace. His mouth, hot and urgent, had haunted her ever since their wedding night. And she was deathly afraid that she would succumb to his desires.

'If you have need of a woman, you can go to your mistress,' she said. The very thought of the unknown woman infuriated her, for it brought back memories of Daniel's death.

'I've already told you. I don't have one. Patricia and I haven't been together since last autumn. And why would I need a mistress when I have a wife?'

She wavered, unsure of whether to believe him. But even if he hadn't been with his mistress, she wasn't about to share his bed again. Not if he was going to leave her.

'I won't be a wife to you. You'll have to force me first.'

His grey eyes hardened like the barrel of a gun. 'I would never force a woman.' There was fury in his gaze, and Emily struggled to remain rooted where she was.

Stephen reached out and, with a single finger, brushed the tip of her breast. Instantly, her nipple hardened beneath the cold fabric. He used his finger to toy with the cockled nub and a hot aching grew, deep inside her womanhood. Her breath shuddered as he rubbed excruciating circles of heat.

Memories of loving him came flooding back. Her hands fell upon his shoulders, reaching for him.

Then abruptly he drew away. Emily could hardly breathe, her body completely aroused by just a single touch.

'Goodnight.' Stephen turned and walked away, leaving her behind.

She wanted to cry out in frustration, but she knew he had done it deliberately. He had intended to stimulate her senses, to make her beg him for more.

She was made of stronger stuff than the Earl could ever imagine. Let him try to make her feel passion. She would never forget the way he'd abandoned her and Daniel.

Never would she let him close to her again.

Stephen avoided Emily over the next week, only offering brief conversation now and then. They slept in separate bedrooms, and he was careful not to spend too much time with her. It would be easier to send her back, if they remained distant to one another.

But then the proof of his marriage arrived.

That morning, Stephen read the letter at least seven times, still in disbelief. Married. It was irrevocably true, every word that she'd said.

His father had invited him to a late breakfast, and Stephen brought the letter with him to Rothburne House. He picked at the toast and jam, his mind spinning.

He and Emily had wed in mid-February, a few miles past Gretna Green. His messenger had verified that he had seen the marriage recorded. Emily possessed a copy of the certificate, which she'd shown him earlier in the week. Everything was in order.

And yet he felt uneasy.

It opened up even more questions that begged for answers. Why had he married her? Had he wanted to protect her? Had he cared for her? Or had it simply been an act of defiance against his father?

There was no doubt she fired his blood, but could there have been more between them? Each time he tried to reach back, the memories of her remained clouded. Only events from ten years ago came to mind.

Emily, climbing a tree, laughing when he'd tumbled from a branch. Her blonde hair spilling over her shoulders, dry leaves tangled in the ends.

The way she'd felt in his arms, so many years ago. Those memories were easy to grasp while the new ones remained veiled.

He re-read the letter another time before his younger brother entered the dining room. Though they looked alike with a similar build, Quentin's hair had a touch of auburn in it. His brother also tended to wear more flamboyant clothing, today's selection being a bottle-green frock-coat with a tartan waistcoat and tan trousers.

'I didn't expect to see you here,' Quentin said, by way of greeting. 'Mother said you'd returned.'

'Father invited me for breakfast. I suppose he's

planning another lecture. He mistakenly believes that I haven't aged beyond the tender years of six.'

'At least you have another place to live.' Quentin's face tightened with distaste.

Stephen sensed the trouble behind his brother's words. 'In other words, you have no money.'

'Not a bean.'

The last time he'd seen his brother, Quentin had been sent away to Thropshire, one of the lesser estates. When was it? He struggled to think.

January. It had been the end of January when Quentin had gone. Another piece snapped into place, granting him a brief sense of satisfaction.

'When did Father allow you to come home?' Stephen asked. Quentin's spending habits had always been a source of contention, and the Marquess had removed his youngest son from temptation's way.

'Two days ago.' Quentin helped himself to shirred eggs garnished with mushrooms. He added a large slice of ham to the plate. 'But you're the black sheep now, aren't you?'

'As it would seem. You heard nothing of my marriage, I take it?'

'Not a word.' Quentin set across from him and dived into the food. 'But it won't be long before all of London knows.'

Stephen picked at his own plate, finding it difficult to concentrate. It should have been easy, sliding back into his old life here. Instead, the void of memories distracted him. So much had changed in just a few short months.

'What about Hannah? Is she still off at school?' He hadn't seen his sixteen-year-old sister since last winter.

'She is. Mother is already scheming potential matches for her.'

The idea of any man laying hands upon his innocent sister appalled him. 'Hannah isn't old enough for that sort of thing. She hasn't even had her first Season.'

'Our mother has great plans, don't you know. She's still upset that you didn't let her mastermind your own marriage.'

Stephen grimaced at the thought.

'Is she that terrible?' Quentin teased. 'Your wife?' At Stephen's confusion, he added, 'You're looking rather glum.'

A mild way of putting it. Glum didn't begin to describe his frustration and annoyance.

'There is nothing wrong with Emily.' Except that he had no idea why he'd married her. In the past week, he'd spent little time at his town house, and Emily seemed to be avoiding him.

He set his fork down, absently rubbing the back of his neck. The prelude to a headache edged his temples. 'Were you there, the night I—' He almost said disappeared, but amended it. 'Left? Or were you still at Thropshire?'

Quentin poured himself a cup of tea. 'I was. Mother dragged me back to London for a few days. She seemed to think you were going to announce an engagement to Miss Hereford and demanded that I be there.' His brother smirked. 'You certainly destroyed Father's plans for the next Chesterfield dynasty. When Mother mentioned your marriage at dinner last night, I thought he might need smelling salts.'

It didn't seem to matter that Stephen had never once given any indication of interest in Miss Hereford. But both of their parents had wholeheartedly embraced the prospect of matchmaking. He pitied the poor woman for what she must have endured.

'Tell me more about what happened at Lady Carstairs's ball,' he said, switching back to their earlier topic.

'You speak as though you don't remember it.' Quentin's gaze narrowed.

His brother was far too perceptive.

'I don't.' Stephen poured a fresh cup of tea, adding cream. 'It's like a cloud blocking out the past few months. I know what happened in January, and I remember waking up at Falkirk a few weeks ago. Everything in between—February,

March, April, even part of May—seems to be lost. I'm trying to find out what happened.'

Quentin rubbed his beard, nodding. 'I'll do what I can to help. What do you want to know?'

'Anything.' He needed a starting place, somewhere to begin filling in the past.

'You were looking for your wife's brother, Lord Hollingford.' Quentin's face turned serious. 'When you couldn't find him, you left. That was the last we heard. Father sent word to all the estates, but you were nowhere. Mother worried that something terrible had happened.'

As far as Stephen was concerned, something terrible *had* happened. The vicious scars upon his chest weren't imaginary wounds. And yet he had no memory of the pain. Whether they were caused by common thieves or something more sinister, he couldn't know.

'Someone tried to kill me,' he admitted. 'And I don't know why.'

A flash of concern crossed Quentin's face before his brother mustered a teasing smile. 'I'll admit, I've wanted to murder you a time or two. It isn't so difficult to imagine.'

'I'm being serious.'

'I could be the heir to all of Father's fortunes,' Quentin continued, gesturing grandly at the breakfast table.

'You are welcome to them.' Despite Quentin's joking claim, Stephen knew his brother far preferred the freedom of being the youngest son. He himself had known the same independence until the tender age of nine.

'But there's something else.' Glancing at the door, Stephen removed his coat and loosened his shirt. 'Would you have a look at this?' He revealed the tattoo beneath his collar.

At the sight of the symbol, Quentin's face grew concerned. 'What is it?'

'I haven't the faintest notion. Do I look like the sort to get a tattoo?'

Quentin laughed, but there was uncertainty in it. 'Perhaps you lost a wager.'

Stephen righted his clothing. 'Perhaps.' But he didn't think so.

'It looks like an Oriental language. Possibly Sanskrit.'

Had he travelled to India? Or had his attackers done this to him? He intended to question several sources until he learned what it meant.

Stephen turned the conversation to a more neutral topic, and his brother filled him in on the details of a particular shipping investment.

'The profits from the cargo were stolen,' Quentin admitted. 'We lost a great deal of money.'

Stephen fetched a pen and paper and began taking notes. 'What was the name of the ship?'

'*The Lady Valiant.*'

At the mention of its name, he'd hoped for a flash of memory. Something that would point toward answers. Instead, there was nothing. He recalled making the investment, but nothing struck him as different from any other ship.

He began jotting down names of the investors who might have been affected by the loss. The Viscount Carstairs was one. Himself.

And Hollingford. Emily's brother had also invested in *The Lady Valiant*. Somehow, he was sure of it.

'Not another of your lists,' Quentin protested. 'This is a conversation, not the time for record-keeping.'

'I prefer keeping detailed records.'

'And thank heaven you are the one to manage the estates and not me. If I had to keep the number of lists you did, I should run screaming from the room.'

'You would simply pay the bills and not worry about where the money came from,' Stephen said.

'Precisely. As long as you and Father support me, that is all that matters.' Quentin raised his cup of tea in a mocking toast.

Stephen frowned. In two lines he estimated profits and potential losses for each ship, the numbers flooding through him. Thank God for something familiar. Orderly and logical, just as he liked them.

He sobered, thinking of how Emily had taken his orderly life apart. He'd never expected to be responsible for a wife and children. Not so soon.

'Does anyone else know I am married?' he asked suddenly, looking up from his list.

'Possibly,' Quentin replied. 'The servants do talk. But Father wants to keep silent about it.'

If the servants knew, then it was likely that half of London knew it by now. Stephen grimaced, just imagining the gossip.

'We've been invited to attend Lord Yarrington's musicale,' Quentin continued. 'And I'd best warn you—Miss Hereford will be there.'

Stephen held back a curse. If he attended the musicale, he couldn't possibly avoid Miss Hereford, despite his desire to do so. She had somehow fallen into the belief that he cared for her, after he'd done little to encourage her. He blamed his parents for leading her astray.

If he arrived with Emily at his side, it would put matters to rest, however. He tried to envision his wife in a ball gown, her fair hair twined with pearls and diamonds.

Instead, it was easier to see her with hands covered in flour, an apron tied about her waist. Tight desire wound up inside him, for he didn't remember making love to her. Was she still a virgin? Had he known the softness of her body beneath him?

Right now, finding out the answer to these questions seemed far more important than meeting with his father and enduring another lecture.

'If you will excuse me.' Stephen rose and bid his brother farewell.

Before he could leave, James Chesterfield entered the dining room. The Marquess raised his hand to halt Stephen. 'Where are you going?'

He met his father's accusing eyes. 'I am returning home to my wife.'

'She cannot remain your wife for long,' his father warned. 'Emily Barrow is an unsuitable Countess. Her family was penniless, and after that scandal—'

'Enough.' Stephen's fists curled, and he kept a firm rein upon his temper. 'It is a legally binding marriage. You can do nothing to end it.'

He didn't know why he was defending Emily or the impulsive move he'd made. A part of him still questioned whether he even wanted her to remain at his side. He hadn't decided whether he wanted a wife at all.

But he'd never let his father know it.

The Marquess's face turned crimson with fury. 'If you persist in this farce, I shall cut off your funds.'

'I have investments of my own.' Stephen kept his voice deliberately calm.

'Do not presume to introduce her into society as your wife. I am warning you. You will not like the consequences.'

'Good day, Father.' Stephen brushed past the Marquess, not bothering to hide his anger. James thrived upon authority and controlling others. He enjoyed arguing, which was precisely why Stephen refused to engage in it. It was his own small measure of power.

For now, he would return home to Emily. Now that he knew the truth, there were decisions to be made.

Namely, whether or not he wanted to remain married to her.

Emily strolled into Mayfair, enjoying the late morning sunshine. She had coerced two footmen into escorting her instead of her maid, preferring their protection. Stephen had left her funds to purchase whatever she might need, but the coins made her uncomfortable.

It reminded her of how much she was bound to him. He truly had rescued her family, providing for Royce and Victoria. Her throat constricted, even as she stiffened her spine.

She'd been so distraught when the men had delivered Daniel's body. And then to learn that her husband was missing, after being seen last with his mistress… It had been too much to absorb.

She'd lived in a state of numbness, not knowing whether Stephen was alive or dead.

I won't let myself fall under his spell again.

She'd been weak before, letting herself dream of him. She knew better now, didn't she? He hadn't loved her. He didn't even remember her.

Don't cry, don't cry, don't cry.

She gripped her reticule, pushing her mind back to the task at hand. Today she would go shopping. The children needed new clothes, and it would take her mind off her worries.

Stopping in front of Harding and Howell, she decided to purchase fabric for Victoria and Royce. The vast array of costly goods was dizzying.

She glanced behind her, to see if anyone had followed them. *Don't be silly*, she told herself. Whoever had attacked her at Falkirk wanted Daniel's belongings. He wouldn't come after them in London.

Even so, it made her uneasy to think of it. Best to carry out her shopping and return home as quickly as possible.

She had worn her faded black bombazine gown, the one Stephen despised. In the simple dress, she was less noticeable than the more affluent women and a less likely prey for thieves. She had ordered the footmen to maintain a discreet distance while she visited the linen draper's.

Upon her return, she passed by rows of stores with glass displays. Confectioners made her stop to inhale the luscious scent of fresh chocolates, while the hot, delicious smell of pastries emerged from a nearby bakery.

But it was the fruiterer who tempted her the most. Behind a large glass-window display of pineapples, figs and grapes, she spied baskets of fresh strawberries.

Oh, heaven. She imagined a strawberry shortcake, with the juicy berries soaking into the cake, topped with cream. It took only moments to part with the coins. Likely she could have gotten a better price at Cheapside, had she bargained for them. But she wanted to remain in Mayfair, where it was safer.

Outside, she strolled along the street before a male voice shouted a warning. Horses reared, and her footman pulled her out of harm's way.

The driver gained control of the animals and pulled the carriage to a halt. Someone bumped against the footman and he knocked Emily into a patch of heavy mud.

'Beggin' your pardon, mum.' The footman turned crimson with shame, assisting her to her feet while the other servant collected her purchases.

A well-dressed gentleman emerged from the

carriage. 'By Jove, it's Miss Barrow. What on earth are you doing here?'

Emily flushed as she saw Mr Freddie Reynolds. Freddie was a peacock of a man, but he had a decent heart. A few years ago, Daniel had permitted her to attend a family gathering at the Reynolds's country estate. Afterwards, Freddie had made Emily the object of his worship. He never failed to send tokens of his affection, a gesture that touched her though she had no feelings toward him.

'Miss Barrow, I am devastated by the accident. No amount of apology is sufficient. Please allow me to escort you home.'

'No, really, I'm fine.' She tried to brush the mud from her gown, but it only made matters worse.

'My dear Miss Barrow, it would delight me no end to have you call me Freddie.'

Emily was not at all comfortable with the idea. It would only start up the courtship again. And now that she was married, he needed to understand that it would be entirely inappropriate. 'Mr Reynolds, thank you, but I…believe you may not have heard of my recent nuptials. I am Lady Whitmore now.'

'Really.' His voice transformed, with a hint of irritation. 'I hadn't heard.'

Her cheeks flooded with colour, and she managed a nod. 'Yes. Well, I really must be going now. It was a pleasure to see you again.'

Freddie's face became a mask, as if he'd suddenly realised the angry tone. 'Forgive me. It was rather a shock to hear of your marriage.'

With a warm smile, he opened the door to his barouche and bowed. 'Please. Since it was my fault you fell into the mud, you must allow me to make amends.'

'I do not wish to soil the inside of your carriage.' She held up her muddy skirts. 'I had best walk home. It isn't far.'

'I wouldn't hear of it.' Freddie removed his cloak and set it upon the seat beside him. 'There. Your throne awaits, my lady fair.'

He wasn't going to relent. Though she winced at the thought of leaving muddy traces upon the fine cloak, another refusal might cause greater embarrassment.

She decided there could be no harm in accepting a ride, so she gathered up her purchases. One of the footmen rode with the driver as an escort, while she sent the other man home.

'Seeing you again does my heart good,' he insisted. 'The beauty of your perfect face and the sweetness of your deportment have haunted my dreams.'

Emily nearly choked. She doubted if her

husband would call her deportment sweet. And hadn't Freddie heard her when she'd said she was married? What were his intentions?

'May I call upon you?' he asked. 'I would cherish the pleasure of your company.'

Oh, no. That would not do at all. Not with her marriage in such a delicate state. The Earl would be furious.

'Mr Reynolds, I am flattered, but as a married lady, I—'

Freddie held up his hand. 'I shall adore you from afar, then. Say no more, my lady.'

It wasn't quite what she'd wanted, but she let it go. Freddie's smile faded into melancholy a moment later. 'I should like to extend my sympathies upon the loss of your brother.'

Emily nodded. It still hurt to think of Daniel. 'Thank you.'

'Were you—with him, the night he—?' Freddie's voice broke off, embarrassed at his question.

Emily shook her head. 'No. I found out when they brought his body, and…' She broke off, not wanting to remember. 'I'd rather not speak of that night.'

'I understand. Please forgive me for asking.' He coughed and then asked her for directions to the house.

Emily told him the way; within minutes, they

had arrived. Freddie's expression darkened at the sight of her residence. 'It is my fervent hope that your husband brings you the greatest happiness, Lady Whitmore. And if ever there is a time when you need a friend, please know that I am your most humble servant.'

He meant that, and so she exhaled a sigh of relief. 'Mr Reynolds, it really has been good to see you again.' She smiled and offered her hands.

Freddie gave her an answering smile, and as he helped her from the carriage, his gloved hands lingered upon hers. 'The pleasure was mine, dear lady. I shall waste away, pining for the moment when I may look upon your face once more.' He gave a gallant bow, tipping his hat. Emily watched him ride away, the packages still clutched in her hand.

It really was not good form to laugh, though she longed to release the mirth bubbling inside her. Emily bit her lip instead while the footman opened the door for her. 'My lady, may I take those for you?' he offered.

'I will see to them, thank you.'

Inside, she found the Earl pacing the floors, a scowl lining his aristocratic face. 'Where have you been?' He didn't wait for a reply before he frowned at the condition of her clothing. 'What happened? You look as though you've been rolling in the gutter.'

'Perhaps I have,' she retorted. 'Forgive me while

I change my gown.' His arrogant tone annoyed her. Did he think she'd fallen in the mud on purpose?

'Where is your maid?' Stephen asked. 'She can burn that wretched dress while you bathe.'

'She is busy taking tea with the Queen.' Emily thrust her purchases into Stephen's arms. 'I took the footmen instead.' She pointed towards the kitchen and held out her packages. 'Put these away, if you do not mind.'

Stephen handed her purchases to the waiting footman and followed her upstairs.

'Where do you think you're going?'

He reached over and turned the doorknob. 'We need to talk. Alone.'

'We can talk in the parlour, like most civilised people do.'

'I don't want the servants listening to our conversation.'

The blood within her body grew cold. If he wanted to be alone with her, the conversation would not be a good one. He would annul the marriage. Or divorce her. All the breath seemed to leave her lungs at the thought of being alone again. She hadn't forgotten the hard times they'd endured before.

Was there a way to convince him to…keep her as his wife? As she followed him up to his bedchamber, she fought against her instincts to flee.

His hand captured hers, warm and imprisoning. She kept her eyes wide open to hold back the emotions threatening.

He claimed he no longer had a mistress. And so far, he'd given her no reason to believe otherwise.

Let it not be true that he was with another woman. Let it all be a lie.

But perhaps she would never know. He couldn't remember the truth of what had happened. And though she should presume his innocence, there were too many shadows upon their impulsive wedding.

He'd never claimed to love her, though he'd courted her over the course of a week. He'd vowed to take care of her and her family, and it had been enough. But oh, she had hoped for more. She'd wanted him to love her, wanted to bring back the heady excitement from their adolescence.

It hadn't happened. Even after the brief ceremony was done, she'd noticed his distractedness. After another week, he'd returned to London, claiming he would find Daniel and bring him home.

Stephen closed the door behind her. 'Sit down.'

But the only place to sit was upon his bed. She wasn't about to let that happen. 'I'll stand.'

'I owe you an apology,' he began. 'I accused you of lying. But you were right about our marriage.'

She didn't answer, her heart still uneasy at the

thought of what he would do. Surely he would end their union.

'Did you remember anything about it?' she asked.

'No.' He neared her, resting a hand upon the wall. Emily forced herself not to move away, to let him say what he wanted. 'But I don't know if we should remain together. It isn't fair to you.'

She lowered her gaze, feeling so terribly alone. She wouldn't beg. No matter what happened.

'Say something, Emily.'

'What do you want me to say? That I never should have married you? That I was foolish to follow my heart instead of understanding that this was nothing but an arrangement?' A tear broke free, and she pushed it away, furious with herself.

'I didn't want to hurt you.'

She wanted to strike out at something, to release the hot anger at herself. 'I know it.'

He reached out to touch her shoulder. The gentle brush of his hand brought shivers to her flesh. It was meant to bring comfort, nothing else.

She could smell his shaving soap, and a part of her wanted him to draw nearer. Another part chided her for her weakness.

He doesn't want you.

But she found herself saying, 'We should begin again.'

'What do you mean?'

'I mean that we don't even know each other. You're already wanting to end a marriage that never started.'

Her words silenced him. He didn't respond, seemingly turning over her suggestion in his mind. The opportunity was here, laid bare.

She took a step forward. Then another, until she stood so close, they were almost in an embrace. He reached out and took her hands in his. 'Come with me tonight, then. My family was invited to the Yarrington musicale.'

The very thought of entering society as a Countess made her knees tremble. She couldn't. The Marquess and society would cut her to shreds.

'I—I can't go.' She fumbled for an excuse. He would never understand her fears. 'It isn't proper for me to attend a public gathering. I'm still in half-mourning.'

'You're hiding.'

Of course she was, but she wasn't about to admit that. 'This is about respect for my brother.'

'You've mourned him long enough.' He drew her closer, resting his hands upon her waist. 'If you truly want to try again with our marriage, you cannot remain at home.'

'I don't have a dress. Everything I own is black.'

'I'll order a gown for you and have it sent to the house.'

'It's not possible to make a gown so soon,' she protested. 'No seamstress alive could do it.'

'With enough money, any gown can be altered to suit you. Or you can borrow one of my sister's. Hannah has gowns she's never worn.'

Though his offer was kind, she rather be flayed alive than attend the musicale. If she ever chose to set foot in society, it would be on her terms, not his.

But Whitmore appeared unaware of her fears. Instead, he touched her cheek. 'I will see you this evening.'

Chapter Six

Whilst a man's heart may be governed by his stomach, a woman's heart is far more complex. A recipe for female happiness would require far more than cake...
—Emily Barrow's *Cook Book*

'Look at these, my lady!' Her maid Beatrice carried several large boxes with her, beaming as she entered the parlour. She laid the boxes upon a velvet-upholstered sofa, bubbling with youthful excitement. 'The master asked me to help you prepare for the musicale tonight. He sent you these.'

Emily reached inside the largest box and found a modest gown of lavender tarlatan. White panels of intricate scalloped lace overlapped the skirt and the waist ended in a sharp vee. The sleeves would leave her shoulders bare, while the bodice consisted of swags of more white lace. As she ran her fingers across the delicate fabric, she remembered how she had once sewn a gown such as this. She had remade her mother's gowns, bringing up the hemline. As the years passed, she'd lowered the hems until she gained the height of a young woman. It had been so long since she'd had a new gown of her own.

This was a gown worthy of a princess. And yet, the idea of wearing it out in society made her feel sick. She'd never had a Season, didn't have the slightest idea what to do.

Opening the other boxes, Emily found silk stockings, petticoats, gloves and, last, a pair of fine kid-leather slippers.

Never had Emily owned a pair of shoes as fine as these. She touched the leather, marvelling at its buttery softness. Unable to resist the urge to try the shoes on, she was dismayed to find them too small. She could squeeze her feet into them, but the toes pinched her.

It was just as well. She could not attend the musicale, even wearing the new dress. It would only make Stephen more aware of her shortcomings. The Earl mistakenly believed that if he gave her a beautiful dress and brought her into his world of affluence, she would metamorphose.

He might clothe her in the gowns of a future Marchioness, but inside she felt like the same

Emily. No one would forget her family's scandal, and they would be quick to shun her.

And what if she happened upon Lord Rothburne? The Marquess despised her.

No, that wasn't right. She was nothing more than dust to him, something to be ignored and swept away. Only now, when she threatened his son's future, was she a danger.

It chilled her to think of it. She didn't fear her husband, but Lord Rothburne's power was far greater than Stephen's. If she attended the musicale, she would invoke his fury.

She dismissed her maid and sat down, touching the gown with her fingertips.

If only…

Stephen drummed his fingers against his thigh as the Yarrington daughters performed, one by one. He'd waited for over two hours, and there was still no sign of Emily.

He never should have agreed to go on without her. She'd claimed she needed more time to alter the gown he'd sent. Now it seemed she had no intention of coming.

He was barely aware of Miss Julia Yarrington's rendition of Mozart's Sonata in C upon the piano, to great applause. Beside him, Miss Hereford sent him a quiet smile. He didn't return it. Though he would not humiliate her by avoiding her, he could not encourage her thoughts of marriage.

And what of his own? Emily claimed she'd wanted a new beginning. He'd invited her to attend, as a way of becoming better acquainted. Though she'd protested the event, he'd believed she would succumb to the temptation of a beautiful gown and an evening spent together.

Instead, she'd lied, remaining at home. This wasn't the old Emily he was used to. She'd never been frightened of anything, a daredevil who had called him a coward when he wouldn't climb upon the roof of her father's house.

When had she changed? What had happened? He'd heard the whisperings about the family scandal surrounding her father's death. But had that truly been enough to transform her?

The Yarrington sisters paused for a brief intermission, and he thought about returning home. He wanted to understand why she'd married him, why he'd married her.

What if he kept her as his wife? Could they make the most of their arrangement?

He rose from his chair, intending to find out. Before he could leave the room, the Marquess blocked his path.

'The evening has not yet concluded.' A threat underlined his father's tone.

'I am aware of that,' Stephen said, keeping his voice low. 'But I have decided to return home to my wife.'

'This impulsive wedding was a ridiculous idea. William would never have done something so foolish without thinking of the consequences.'

'You are right,' Stephen conceded. 'William would have married any woman of your choosing.' His brother had been the perfect son, the perfect heir. Stephen was the disappointing spare.

His father suddenly brightened, his attention focused behind Stephen. 'Miss Hereford. Are you enjoying yourself?'

The young woman blushed, lowering her eyes and dropping into a curtsy. 'Yes, my lord. I am enjoying the evening very much.'

The silent message from his father said: *This is the woman you should have married. She is far more suitable.*

Stephen bowed politely and made his excuses to Lady Yarrington. With a tight smile to his father, he departed.

Emily's maid was unlacing her corset when he opened the door to her bedchamber. He didn't apologise for the intrusion, but ordered the maid, 'Leave us.'

The maid fled, closing the door behind her.

Emily tried in vain to cover herself. It did no good—he could easily see the curves of her breasts rising from the chemise, the small waist accentuated by the corset. Thankfully, she had already discarded the heavy crinoline and several petticoats.

With each step closer, she took another step back. 'What are you doing here? This is my room. You shouldn't be here.'

'I am your husband. I've every right to be here.' His tone came out sharper than he'd intended, but he was completely distracted by her state of undress.

Her golden hair was unbound, falling to her waist. He needed to touch it, to wind it around his wrist while he captured her sweet mouth.

'Why didn't you come tonight? I thought you wanted to begin again.' He reached out to her waist and turned her back to him, revealing her partially unlaced stays. Slowly, he drew another lace out.

'I did—I mean, I do.' She lowered her chin, and he moved her hair over one shoulder while continuing to unlace her. 'But I couldn't go.' She shuddered at his touch, trying to push his hands away.

He lowered his mouth to her nape, not really caring how discomfited she was. He wanted to taste her skin, to know if it was as soft as he suspected. At the touch of his lips, gooseflesh rose upon her skin.

'Stephen, please don't,' she whispered. But he kept her trapped, using his mouth to trail a path of heat across her collarbone.

'Why did you stay behind?' he asked again.

'I told you. I'm in mourning for my brother.'

'I don't believe you.' He removed the corset until only a thin layer of fabric covered her body. His groin tightened, and he pulled her against him, caressing her with the cloth between them. He spanned her waist with his hands, tantalisingly close to her breasts. 'What are you afraid of?'

'I cannot be your wife in front of everyone else.'

'Why?'

'Your father won't allow it. Did you forget that he tossed us into the streets? What do you think he would have done tonight? Embarrassed both of us in front of everyone, that's what. I would never humiliate you like that.'

He didn't want to admit that she was most likely correct. But he would have defended her, if anyone had dared to insult her. It was a matter of pride. 'You should have had more faith in me.'

'There's nothing you could have done.' She turned to face him. 'It's better for everyone if I just stay out of society.'

'Then you've already given up, haven't you?' There wasn't any hope of starting over again if she wasn't going to try. He wouldn't force her to stay here against her will. 'I'll send you back to your brother's home with the children. We'll end the marriage and go our separate ways.'

'There's nothing for me to go back to. I can't take them home again. There's hardly any furniture, and I need money for food. Royce has outgrown his shoes and he needs a new coat. Victoria will need dresses, soon enough.'

'I'll give you the funds you need.' When she remained silent, he prompted, 'Isn't that what you want? Your freedom and a means of caring for them?'

'Yes. No. I don't know.' She hugged her waist, fighting back tears.

'Which is it, Emily?'

She shook her head and crossed the room to the door. With her hand resting on the knob, she said, 'I want you to go.'

Her indecision made him question what it was she truly meant. He needed to break through her shield of indifference, to find the Emily he'd known before.

He pulled her mouth to his, kissing her with all the pent-up frustration he felt. Her lips were slightly open, and he stole her mouth, tasting the warm sweetness of her.

Unexpected desire blasted through him. She tried to push him away, but within seconds her hands relaxed until she was kissing him back. It was the innocent kiss of a woman who had not been kissed in a long time. The years seemed to fall away until she was once again the young girl he'd practised kissing in a stable. Only now, he held a woman in his arms. A beautiful woman who made him lose his sense of reason the moment he touched her.

He drew her against him, moulding the base of her spine while his body ached to claim her. He cupped her firm backside, pressing himself against the juncture of her thighs.

He broke away, his pulse pounding. He wanted to strip her bare and make love to her. He'd been married for nearly four months now, and he'd never seen his own wife naked.

There was something inherently wrong with that.

'Do you still want me to go?' he breathed against her mouth. Her face was flushed, her breathing unsteady.

'Please. I can't bear it when you touch me.'

He let her go, unable to say anything. He didn't bother to look at her before he slammed the connecting door shut.

Wrenching tears broke from her, and she longed to throw something at the wall. It was just like before. He'd driven her into wild need, her body aching to receive him.

If there were any way to leave London, to hide elsewhere, she'd depart immediately. Being here with Whitmore only dredged up the feelings she'd tried to bury.

He wanted to share her bed. She knew it, and even now, she wanted to feel his body against hers. But it would be wrong. To him, it would be nothing more than an act of passion. While to her, it would reopen the past.

More than ever, she wished she'd never married him. She hadn't thought about the future, of what it would mean to be a Countess. She would have to host parties, to assume the duties of being his wife. His position demanded more than she could manage.

She didn't want to leave him, though it was the right thing to do. He deserved a better wife than she could be. With a sigh, she finished undressing and donned a nightgown.

And tried not to think of her husband in the next room.

Stephen tossed back a second brandy, his fury rising. What did she mean, she couldn't bear his touch? Her rejection cut him deeper than the knife wound across his ribs.

Tonight she had proved that she didn't want him at all. As a husband, he was failing miserably.

What would it be like to have her willing? He pictured her full of fire, as passionate as he. Long ago, it had been that way between them.

A flash of memory took hold, and he saw a vision of Emily laughing, pulling him into her arms. Only it wasn't the young girl whose face he saw.

It was his wife's face. A recent memory, one he'd never seen before. He fought to hold on to it.

In the vision, he saw a breathtaking woman who hugged him while snowflakes fell from the sky, lightly dusting her hood. One flake fell upon her lashes, drawing his attention to her brown eyes. Her cheeks were bright from the winter chill, her smile welcoming.

While icy snow dampened his shoulders and hair, she tempted him with the spicy darkness of her kiss. He could see the love in her eyes, feel it from the warmth of her embrace.

A cloak of guilt shadowed the memory. He'd given her the security of his name, an arranged marriage to bring her out of the hardships she was enduring. In return, she'd helped him to break free of his father's interference. She'd asked only one thing of him—-that he would find her brother and bring him home again.

And in that, he'd failed.

The memory faded, and Stephen stood from the

chair. Quietly, he opened the adjoining door to his wife's bedchamber. She had extinguished the candle, and the room was too dark for shadows.

'Emily?' he whispered.

There was no reply. But really, what had he been expecting? She didn't want him to touch her, that was clear.

What he didn't know was whether or not to remain married to her. The simplest solution was to let her go. She deserved a second chance at happiness.

She intrigued him in a way no woman had before. He couldn't reconcile the two parts of her—the headstrong adolescent girl and the fiercely protective woman who was terrified of society.

And then, it struck him why. She hadn't received the necessary training a Baron's daughter deserved. She hadn't had the years of dancing lessons and etiquette. From her own mouth, she'd confessed her reluctance to embarrass him in public.

What if he gave her what she'd been missing? Gowns and jewels, and the tutors she needed. Perhaps it would atone for what he'd done.

In the morning, he would send word to the dressmaker's and the jeweller's that Emily was to be outfitted with the finest clothing and pearls to befit her rank.

And as an afterthought, he decided to order new shoes for Royce and clothing for the baby.

Chapter Seven

*Always use the greatest care when preparing
a meal for your husband. Most do not take
kindly to raw meat, burned about the edges.
But all may be forgiven with a kindly smile
and a sweet deportment...*
—Emily Barrow's *Cook Book*

The first flowers arrived on Monday. Stephen disregarded the bouquet of yellow tulips. On Tuesday, lilies of the valley were delivered. Wednesday and Thursday brought daisies and lilacs. By Friday, a dozen roses had arrived in every shade from the most delicate pink to the deepest ruby red.

They weren't from him.

Exactly what was going on? Had his wife entertained gentlemen callers while he was visiting his family? He'd like to find the fop who'd sent them and wrap the long-stemmed roses around the gentleman's neck.

He discovered Emily arranging the blooms in the parlour. She wore the dress he hated, the black one with the frayed hem. Why she insisted on wearing the Dress of Martyrdom when he'd presented her with a dozen dresses in every colour, he didn't know. At the very least she could wear a gown that didn't look as though it had been dragged through the ashes.

'Who sent these flowers?' he asked.

Her cheeks flushed. 'Freddie—I mean, Mr Reynolds did.'

Freddie Reynolds? Damn it all, now what was that little weasel doing in London? He'd never liked Reynolds, even when his father had invited their family to share in a country dance or an evening supper.

Short of stature, and dressed like a dandy, Reynolds was the sort of man to charm the ladies with the most inane conversations about hothouse flowers and the latest fashions.

Stephen glanced at one of the cards.

Your eyes are like the bluest ocean,
Your lips as red as my heart's blood
Which I would gladly shed
If I could but walk upon the same grains of sand
Tread upon by your feet.

'Good God. What is this?' he demanded. The verse held some of the most ridiculous lines he'd ever read.

'Poetry, I believe.' Emily sniffed one of the red roses before arranging it with the lilies.

'Your eyes aren't blue. They're brown,' he pointed out. 'He's got it all wrong. And what's this bit about sand? We're in London, not the Sahara.'

Had his wife lost her mind? *He* had sent her pearls and the finest ballroom attire that she still hadn't worn. But when Freddie Reynolds sent her flowers, she was beaming and snipping the stems?

Not likely.

'You will not accept flowers from other gentlemen.' Stephen grabbed the bouquet of roses and tossed them in the hearth. When the blossoms scattered with a soft thump, he felt better.

She sighed. 'I told him I had married you. But I've known Freddie for years, and he's not a man who abandons a courtship easily. I suppose you don't remember him from when we grew up together.'

'I remember him well enough, and if he doesn't cease this nonsense, I'll shove the damned roses down his throat.'

Emily shrugged. 'It's harmless, really. He told me…what was it? He is adoring me from afar.'

'What utter rubbish.'

'I think it is rather flattering, actually. Like an unrequited lover, pining for me.' She picked up another bloom and adjusted it in the vase. 'And, I suppose I should keep my options open.'

'What do you mean by that?'

'In case you divorce me, and I decide to remarry.'

'Absolutely not.'

She broke the head off one of the roses and laughed, reaching up to tuck it behind his ear. 'Jealous?'

'Not at all.' It was then that he realised she'd been teasing him. Though it eased him to know it, the idea still disgruntled him.

He could certainly buy nicer flowers. And the poetry…ye gods. Shakespeare or Tennyson would be far better.

Stephen removed the offensive flower and threw it on to the fire. He took savage pleasure in watching it wither up into flames. 'I could do far better than him at courting.'

'I wouldn't know.' She went back to arranging the flowers while he tried to make sense of that remark.

'I courted you before I wed you, didn't I?'

She shook her head. 'Not really. You escorted me home, and we talked. I made you ginger biscuits.'

'I must have brought you a gift.'

She held up her wedding ring. 'You gave me this.'

It didn't seem possible that he'd made such a momentous decision without even courting the woman he'd married. 'In all the time I spent with you after I returned to Falkirk, I never gave you anything?'

Her face turned pitying. 'It wasn't that long, Stephen. Only a week before you proposed. Then after we got married, you left me for London.'

'I don't understand. Why did you marry me if I gave you nothing except the ring?'

She lifted her shoulders in a shrug. 'You rescued me from the life I had. And we were friends, once.'

'Once?' She spoke as if that were no longer the case.

'It's been a long time, Whitmore.'

He took her hand and raised it to his lips. Pressing a kiss against her skin, he held her fingers far longer than was proper.

She eyed him with suspicion. 'And just what are you doing?'

He gave her a wicked smile. 'Courting you.'

Victoria grasped Emily's fingers and, with a determined look, trod her first wobbly steps around the parlour. Emily helped the baby balance, unable to stop her smile when Victoria reached out to clutch the sofa. There was something magical about watching a child learn to walk.

A light knock sounded at the door. 'Yes?' Emily turned just as the door opened.

Harding held out an enormous array of flowers. Roses, gardenias, hyacinths, tulips and every spring flower imaginable had been stuffed into the arrangement. It was easily three times the size of any bouquet she'd received thus far.

Once again, they were from Freddie. The ostentatious display made her uncomfortable, as though he were trying to prove his affections. More wasn't necessarily better.

Emily pointed to the piano, for it was the only surface large enough for the monstrosity. 'Please set it down over there, Harding.'

'There was, er, another arrangement of flowers for you as well,' Harding added. The young butler folded his hands behind his back and rocked to his heels.

Another one? Was Freddie trying to purchase every flower in London? She held back her irritation, wishing that the man would just stop. Like a clinging vine, he was smothering her.

'You may put it beside the other flowers. If there's room.'

Harding bowed and returned a moment later with a simple posy of daffodils tied up in white ribbons. The bright yellow of the cheerful flowers lifted her spirits.

They were from her husband.

Touched by their simplicity, Emily fingered the

blooms. He'd plucked a daffodil for her once before, when she was but a girl. And, oh, the scolding he'd received from his mother. She smiled, remembering it.

It hadn't mattered then that he was an Earl. He'd been the first boy she'd kissed, the one she'd fallen completely in love with. He had been everything to her.

And now? She didn't know. A note of melancholy drifted over her, trouble encircling her spirits. She'd made such a mess of things.

Abruptly, she seized the large arrangement and threw the blooms onto the hearth. To encourage any other man was wrong. She was using Freddie to make Whitmore jealous, and that wasn't fair.

Victoria began to fuss, so Emily picked her up and took her to Anna. The nursemaid opened her arms for the infant, and Victoria snuggled in, her eyes drooping shut. Emily's heart caught at the sight of the baby. Victoria and Royce were her children now. She would do anything for them.

Their futures rested on her shoulders, and she had to ensure that they were cared for. Her nerves wound tighter. What if the society gossips resurrected the past scandal? They would not have forgotten her father's unspeakable death. She couldn't bear it if those secrets were revealed.

The matrons would ply her with questions, questions she didn't want to answer. She was desperately afraid of the glittering world far beyond her reach.

Playful shouts of delight sounded from Royce's room. When Emily reached the door, she peered inside. The room was in shambles. Her nephew had stripped his bedding from the mattress, and one sheet dangled from a sconce upon the wall, perilously close to the gaslight.

'Ahoy, matey!' Royce yelled as she walked inside. His ash-blond hair flopped across his shining brown eyes as he bounced on the bed. 'I'm a pirate!'

'Are you?' She reached up to untie the sheet, which had served as a main sail. 'Do not tie these to the gas lamps, sweeting. Else you'll set fire to us all.'

A gleam of mischief crossed his face. 'I could burn the house down. Then we'd be rid of the Earl.'

'Royce, how dare you say such a thing?' she scolded. 'Without the Earl, we'd be out on the streets.'

'But I want to live on the streets,' Royce said, slashing his shoe toward Emily, as though it were a sword. 'We could rob the rich and give to the poor,' he said. 'We'd be outlaws like Robin Hood.'

'And where would you sleep at night?' she asked, taking the shoe away.

'I'd sleep in a tree, of course.'

'In the park?'

He bobbed his head again, falling backwards on to the bed, his arms and legs spread wide. Emily began picking up the tin soldiers where Royce had left them strewn about the room. One of the soldiers had numerous dents and barely resembled its original condition. She scooped the rest up and set them upon a desk.

The battered leather shoes suddenly caught her attention. Royce had used one as a sword while he wore new shoes made of fine leather.

'Where did you get these?' she asked.

'They were here this morning upon my trunk.' Royce snatched a pair of tin soldiers and began a mock fight. Then he paused a moment. 'Didn't you buy them?'

Emily shook her head.

'It must have been the elves,' Royce said, nodding. 'Like *"The Shoemaker and the Elves"*.'

Emily gave a pensive smile at his mention of the story. 'Yes, you're right. It must have been the elves.' Yet she knew who had bought them—Stephen. He really had been listening to her last night.

The thoughtful deed meant more than she wanted to admit. Tucking the sheets back on to the bed, she said, 'The day is lovely. Shall we go for an outing?'

Royce beamed at her suggestion and within moments helped her put the room to rights. After donning a cloak and bonnet, she asked Harding to send along a footman as a chaperon.

As Royce struggled with the buttons, she noticed that once again, the 'Elves' had gifted the boy with a new coat. The black wool was perfect for a boy of his size, and Royce put on a new straw hat. He beamed at her as he showed off his finery.

'Where did these come from?' Emily asked.

Royce grinned. 'Harding bought them.'

The butler shook his head discreetly, and Emily tried to push away the feeling gathering around her heart like a warm blanket.

She followed Royce outside, wondering how to reconcile herself to this new side to her husband.

Stephen set his spectacles to one side, rubbing his eyes. He'd spent hours poring over ledgers in his study. Endless accountings of estate figures, harvest yields and rents paid lay before him in his own familiar script.

He had a sudden urge to set it all on fire.

He hadn't come any closer to finding a reason why anyone had attacked him. There were no records about *The Lady Valiant*, regarding any sort of stolen profits. It was as if the ship had never existed.

He wanted to believe that the scars he bore were nothing more than the result of common cutthroats. But the tattoo on his neck and the missing memories suggested otherwise.

Start at the beginning, he thought. He struggled to remember why he'd left London at the beginning of February. Had he merely needed an escape from his life here? Had he run away, intent on avoiding his father's interference?

Or had Hollingford asked him to come? He hadn't considered that possibility before. Emily's brother was an acquaintance, not a friend. But Stephen suspected that perhaps there was a connection between himself and Hollingford.

Closing his eyes, Stephen struggled to remember. He inhaled slowly, trying to keep his mind relaxed. He allowed his imagination to wander, and it settled on an older memory.

It had been winter, and a sixteen-year-old Emily was shoving handfuls of snow down his collar. He'd thrown her down upon the hillside, both of them laughing as he smashed snow into her own face.

Emily had flung her arms about him, and his body had risen to her innocent call. For a brief, frozen moment, her lashes stilled, her amber eyes catching him with a look of intensity. Her hands had paused upon his shoulders, waiting for him to lean down.

He'd kissed her cool mouth, a touch that had left him reeling. When she pulled back, she smiled.

Then she'd shoved his face back into the snow, until his own clothes were sodden.

The vision faded, and though he fought to reach one of the hidden memories, he couldn't grasp anything.

Was Emily still the same laughing girl he'd known? He couldn't deny that he wanted her in his bed. He wanted to peel away each layer, each petticoat and chemise until he found the woman beneath. She had a passionate nature, one that heated his blood just to look at her.

But she was afraid. Although she had thanked him for the flowers and the gowns, she seemed apprehensive, as though she expected everything to vanish.

Perhaps it would. Everything about their union had been a mistake. And he still didn't know if there was any chance of a successful marriage between them.

Chapter Eight

Mix two eggs, 8 oz sugar, 1 tablespoon melted butter, 4 oz milk, 12 oz all-purpose flour, 1/2 teaspoonful bicarbonate of soda, 1 teaspoonful cream of tartar, 1 tablespoonful of marmalade, 1 tablespoonful orange juice, and a little of the grated rind in an earthen bowl. Bake in two round shallow pans, but take care not to stoke the fire too hot...

Recipe for orange cake from Emily
Barrow's *Cook Book*

A knock sounded at the library door. James Chesterfield disliked being disturbed, especially when he'd asked the servants to keep everyone out.

'Enter,' he commanded.

Frustration curled up within him at the sight of his son. He had tried reasoning with Stephen, tried to make his son understand why he could not remain married to Emily Barrow. She knew nothing of the *ton*, never would, despite her birthright. One had to be bred among the Quality to understand. As a woman who had never been presented before the Queen, she was utterly unsuitable. But Stephen did not grasp the true meaning of duty, not the way he should.

James feared it was too late. The scandal of divorce far outweighed the scandal of wedding someone inappropriate.

His son remained standing, an inconvenient behaviour because it forced him to look up. 'I came to ask you about the night I left London, several months ago.'

James stood to meet his son eye to eye. He leaned upon the desk, taking some of the weight off his bad leg. 'When? The time in February when you ran off to marry an improper young lady? Or when you disappeared from the Carstairs's ball, two weeks later?' He made no effort to conceal his irritation. His son had a duty to behave in a manner befitting the family name.

'The second time,' Stephen responded. 'I have no memory of what else happened that night when I was hunting Hollingford. Did you hear anything about it, after I disappeared?'

'No. Nor do I care about the reasons why you shirked your responsibilities.'

'A man tried to murder me,' Stephen stated. 'And unless you help me to understand what happened that night, it could happen again.'

James didn't believe it. Likely his son had run into thieves, if anything. 'Exaggeration does not become you.'

At that, Stephen pulled up his shirtwaist and revealed a deep red scar. 'Does this look like an exaggeration?'

The jagged wound struck him silent. Stephen continued talking about theories of what had happened and talk of danger, but James heard none of the words. He saw only the physical evidence that someone had tried to take another son away from him.

The emptiness of loss shadowed him as he thought of William, his first-born. A father was not meant to outlive his son.

Although Stephen had done a tolerable job as the new heir, James had never been close to his rebellious second son. A part of him wished that it had been William who had disappeared, only to resurface months later.

With effort, he forced his thoughts back to the present.

Stephen added, 'I intend to lure him out into the open so I may deal with him. I want your help. And—' he narrowed his gaze '—I expect you not

to meddle with my marriage. I would rather concentrate on finding my enemy than worrying about
what you've done to Emily.'

Steeling himself, James set down his pen. 'What
do you wish to know?'

'Tell me of my dealings with her brother. I
remember Hollingford in a vague manner, but aside
from his gambling habits I don't recall much.'

Hollingford had been a desperate man who'd
spent most of his hours at the gaming tables instead
of earning a proper living. 'The man had no
money,' James answered. 'Disgraceful, really, the
way he gambled every penny.'

'Did he owe any debts to me?' Stephen asked.

'If you loaned him money, it was charity.
Hollingford never repaid any debts.'

'I'll have to bring him out into the open, then,'
Stephen murmured.

'Who?' Obviously he was not speaking of
Hollingford, since the man was dead and buried.

'The man who's trying to kill me.'

James let out the breath he'd been holding.
Words of protest died upon his lips, smothered by
denial. 'What do you intend to do?'

'I want to host a ball and invite all of our
acquaintances,' Stephen said. Grimly, he added,
'If someone is trying to murder me, I want him to
know I am back in London.'

James did not care for this tactic at all, though he recognised the logic. 'What if he tries again?'

'I will be ready.'

In the past three nights, her husband had seemed more distracted than usual, as though he had lost interest in the courtship. It was starting to bother Emily, and she wished she could somehow make things better between them. But she was afraid Whitmore would turn her away.

She sometimes woke up in the middle of the night, reaching towards the other side of the bed. The sheets remained empty and cold. The connecting door between their rooms might as well have been made of stone.

This afternoon, her fingers itched to do something, so Emily retreated to the kitchen. The familiar warmth of the space and the aroma of freshly baked bread relaxed her.

She shooed the servants out and gathered ingredients for a pound cake, creaming butter into sugar and cracking each egg into the bowl. With each broken eggshell, her uneasiness grew.

Though her husband behaved as though nothing were wrong, that they were friends, it was starting to wear upon her nerves. They shared meals and conversation together, speaking about dull topics such as the weather. And what she really wanted to know was when he would kiss her again.

If he would kiss her again.

Her arms ached from beating the eggs, but she continued. Now, more than ever, she was beginning to believe him, that he hadn't been with his mistress. Not in all the weeks since he'd returned had he spent time with another woman. The realisation embarrassed her.

She'd blamed him for her brother's death, but that wasn't fair. He couldn't be with Daniel at every moment. And though she might never know what had happened that night, she needed to let go of the anger or else their marriage would not have a chance.

The door to the kitchen opened, and the Earl entered. His dark hair was combed back, his cheeks shaved. He rested his palm against a wall, watching her. 'I thought I might find you here.'

Her knuckles curled over the wooden spoon as she met his gaze. 'What is it?'

His eyes watched her with interest. She became aware of just how warm the kitchen was, and moisture dampened the back of her neck. He was eyeing her the way he might stare at a piece of chocolate before he devoured it. 'Do I need an excuse to speak with my wife?'

Emily cracked another egg into the bowl, the shells crumbling under her shaking hands. 'N-no.'

Honestly, what was the matter with her? She hadn't meant to add that egg. To cover her flustered mien, she focused on blending the batter.

'Ten eggs?' he remarked, glancing at the fallen shells. 'I suppose we should fashion a hen house in here somewhere.'

'It's for a pound cake,' Emily said. 'And—and— I've some strawberries, too.'

'I look forward to tasting them.'

The deep timbre of his voice suggested he had other items in mind for tasting. Emily beat the eggs so fast, it was a wonder she hadn't scrambled them.

Stephen reached in to taste the batter. His finger disappeared inside his mouth, and, God help her, it only reminded her of his sensual kiss. She imagined his mouth capturing hers, asking her to bend, to yield to him. Closing her eyes, she wrenched her attention back to the cake batter.

He dipped his finger into the mixture again and held it out to her. 'Want a taste?'

The idea of licking his finger made all the blood rush to her face.

'No, thank you.' She beat the helpless batter, even though it was already well blended.

'Too bad.' His finger disappeared into his mouth. Oh, he knew exactly what he was doing, embarrassing her in such a manner. She turned her back, but he trapped her against the table.

His hands surrounded her waist, and he drew her against his chest. She could smell the spicy male scent of him, of shaving soap and pine. With his fingertips beneath the curve of her breast, her breath hitched.

'I'm hosting a ball tomorrow night, at Rothburne House.'

She was completely distracted by his physical presence. His words hardly meant anything, but she managed to nod. 'All right.'

'It isn't necessary for you to attend. You may remain here, instead.' He released her, and she turned her attention back to the cake.

'Oh.'

It wasn't necessary? Confusion filled her up inside, and she didn't know what to think. This ball was a second chance, after she'd declined the previous invitation, staying home during the musicale. Why wouldn't he want her there?

Her stomach tightened with fear. Maybe he didn't want anyone else to know about their marriage. But, no, that wasn't possible. She'd lived here for nearly a fortnight, long enough for London to be well aware of her presence.

Did Whitmore still want her to remain his wife? She didn't know his intentions. He'd sent the flowers and numerous dresses that she hadn't worn. But perhaps that was only to compete with

Freddie Reynolds's courtship, not because he cared for her.

If she were a better wife, she'd attend the ball at his side. She'd face her fears and fight for their marriage. But she hadn't the slightest idea of how to conduct herself. It was impossible.

Not to mention he didn't want her there. No, that wasn't right. He'd said it wasn't necessary for her to attend. But what if she did come?

Think, Emily. There was only one day. Not enough time to prepare herself. Her mind whirled while she began pouring the batter into greased pans. She picked up a tin of candied almonds for the cake tops, and Stephen filched one. Out of instinct, her hand covered his to stop him.

He halted, amusement in his eyes. 'Am I not allowed to have one? Or did you want it for yourself?'

His teasing startled her, and she didn't protest when he slipped the candied almond into her mouth.

The act made her body tighten, made her want to drag him closer for a kiss. But no, she couldn't do that.

Emily dried her hands on her apron, masking the sudden pulse of trepidation. Self-doubts multiplied, making her wonder why she was even considering this. The Earl couldn't know how cruel society could be. As his wife, she would be scrutinised and found wanting.

'I'll see you at dinner.' He took a handful of candied almonds with him, striding away. Another dinner, another conversation. Another empty bed.

Emily closed her eyes. It was time to take a chance on what she really wanted.

Chapter Nine

In a cup, mix the juice of one orange with 1 tablespoonful of lemon juice. Fill the remainder of the container with cold water. Strain through a cloth and put on to boil. Add 1 tablespoonful of corn flour, wet in cold water, and then the rind of half an orange. Stir till thick, then cook in a pan over hot water for ten minutes...

Filling for orange cake from Emily Barrow's *Cook Book*

Someone was following him. Though it seemed an unreasonable suspicion with all the hired hacks and other carriages out on the road, Stephen couldn't shake the heavy premonition.

The evening air held the coolness of spring, and a low fog obscured the road. Flickering gas lights shone through the mist, while another carriage drew closer.

Stephen ordered his driver to take them past Grosvenor Square towards Hyde Park. The man was one of the newer servants sent over from Rothburne House, but he was a friendly enough sort. They rode in silence for half a mile, perhaps more. No one appeared to be traversing the same path. In time, he was forced to admit he'd been wrong. When they reached an area towards the lake, the carriage slowed to a stop.

'Take me to Rothburne House,' he told the driver.

Instead of following his command, the driver turned. A revolver glinted, and out of raw instinct, Stephen threw himself sideways. The shot exploded inches from where he'd been sitting.

Damn. Survival instincts took over, and he seized his assailant's arm. Muscles burned and perspiration slid down his forehead as he held the revolver away. The man's finger eased across the trigger, ready to fire.

Stephen slammed his head against the man's nose, twisting his body to gain control of the weapon. Caught off balance, the driver lurched forward, and Stephen fired the gun. Blood spread across the driver's shirt, and he slumped against the door.

With the dead man lying at the bottom of his

carriage, Stephen stilled. Though outwardly he showed no sign of exertion, his pulse pounded with energy. He had hoped to draw his enemy out, and now it had happened.

He felt no remorse for the assailant's death. Nor did he believe this was the same man who had tried to murder him back in February; likely the man was only a hired killer.

He had been careless, too trusting, and it had nearly cost him his life. Stephen withdrew his handkerchief, wiping the blood from his hands.

He had achieved his goal, it seemed. His attacker now knew he was back in London. And he wanted Stephen dead.

Emily searched the glittering ballroom for a sign of her husband. She wore the lavender gown Stephen had given her. Though it was old-fashioned, Emily liked its simplicity. Her maid Beatrice had laced up her corset until Emily could barely breathe, but the results made her waist tiny. Her petticoats and crinoline swelled the skirts around her like the gown of a princess. The effect was lovely, except for the shoes. She had nothing else to wear, save the dancing slippers Stephen had purchased for her. The terrible shoes pinched her toes like a vice, yet she had no choice but to suffer.

Beatrice had taken charge of her hair, placing white roses behind the knot. She had loosened stray tendrils to float around Emily's nape.

For a moment, Emily hesitated at the door, afraid of disgracing herself by either fainting or heaving up the contents of her stomach. She had arrived separately from Stephen, since she hadn't told him of her intention to attend. Her maid Beatrice stood behind her as a chaperon.

Already she was breaking so many rules of good manners. She should not have come without her husband at her side. But then, did anyone know she was married? She wasn't certain whether Whitmore had revealed it to anyone. Heaven knew, the Marquess would not speak a word of it.

Nervously, she twisted her gloved hands, terrified of what they would say. She recognised Phillips, the footman who had tossed her into the streets some weeks ago. Across the ballroom, she saw Lady Rothburne signal to the footman, shaking her head slightly. The acerbic feeling in Emily's stomach worsened as Stephen's mother did not come forward to welcome her.

The footman stared at her as though she were an unwanted insect. 'I do not believe you were invited, madam.'

Emily struggled to maintain her composure. A deep flush suffused her cheeks, and she forced herself to hold her head high. *Do not let them see your feelings.* 'I am the Countess of Whitmore,' she murmured. 'I rather think my husband would be offended if you deny me entrance, don't you?'

Where was Stephen? She looked around, but did not see him anywhere. Without him as an escort, she felt the curious eyes of the crowd watching her. A wall. She needed a wall where she could blend into the background and await her husband.

Then, a voice rescued her, calling out, 'Miss Barrow! By Jove, it is *such* a delight to see you again.'

Freddie Reynolds beamed as though she'd handed him the sun on a silver platter. He wore a crimson frock-coat with a matching waistcoat and black trousers. His brown hair was combed back, his beard and mustache neatly trimmed. In spite of herself, Emily couldn't help but answer his smile.

'Oh, forgive me, I mean Lady Whitmore. I was hoping to see your face again, and now that I have, my life holds meaning again.'

His exaggeration made her smile. In all honesty, she replied, 'Mr Reynolds, it is a pleasure to see you as well.'

'But where is your husband? Surely you did not come alone?'

Before she could fabricate an explanation, he waved his hand. 'You must allow me to be your escort, if I may be so bold. It would be an honour, Lady Whitmore. Quite an honour.'

'Well, actually, I—'

'Did you like the flowers I sent to you?' he interrupted.

Before she could answer, he held up a hand. 'No. If they were not to your taste, I would rather not know.'

'They were lovely, but really, you shouldn't—'

'Perfect! I shall see to it that you receive more this week. I intend to woo your heart yet, my lady.'

'Not now, you won't.' The sharp voice of the Earl intruded. Her husband wore all black, except for the snowy white cravat that was impeccably tied. Tall and imposing, he eyed Freddie with distaste.

Freddie jerked with surprise at the Earl's unexpected arrival, but he quickly recovered. 'Lord Whitmore. It has been many years, has it not?'

'It has. Thankfully.'

Emily couldn't believe Whitmore's rude behaviour, but at last she managed to find her voice. 'Reynolds, I am grateful for your offer, but now that my husband is here, I do not need an escort.'

With a false cough Freddie said, 'Lady Whitmore, perhaps I should be going.'

'An excellent idea,' the Earl interrupted. 'You might take an extended tour of the Continent starting in the morning while you are about it. And stop sending flowers.'

After Freddie beat a hasty departure, Emily snapped open her fan, suddenly feeling not at all sure she should have come. 'That wasn't very nice.'

Whitmore didn't seem to care. 'Why are you here?' His voice was edged with anger, cutting down her fragile courage.

She stared at one of the potted plants, taken aback by his tone. 'You said that it wasn't necessary for me to come, not that you didn't want me here. Should I return home?'

'We'll talk first. Meet me by the stone urns near the garden.' Stephen did not wait for a response, but strode away. Emily glanced around, and saw several women staring at her, whispering.

She didn't know what stories were coursing about London, but she was sure their gossip was not at all flattering. One of the matrons stared at her, before turning her back.

It cut her apart to see it, but she didn't know if her father's scandal or her marriage was the reason.

She waited endless minutes, trying to avoid notice. She ordered her maid Beatrice to maintain a slight distance. Eventually, she made her way to the terrace and located the stone urns Stephen had mentioned. The light fragrance of verbena drifted from the soil.

Her husband emerged from the shadows, gesturing. Emily moved forward until she stood beside a tall boxwood. From the ballroom, no one would see her speaking to the Earl.

Stephen lowered his voice so as not to be heard. 'Someone tried to kill me tonight just before the ball. He took the place of my driver. I left his body near the park and alerted the authorities.'

Though he had tried to push the memory out of his mind, it lingered. The smell of gunpowder, the slick feeling of a man's lifeblood, haunted him. It intensified his need to understand why his life was in danger. And he regretted bringing Emily into this.

Emily said nothing at first, her silence damning.

'Did you wish they had been successful?' he enquired darkly.

'I thought the danger was over,' she admitted. 'Why would anyone want you dead?'

'I have my suspicions. It may be related to a shipping venture I made several months ago.'

'What does that have to do with the attacks?'

'According to Quentin, the investment was a loss. All of the cargo profits were stolen. Your brother was involved with the shipment,' he continued, 'along with Carstairs and myself.'

A guilty look crossed Emily's face. 'Daniel did nothing wrong.'

'I did not accuse him. But the man who murdered your brother is likely the same person who is trying to kill me.' There were too many connections, and he needed to fit the pieces together before the man could strike again.

'I thought you said he was dead.'

'I don't think it's over. He was a hired man, likely.'

Emily took a deep breath, her eyes cast downwards. 'Someone attacked me as well. Just after you left for London, while I was at Falkirk.'

Her words stunned him. He listened to her explanation, while his mind seized the logistics.

Why hadn't she told him sooner? Damn it all, he was her husband. He had the right to know when someone was threatening those under his protection. 'Did he hurt you?'

'No. He pushed me down, but that was all.'

His fist clenched, along with his gut. 'Did you speak of this to anyone else?'

'Only you.' For a long moment, she stared at him, her face bathed in moonlight.

'I cannot protect you if you keep holding secrets from me.' His voice sounded more irritated than he'd intended. 'You should have told me about the attack.'

'I've told you everything I know.'

He didn't believe her. She'd waited this long to confide in him—what else did she know? Getting her to let down her defences, to trust in him, would take time.

If that was what he wanted.

He studied her for a long moment, her blonde hair silvery in the moonlight. She wore the strand of pearls he'd given her, and the beads rolled against the curve of her breast.

'Why are you looking at me that way?' she whispered.

He palmed her waist and pressured her toward the darkness. Without a word, he pulled her against the boxwood. Her breath hitched, her shoulders rising. With a single finger he twisted the pearls, drawing them taut against her bodice. Her mouth opened with a hush, her nipple tightening as he drew the strand over the hardened tip.

'I think you know why.' His own breathing grew harsh, but he continued the game. Teasing her. Tempting her. Leaning close, he kissed the softness beside her ear. She shivered, balancing her gloved hands upon his shoulders.

'Whitmore, anyone could see us—'

'Stephen.' He brushed his mouth against her cheek, moving toward her lips. 'You used to call me Stephen.'

Before she could protest again, he stole her mouth, tasting the sweetness of the girl she'd once been. And the woman, the innocent beauty who was slowly captivating him.

'You kissed me like this when we were younger,'

he breathed, grazing her breasts with the pearls once more. 'Do you remember?'

'In the stables,' she whispered. 'I was sixteen.'

When he tried to kiss her again, she stepped back, tangling her hair in the hedge. 'Do they know about our marriage?'

'Probably,' he acceded. 'I've heard the gossips whispering.'

'And what will you tell them?'

'Nothing. It's best if they think I didn't want a wife. It will protect you from my enemies.'

Had he struck her in the face, it couldn't have hurt any worse. 'You want me to go back inside, letting them think I trapped you into marriage?' She disentangled herself, stepping free of his embrace. 'No, thank you.'

It wasn't what he'd meant at all. 'Just stay away from my side for tonight, Emily. Let me worry about the details.'

'And that very small detail that you *chose* to marry me?'

'It would not be for long,' he added. 'You need only keep out of society until the man is caught. After that, I'll reveal everything.'

'Don't make me a part of your games.' She took another step backwards. 'If you won't admit the truth, then don't cast the blame upon me. I'd just as soon keep our marriage a secret, if it's all the same to you.' She strode away from him, not looking back.

But it was far too late for secrets. Stephen let her go, biding his time. Tonight, when they were alone, he would make her understand. And perhaps then, he'd demonstrate exactly what he wanted.

Her. In his bed.

Emily danced with Freddie and endured the fascinated glances of strangers. Beneath her stiff posture and masked smile, she was drowning inside. Her husband was tearing her apart, one moment making her feel hope, and then another pretending as though she didn't exist.

She did want Stephen back in her life, but not as his convenient wife. Not as a woman cast aside whenever he chose. If he could not acknowledge her, she didn't want him at all.

Her dance with Freddie ended, and she curtsied. After he departed to pay his respects to their hostess, she stood among a group of young ladies drinking lemonade. Beyond polite responses, they made no further conversation. It was as though the Marquess had branded her as an Untouchable. Likely the only reason she had not been removed from the ballroom was due to her avoidance of the Earl.

A bitter taste rose in her mouth at that. Stephen had said it was to protect her, and maybe it was true. His earlier revelation had shaken her. A man had tried to murder him, and she hadn't let herself think about it. If that man had succeeded, she truly might have been widowed this night.

A coldness slid beneath her skin, like a blade. She didn't want to think of being alone again. Not after all that had happened.

She stumbled into Lady Thistlewaite. The grey-haired matron wore a saffron silk gown that made her look like a large dandelion.

'Miss Emily Barrow. What a surprise to see you here.' Lady Thistlewaite studied her with eyes eager to pry out the story. 'Or should I say, Lady Whitmore?' Her tight smile gleamed, as though she had claimed the greatest gossip prize in all of London.

'Lady Thistlewaite,' Emily responded, with a light nod. She remembered her mother speaking of the dowager Viscountess. One of the worst rumour-mongers in society, she could shred a woman's reputation faster than a pair of scissors.

'After your father's tragedy, why, I can hardly believe you are here. Such a scandal, it was.'

Emily said not a word, but the barb had struck true. Lady Thistlewaite knew it, too.

'And you captured the Earl of Whitmore.' The Dowager shook her head in disbelief. 'I can hardly believe he would marry a woman such as yourself.'

'We are married, yes.' Though the matron was fishing for more information, Emily refused to give it. She searched the ballroom, desperately hoping for an escape.

'Well…' Lady Thistlewaite paused, her gaze sweeping over Emily. 'I do not wish to be the bearer of bad news, but I know you would wish to put the stories to rest. They are saying that you were caught in a compromising position, and the Earl wed you to preserve your family honour.'

'That is not true at all.' Emily clenched her gloved hands around her fan, trying hard to hold back her temper. 'And I do not believe our marriage is any of your business.'

Lady Thistlewaite stared back as though Emily had slapped her. With a huff of air, she continued on. 'My dear, I was only trying to help. You will want to put the stories to rest, won't you? And how can we ever do that, if you do not tell us *why* the Earl married you?'

'You may ask him that yourself.' Her voice came out harsher than she'd intended, and she tried in vain to escape the matron.

'Now, now. There is no need to take offence.' Lady Thistlewaite placed herself directly in Emily's path. 'But I did think you should be warned. No one else would dare to tell you about this, but I should hate for you to have your feelings hurt. It would be a most awkward situation.'

Emily wasn't sure which of her feelings hadn't already been crushed by the woman's meddling gossip, but she waited.

'The Earl intended to wed Miss Hereford, long before he met you. This scandalous marriage has quite broken her heart.' Lady Thistlewaite fanned herself, tut-tutting. With a sly smile, she added, 'You really shouldn't have chased after the Earl, you know. It speaks of ill breeding.'

Emily gritted her teeth. 'I never chased after him.'

Lady Thistlewaite offered a sympathetic smile. 'It isn't obvious to you, I'm sure. But the Earl has kept his distance from you tonight, hasn't he?'

Emily squared her shoulders. 'He did not know I planned to attend.'

The matron shook her head sadly. 'My dear, it is obvious that you are in desperate need of advice. For instance, the dress you are wearing is far too plain for a gathering such as this. Lavender does not flatter your complexion. You look as though you are wearing half-mourning. Blue or rose would be better.' The woman lowered her voice as though she were about to impart the secrets of warfare. 'I have a dressmaker whom you should see.'

Emily counted to five before answering. Losing her temper in front of the Whitmore household would not precisely endear her to the Marquess. She managed to nod. 'Thank you. Now, if you'll excuse me…'

Lady Thistlewaite lifted her hand. 'Call upon me in the morning, and I would be happy to advise on proper attire. You are the daughter of a Baron, after all. Since your departed mother cannot be here for you, I shall take it upon myself to instruct you. It would be my Christian duty to help you understand the necessary etiquette.' With a pat to Emily's shoulder, the matron sailed across the ballroom to find another target.

Emily said nothing, tears pricking at her eyelids. From the stares directed toward her, no doubt most people sided with Lady Thistlewaite in believing that Stephen was embarrassed by her.

She watched her husband mingle with the guests and dance with simpering young misses vying for his attention. He didn't look at her once, though she watched his every move.

It hurt to see him pretending as though she didn't exist. She went over to stand by the refreshment table, wishing she had never opened her mouth.

'I suppose you think to worm your way into our lives,' a deep voice said.

It was her father-in-law. And here, she had thought the evening could not get much worse. He had come to finish her off and pick his teeth with her shattered feelings.

Lovely. Just what she needed.

The Marquess of Rothburne stood just behind her, behaving as though he weren't speaking to her. But Emily knew the remark was aimed at her.

'You do not like me,' she said, keeping her voice calm. 'I am aware of it.'

'You don't belong here. You could never dream of being a part of us.'

'Hide the silver, is that it?' Emily turned to face him and offered the Marquess a serene smile. 'Let me reassure you. I am not after Stephen's wealth or his title.'

'You've blinded him. Like a common lightskirt, aren't you? He isn't thinking clearly.'

'I am not a lightskirt, my lord. Nor will I be a target for your ill-aimed insults. I am the Countess of Whitmore. You had best get used to it.'

It would have been a rather grand exit, had her hands not been shaking so badly she had to set down her glass of lemonade. No matter what, she promised herself she would not cry.

Especially when she caught the triumphant smile of Lady Thistlewaite.

Chapter Ten

When roasting beef, consider using only salt and pepper. Often, the greatest cooking success may be found in keeping the dish simple.
              —Emily Barrow's *Cook Book*

Emily held a plate of lemon cream moulded in the shape of a fish. She gripped the plate hard enough to stop her shaking hands. Tonight had been beyond her worst nightmares. Not only had she endured the stares and gossip, but her own husband had abandoned her. Would this evening never end? She cast a longing look towards the door, hoping to escape.

Perhaps if she kept her back to the wall, slowly moving towards it, she could slip away without Stephen noticing. She started moving, but when she passed by one of the corridors, she heard the sound of weeping.

She really shouldn't interfere. It wasn't her

business, after all. But someone else was having an even worse evening than her own, by the sound of it.

The noise led her to a young woman, who was crying just beyond the ballroom. She wore an ice-blue satin gown trimmed with matching ribbons and her hair was a lovely auburn colour. Glittering diamonds sparkled about her neck.

'Are you all right?' Emily asked.

The young woman tried to dry her tears, nodding and waving her hand. 'I am fine.' When she looked up and saw Emily's face, her expression transformed into hatred. 'Oh. It's you.'

Emily didn't know what to say, but the woman continued. 'Lady Thistlewaite warned me that you were here.'

'Have we met?' Emily asked, uncertain of why the girl would hate her so much.

'I am Lily Hereford.'

Ah. The spurned maiden. 'I am Emily.' She deliberately did not give her surname, because really, what was the point in upsetting the woman further? Already the young woman knew that she had married Stephen.

'You stole Lord Whitmore from me,' Miss Hereford said in a tight voice. 'We intended to marry.'

Whether or not it was true, the woman certainly believed it. Emily held her dessert spoon like a weapon, even as Lily advanced upon her. 'This is not a battle between us,' she said. 'If you have a quarrel, you should discuss it with Lord Whitmore.'

'You should be ashamed of yourself,' Miss Hereford reproached. 'How can you call yourself a lady, believing he would want someone like you? What did you do? Place yourself in his bed?'

Emily bristled and she bit back a nasty retort. Oh, she could easily argue with Miss Hereford, but this was a battle of words not worth fighting.

'I believe there is nothing left for us to say to one another.' With a curt nod of farewell, she returned to the ballroom.

She found an empty spot against a wall and took deep breaths to calm herself. Miss Hereford's spiteful words were meant to wound her, to make her doubt herself. And they raised questions she'd tried to avoid.

Why had Stephen married someone like her, when there were so many other women to choose from? Miss Hereford embodied everything a lady should be: graceful, poised and completely at ease in society.

Emily, on the other hand, couldn't imagine feeling comfortable amongst the *ton*. Like vultures, the society matrons would peck at her confidence until there was nothing left.

Stephen crossed the ballroom, heading straight

towards her. And though he made brief eye contact, he did not speak to her, as if she weren't there. His deliberate evasion made her anger rise another notch.

He kept walking past her, until she heard his voice saying, 'I believe the next dance is mine, Miss Hereford?'

No. He was not going to dance with that woman, was he?

As they passed, Miss Hereford shot her a triumphant gaze. Emily was sorely tempted to throw something. The dessert spoon, perhaps, or better, the remains of the lemon cream.

But then, a true lady would never cause such a scene in public, even if it did wound her feelings, watching them.

That was it. She wasn't going to stay a second longer. Stephen swept Lily into a dance, but even as he moved her across the ballroom, his gaze remained upon Emily. She recognised the look of possession, but she took no comfort from it.

Instead, she saw Miss Lily Hereford at ease among the gentry, gliding across the floor in Stephen's arms. She saw the Marquess's nod of approval.

Would anyone notice if she drowned herself in the lemonade bowl?

She handed a servant the remains of her dessert and strode towards the terrace. Never again.

Though she'd mistakenly believed she could fit in, it was useless. She was not, nor would ever be, a woman who could belong at such a gathering.

Her imagination conjured up a vision of what it would be like to have gentlemen vying to dance with her. What must it be like to receive pretty compliments instead of warnings that she needed a better dressmaker?

She wanted to dance in the Earl's arms, to wear an ice-blue satin gown with jewels, knowing that she belonged. And if he dared court another woman, his toes would suffer for it.

Her own feet had begun to ache, so she located a quiet area leading to the terrace. She stuffed the tight dancing slippers behind a large fern, grateful that her long skirts hid the evidence of her stocking feet.

She planned to walk through the gardens and along the side of the house to make her exit. But Stephen caught up to her a few moments later. Concern lined his face. 'What did Miss Hereford say to you before I arrived?'

'She was angry about our marriage.'

He grimaced. 'I feared as much. You looked ready to scoop out her eyes with that spoon.'

She ignored him and continued her walk through the grass. The hem of her gown grew damp from the grass and her stockinged feet itched.

Discarding her slippers had not been an intelligent idea, even if she'd saved her pinched feet.

Stephen continued to follow her, and she didn't bother to ask why. This time, he could say nothing that would convince her to stay. She would throw herself in front of a carriage before setting foot back in that ballroom.

Starlight illuminated the darkened skies, and she inhaled the lush fragrance of Lady Rothburne's rose garden. From the ballroom, the faint strains of music calmed her mood.

'I want to dance with you now,' Stephen said, his hand reaching towards hers.

'I am a terrible dancer.' She kept walking towards the tall boxwoods, wincing as she stepped on a rock.

'Freddie was limping after that first round,' Stephen admitted.

Oh, that was too much. Did he really think she wanted to dance with him, after all that had transpired this evening? 'I might cripple you.'

His answer was to hold out his hand. 'I'll take the risk.'

'Don't say I didn't warn you.'

The music changed into a lively polka. Stephen took her hand, but Emily could not manage the steps. Her feet tangled up in her skirts, and she tripped over the hemline. Stephen almost caught her, but Emily crashed them both into the boxwood hedge.

A laugh escaped her, breaking her terrible mood. What would Lady Thistlewaite say if she saw her now?

My dear Lady Whitmore, it is truly bad form to toss your husband into the shrubbery.

Even when he deserved it.

Stephen lifted her up, plucking a twig from his waistcoat. 'Well, that was interesting.'

'I am worse than I thought I was.' A snort escaped her, and she reached up to remove a leaf from his hair.

'I'll see to it that you receive lessons.'

From the ballroom, a slow, melodic waltz began. Stephen clasped her about the waist, drawing her closer. 'Shall we try it again?'

'We'd best move away from the bushes,' she said.

He led her deeper into the garden, but well away from the hazardous vegetation. With his hands around her waist, he waltzed with her. Emily's heart beat faster, and she swallowed hard. She could smell his shaving soap, and his palm rested upon her spine. His eyes were dark silver in the mists. Were it not for the moonlight, they would have stood in complete darkness.

She accidentally stepped on him, and his eyes narrowed. 'Why aren't you wearing shoes?'

'They didn't fit. I could not tolerate the pain any longer, so I hid them behind a plant.'

He shook his head in exasperation, then lifted her feet to stand atop his. He pressed her close, and memories welled up inside. He had danced with her like this before, only the day before he'd taken her to Scotland for their marriage. At the time, she had believed it to be wildly romantic, and he, the daring hero. Now she saw their impulsive wedding as the mark of fools.

'I am sorry about the way I treated you back there,' he murmured. 'But after tonight, I don't want to put you or the children at risk of attack. I wouldn't forgive myself if they harmed you.'

She didn't acknowledge the apology, but shivered at his warm breath against her cheek. When the music ceased, he held her for a moment.

The faint light of the moon cast shadows over his face. Upon his collar she saw the faint stain of blood, and it bothered her. He had almost died tonight. She found herself watching him, her breath rising and falling in rhythm with his.

Lord help her, she remembered too well what it was to love this man. Her hand moved up to his face, as if to memorise it. The warmth of his skin, the striking features of his face captivated her. His dark grey eyes melted away her inhibitions.

And this time, she kissed him. At first, the lightness of his lips against hers was like a soft breeze, barely there. Then, he slanted his mouth to take her more deeply, his tongue touching hers. The wet sensation made her relive every moment of her wedding night in his arms.

He had been every dream come true, both gentle and passionate. She'd loved him so much, believing that he loved her, too. The memory shadowed her, the past colliding with the present.

Don't think of it. Just be with him now.

The seduction in his eyes held her spellbound, stealing her breath while intense heat spread through her skin. Her breasts tightened against the delicate fabric, as his mouth moved away from hers to trail down to her shoulders.

She closed her eyes. 'You don't remember anything of what it was like, do you?' Her own memories haunted her, of feeling his hardened body atop hers. 'Our wedding night.'

'I want to remember it.' His mouth nipped at her ear while his hands skimmed over her spine. 'Perhaps you can show me tonight.'

She inhaled the crisp spring air, trying not to think of how he'd forgotten her. He hadn't loved her then. And he didn't love her now.

'You married me to escape Miss Hereford,' she said slowly. 'I was a means to an end, not someone you wanted to wed.'

'That wasn't the only reason, and you know it.'

His fingers grasped her wrist, softly tracing a pattern over her skin. 'Don't shut me out, Emily.'

Thoughts of his carnal embrace invaded her mind. She wanted to be with him, more than anything. And yet, if she shared his bed, what if she were nothing but an evening's entertainment?

She wanted to be more. Although he had broken her heart, she still cared for him. And one night would never be enough.

She stepped away, not even knowing the syllables that escaped her mouth before she picked up her skirts and fled. She ran through the gardens to the front entrance where the carriages waited.

Gravel cut into her feet as she hailed the coachman. She climbed inside the carriage, clenching her fan in a death grip. Minutes later, her maid Beatrice joined her, after a footman located her.

All through the ride home, Emily tried to harden her heart. She shouldn't want to be a part of society, or desire a taste of his world.

But when he'd danced with her alone in the garden, in that moment he once again became the man she had fallen in love with. Handsome, strong and capable of fulfilling her every desire, it had taken all of her will-power to resist him.

And worse, was the knowledge that he desired her, too.

* * *

Stephen swirled the brandy in his glass, watching Lord Carstairs pour his own glass. He'd chosen his father's study for their meeting.

'Thank you for agreeing to speak with me, Whitmore. I am glad to see you are well after everything that has happened.' Carstairs sat down, slightly agitated. 'I've not seen you since the night you left my house.'

'I apologise for my sudden departure,' Stephen replied, watching the man for any suspicious gesture.

Carstairs shrugged. 'Understandable, given the circumstances. But honestly, Whitmore, you should have waited for my men to assist you. Going after Hollingford on your own was not wise. I am surprised you lived to tell the tale.' His face turned serious. 'Did he give you the list?'

Stephen wasn't certain what list Carstairs was speaking of, but he played along. 'No. I did not find it.'

'Damn. We need the names of the other investors.' Carstairs took a sip of his brandy.

Stephen kept his face neutral, wondering just why Carstairs was so interested in a list of names. He ventured a guess. 'The investors in *The Lady Valiant*, you mean?'

'Yes, of course.' Carstairs's eyes narrowed.

'Have you any idea of where Hollingford kept his records? Did you send men to his residence?'

'No. I've only just returned to London.' From the desperate tone in the Viscount's voice, Stephen suspected there was more to the stolen shipment. 'Has something else happened?'

'I've received notes of a threatening nature in the past few weeks. He wants a thousand pounds, or he'll harm my family.'

Carstairs slammed down the glass, anger glinting on his face. 'I couldn't pay him if I wanted to. I was relying upon the profits from that shipment.'

The revelation of financial problems made Stephen even more cautious. 'Why would he target you for his blackmail?'

'I suppose he thinks I stole the money.'

Stephen made no comment, waiting for Carstairs to reveal more. The Viscount tossed back the remainder of the brandy.

'One last matter, Whitmore. You should straighten your collar. Someone might see.'

'See what?'

With a twisted smile, Carstairs unbuttoned his cuff and raised his sleeve.

There, upon his forearm, was a black tattoo exactly the shape of his own.

Chapter Eleven

When beating egg whites, be patient and steady. Effort is required for something worthwhile.

—Emily Barrow's *Cook Book*

Stephen handed his cloak to one of the servants and walked upstairs. In his hands, he held the dancing slippers Emily had hidden behind a potted plant.

Ever one to break the rules, that was his wife.

But he'd frightened her tonight, somehow. When he'd shown her his desire, she'd fled, as though he'd asked her to lie with him in the flower garden.

When he reached the landing, he wondered where she had chosen to sleep. Tonight something had changed between them. For the first time, she'd kissed him. It was the last thing he'd expected, especially after such a gruelling night.

He didn't like the way she'd been treated. More than one heartless matron had trod upon her tender feelings. He blamed himself for not interfering. And yet, he couldn't remain at her side the way he wanted to. If he even hinted that he cared about Emily, he endangered her.

For all he knew, the man behind the attacks might have been present at the ball. It might even be Carstairs himself. The Viscount had most definitely played a part in the shipment. But was he a threat? The tattoo suggested he was not.

He heard the low cry of a child from one of the rooms and decided to quiet the guilty party.

Opening the door, he saw a downy head lift from the two wingback chairs pushed together. It was the infant girl. Stephen couldn't remember if Emily had ever mentioned her name. He realised he should have purchased a cradle for the baby, long before now.

The baby grinned, revealing a set of two teeth on her bottom gums. 'Da-da-da.'

'Not a chance,' he warned. 'We'll have none of that foolishness. Now cease this noise before someone hears you.'

Her face crumpled, and she screwed up her face to cry.

Stephen closed the distance and lifted her up before she could shriek. He had no doubt that the young imp would not hesitate to wake the household with her infernal screaming.

The baby buried her face in his neck, snuggling close. Her soft hair smelled of a floral soap. A curious protective instinct curled around him, and he held her at a distance to study her.

She chortled, stuffing a fist in her mouth.

'I don't suppose you'd know where your Aunt Emily is sleeping?'

'Gah,' the baby replied.

'You are a veritable wellspring of information.' He set her down in the wingback chairs, and she whimpered, holding her arms out to him.

'Go to sleep.'

She looked ready to cry, and so he arranged her sideways in order to rub her back. She gave a soft sigh. After several minutes, she succumbed to sleep.

Stephen tiptoed out, wondering whether 'Gah' meant left or right.

The door to one of the rooms flew open, and Emily raced toward Stephen, her face deathly pale. 'He's gone.'

'Who is gone?'

'Royce.' Emily was already running down the stairs to fetch her cloak. 'I went to bid him goodnight, and his bed hasn't been slept in. I think he's run away.'

'Why would you say that?'

'The other day he told me he wanted to look for his father.'

'He'll be looking for a long time, then,' Stephen remarked, but Emily did not react to his dry comment.

He prayed that the boy was only hiding, for a small child would not make it far in the London streets without facing danger. 'How long has he been missing, do you think?'

'I don't know. Perhaps hours. His coat and cap are gone.'

Her fear bordered on hysteria, but he needed to calm her. They would not find the boy without a clear, logical plan. Emily had nearly reached the door when Stephen stopped her. 'Have you searched the house?'

Emily nodded. 'I can't find him anywhere.' Tears spilled over her cheeks and she wrung her hands. 'What if we don't find him?'

'We will. But I want to search here first.'

'He's not in any of the rooms.'

'There are many places for a young boy to hide, Emily.' Stephen led her up the stairs again, even as her attention remained upon the front door. 'What were his favourite belongings?' He wanted her to focus on answering questions rather than panicking. Calm and steady, he took her hand. Though he did not believe his enemies would go after a small boy, he could not know for certain.

'He loves his tin soldiers. But it doesn't matter. They're only toys.'

'Not to him, they aren't. To him, they are his most prized possessions. He wouldn't leave them behind, if he ran away.'

When Stephen threw open the door to Royce's room, neat rows of tin soldiers stood in line. He took her hand, trying to reassure her. 'No boy would leave on a search for his father unless he brought his toys with him.'

'What if someone took him? The man who attacked me in the garden might have…' Her voice trailed away.

She had echoed his own fears, but he wouldn't acknowledge them. Not yet. Stephen studied the room, checking beneath the bed and behind the curtains. When his search came up fruitless, he tried to allay her fears with a lie. 'I doubt if anyone would kidnap him.'

'How can you be sure?'

His lips lifted in a slight smile. 'I cannot. But I ran away a few times myself, as a lad.'

Emily did not appear consoled. 'If anything has happened to him, I won't forgive myself.'

The curtains billowed slightly and Stephen stepped forward, planning to close the window.

He looked for Royce again, this time outside. A tall oak tree grew not far from the house, a long branch stretching out beside the boy's window. Stephen peered out into the darkness.

'Bring me the lamp.' When Emily did, he opened the window wider and held the lamp into the darkness. There, curled against two crossed branches, Royce slept. A pair of linen drawers were tied around his head, pirate-style. He wore his black coat, and under that, his nightshirt bared his legs to the cool air. His cap rested on a smaller branch nearby.

Emily gasped at the sight of him. 'Get him back inside before he falls to his death!'

Stephen handed her the lamp, and she held the curtains back as he prepared to climb on to the branch. It was a precarious balance, but he managed to edge on to the thick limb, holding the windowsill for balance.

'Royce,' he said gently, 'it's time to come inside.'

The boy yawned and blinked sleepily. 'I want to sleep outside.'

'You've worried your aunt.'

'Royce, please come in,' Emily begged. Fear hovered in her eyes. Without waiting for the boy to argue further, Stephen lifted him into his arms and slid across the branch to hand him over to Emily.

When they had both returned inside safely, the boy murmured, 'Is the bad man gone?'

'The bad man?'

'The man who was searching my room. He was trying to take my toys.'

Emily didn't move, didn't breathe. All the blood had drained from her face and she stood as motionless as a statue.

'What did the man look like, Royce?' Stephen asked, helping the boy into bed.

'He was green with tall horns.' The boy yawned. 'He had a red tail, too.'

Emily visibly relaxed. 'It was only a dream, sweeting.' She tucked him in and pressed a kiss to his temple, removing the drawers from his head. Smoothing his hair, she kissed him a second time. 'Goodnight.'

He mumbled a sleepy response, pulling the covers up to his chin. Stephen held the lamp up, waiting for Emily to follow him from the room. When they reached the privacy of the hallway, Emily turned. 'Do you really believe there was someone here tonight?'

Stephen shrugged. 'It sounds like a young boy's overactive imagination.'

'And what if he wasn't imagining things? Someone tried to kill you.'

He hadn't forgotten about that at all. Though he

didn't know why, he suspected it had something to do with Carstairs and Hollingford.

'The man who attacked you at Falkirk,' he began, 'what did he want?' He sensed that there was another connection, something he hadn't foreseen.

'He wanted investment papers that belonged to Daniel.'

The stolen shipment. No doubt the assailant had something to do with the theft. And if he wanted the papers, likely he was trying to cover up his own involvement.

'Did you give him anything?'

'I had nothing to give.' Emily rubbed her arms, as if to ward off a chill. 'But I think he went to my father's house. Daniel had some of his belongings there, before he—' Her voice broke off, and she lowered her gaze to the carpet.

'We need to go back to Falkirk. I think your brother was hiding information. It may have cost him his life.'

She looked so glum at the knowledge, he wondered if perhaps he shouldn't have said anything. It had been a difficult night for both of them. And tonight, he intended to keep a close watch over her. There had been too many dangerous encounters.

He escorted her down the hall and opened the door to her room. Before he could enter, she blocked the entrance. 'Where do you think you're going?'

'I am staying here tonight.'

She glared at him and he could almost see her defences rise up in anger. 'Do you really believe that after tonight I want you to share my room?'

She was angry, he realised. He'd been thinking of her protection, while she still held hurt feelings.

Taking her hand, he pulled her inside her room, closing the door and locking it. He pocketed the key. 'It is my duty to protect my family, don't you think?'

She glared at him, and Stephen knew he hadn't been forgiven for his earlier behaviour. He changed the subject. 'Why did you kiss me earlier?'

'Because I wanted to.'

Her honesty caught him up short. He didn't know what to say next. Instead, he moved behind her, slipping the pins from her hair. It spilled across his fingers in a silken veil of gold. Stephen continued removing pins, using his fingers to smooth the strands of hair.

She turned, biting her lower lip. 'Thank you for purchasing a new coat and shoes for Royce.'

The words weren't what he'd expected. And when her hands rested upon his shoulders, he wondered if she would kiss him again. Her mouth reminded him of a peach tart, sweet and warm. He wanted to nibble at her lips, tasting her until she melted against him.

Stephen drew her closer, resting his palms on her waist. Though she was still fully clothed, an intimacy rose between them, with her hair falling around her shoulders. 'Why did you run from me?'

Colour flooded her cheeks. 'Because I—I was afraid.' She turned her face to the side, but her fingers remained upon him, her thumbs idly tracing a pattern. From the slight blush of her cheeks, he realised she wasn't going to push him away.

'And are you still afraid?'

When she didn't answer, he drew her back into a dancing position. Without asking permission, he moved in a gentle circle, waltzing with her. 'Do you remember the first time we danced?'

She nodded. 'It was in the stables at Lady Woolthrope's house party.'

'Ten years ago,' he said, releasing her. He sat down in a chair before the fire, propping his feet up. 'I was seventeen.'

Emily joined him, sitting within arm's reach. So many memories of their past. As an adolescent, Stephen had trod on her toes more times than she could count. He hadn't wanted to embarrass himself in front of the family at his first public gathering. Emily had known as little about dancing as he did, and they'd crashed into the horse stalls more than once on a bad turn.

'You fell into the muck,' she said.

'I'd been trying to forget that part.'

He edged his chair closer to hers, and she didn't pull away. The fire warmed her stocking feet, and she suppressed a smile. 'That was the best part.'

He pulled off his socks, setting his bare feet beside her. 'What else do you remember?'

Hiding from her parents while they argued over what to sell next. Lying back in the summer grasses next to the boy whom she'd dreamed would rescue her. Experiencing the thrill of her first kiss.

Emily's skin prickled, aware that he was only a few feet away from her. 'You hated your father,' she whispered. 'I remember that.'

He grew sombre at the mention of the Marquess. 'You used to make me laugh. When nothing else would.'

He stood and knelt before her. In his eyes, she saw a hint of the boy he had been, so desperate to win his father's approval. And how many times he had been disappointed.

He rested his hands upon her knees, closing his eyes. Emily almost reached out to touch his dark hair, to kiss him. *Don't*, she warned herself. *He'll only break your heart.* He didn't see when she pulled back.

His hands moved beneath her skirts, to caress her legs. Although a thin layer of fabric protected her from his bare palms, her imagination remembered full well what it was like to feel him caressing her thighs. Dear God, what was he doing?

Heat blazed through her as he reached up to unbutton her gown, lifting it away. Her mind cried out for her to stop him, but her body remained frozen, trapped by her own rising desire. She didn't protest, as she should have. As each petticoat, stocking and crinoline joined the discarded dress, she grew more nervous. Then he unlaced her stays, his hands warm and seductive.

Clad in only a chemise and drawers, she felt completely exposed. Even when they had been intimate, it had always been dark. He had never seen her unclothed.

She didn't move when he lowered his hands and took her foot into his lap. His thumb glided over her arch, his hands squeezing gently as he massaged the soreness from them.

She closed her eyes, wishing she had the courage to pull away. But, oh, his hands felt so good.

Needing to fill the silence with conversation, she fumbled for the right words. 'Thank you for finding Royce.'

'Look at me,' Stephen said firmly. Though she didn't want to, he waited until her gaze met his. 'I know you're still afraid. But I won't let anyone harm the children.'

'Promise me.'

'You have my word.'

Before she could breathe, he drew her legs around his waist in a shocking embrace. His mouth captured hers in a feverish kiss. Mindlessly, she kissed him back, her body remembering his.

'I don't love you,' she whispered when his mouth tugged at her ear. *I can't. I won't.*

He tugged at her chemise, exposing her breasts. Slowly, he circled her skin with his tongue. Her sensitive nipples rose up, aching for his kiss. His thumb grazed the tip and she shuddered.

'You want me. And you belong to me.'

Between her legs, a wetness made her crave him. She hadn't forgotten a moment of the nights they'd shared after their wedding. With each caress of his fingers upon her breasts, a dark need welled up.

He covered her breasts again and tasted her through the soft cambric, scraping his teeth against the taut nipple. She nearly came apart at the rough sensation of wet fabric and his hot mouth.

'Stephen,' she whispered, holding on to his shoulders and trying to urge him closer. Desire battered against her sense of reason. She didn't understand what he was doing when he moved back from her.

He reached inside his waistcoat and withdrew the key. 'If you want to share my bed, you need only open the door.'

He tilted her chin up and brushed a searing kiss upon her lips before pressing the key into her palm. She barely heard the sound of his adjoining door closing.

He was giving her a choice. She could become his wife in body as well as name. And she could not accuse him of forcing her.

Go to him, her body pleaded. *Surrender to the seduction.*

But though he might reawaken her to the sweet pleasure of his bed, the terrible fact remained. He didn't remember making love to her on their wedding night.

And though it wasn't his fault, it devastated her to know that the most perfect night of her life meant nothing to him.

Her hand covered her mouth, as if to stave off the violent tears threatening. She didn't dare go to his bed, for, once again, she would be the lovelorn maiden. And he, indifferent to her feelings.

Not again.

Before she could lose her grasp on sanity, she set the key upon the fireplace mantel and extinguished the lamp.

Chapter Twelve

When serving food, the eye should take pleasure, as well as the stomach. Fresh flowers, fruits or other elements of decoration can elevate a dish from ordinary to sublime. A husband might observe that fine jewellery may also be used to elevate a woman's appearance.
—Emily Barrow's *Cook Book*

'What have you learned?' the voice asked.

'They are leaving for Falkirk. I will follow them and locate the records. The Earl will lead us to them.'

'The Earl is supposed to be dead.' The voice grew frustrated, a note of anger rising higher.

'I will not fail you again, my lord. The records will be destroyed.'

'See to it. Or you will not like the consequences.' The voice paused a moment, then continued. 'Use every means necessary.'

* * *

Victoria Barrow was a traitor of the worst sort. Instead of sobbing for hours on end as she had done on the trip to London, the infant had spent most of the journey happily curled up in Stephen's arms, her face nestled against his waistcoat. He'd given her a pocket watch to play with, and she had entertained herself by chewing upon it.

Emily's teeth were about to rattle their way out of her head from the roads. She prayed they would not have to travel for much longer. Stephen had suggested the train, but her stomach lurched at the thought. She had no desire to inhale soot while travelling at such an unnatural speed.

In time, the children fell asleep. Victoria's body had grown slack against Stephen, her fist curled beneath her chin as she drooled upon his shoulder. The wet nurse Anna had offered to take the baby, but Stephen refused. Emily's heart softened to see him holding the baby as if the child were his own. For a moment, they seemed like a true family.

'Reach into that valise, won't you?' he directed Emily. 'There's something inside that I've been meaning to give you.'

She located the leather valise and unfastened it. 'What am I looking for?' She rummaged around and at last her fingers closed upon a book. 'This?'

He nodded. 'Open it.'

The small volume was filled with a woman's handwriting. At first Emily thought it was a diary, but when she read the first entry, delight blossomed inside of her.

'I can't believe it.' It was a book filled with cooking recipes, everything from currant buns to porridge. 'It's wonderful.' She couldn't help her smile, didn't care if he saw how happy the gift had made her.

'It belonged to my grandmother. I had my mother send it to me.'

Emily skimmed through the pages eagerly, laughing when she found a recipe for Apple Jonathan. There were no fresh apples to be had yet, but perhaps she could use dried apples and achieve the same effect. While she read through the book, she noticed Stephen's leg resting beside hers. The warm heat of him seemed to penetrate her skin like a caress.

The hours passed, and night descended until Emily could no longer read his grandmother's handwriting. Anna had taken the baby to nurse, and in time, both fell asleep with the rocking of the coach. Royce stretched out with his head upon Anna's lap, his eyes closed while one hand firmly gripped a tin soldier.

With everyone else asleep, the interior of the coach grew intimate. Emily was more aware of her husband, of his strong face, his eyes meeting hers with unspoken promises.

Stephen reached out to take her hand. His fingers touched her skin, moving up to cradle her wrist. Though he did nothing more than brush his thumb against the pulse at the base of her hand, the sensation made her breath catch.

'We'll be stopping at an inn soon,' he whispered in her ear.

Heaven help her, but his suggestion tempted her with the proximity of such close quarters. She imagined pulling his mouth against hers until she felt the secret thrill of his kiss. 'I know.'

'There is no need to be afraid. I won't touch you unless you want me to.' His voice captivated her, seducing her with a dizzying need.

His fingers slid up her arm, and she shivered. 'The children,' she reminded him. He acceded to her wishes, drawing back.

Emily's breathing was unsteady, and she pinched herself without letting him see. She needed to distance herself. But more than anything, she wanted him.

She forced her gaze away, staring outside at the blackness of the night. The coach continued onwards, and as time passed, she grew more anxious.

Why was she even considering sharing his bed?

Too much had changed. He'd left her and all but disappeared from her life.

She couldn't let him hurt her that way again. And yet, she could not deny that he tempted her. Could she let him be her husband in body, as well as in name?

The longings rose up inside of her, so deeply. As she watched Stephen lift the sleeping children from the carriage, she was very much afraid of loving him again.

He arranged two rooms for them at the inn: one for Anna and the children; the other for Emily and himself. The innkeeper's wife fed them a delicious stew of chicken seasoned with thyme and garlic. The crusty bread tasted like heaven when Emily dipped it in the stew. While she chatted with the woman about spices and seasonings, Stephen went upstairs to prepare the rooms.

Once Royce and Victoria were asleep, Emily returned to the room she would share with Stephen. She stared at the small bed, suddenly wary of sleeping in the same room with her husband. Anna helped her undress, and when she was clothed in a cotton nightgown, she slipped beneath the covers to await the Earl.

It was like her wedding night, all over again. If she let him make love to her, she risked losing her heart again. And she didn't want the emptiness of such a one-sided marriage.

The door opened, and Stephen entered, fastening the bolt behind him. He removed his frock-coat and waistcoat, lifting his shirt away. Emily buried her face in the sheets, though not before she caught a glimpse of a lean muscular chest and the black tattoo edging his neck.

'Emily?' he whispered, sliding in beside her. His warm body nestled against hers, and she realised in a panic that he wore nothing. His mouth rested against her ear. He reached around to cup her breast through the cotton, his thumb idly stroking the tip.

'You shouldn't,' she managed, her whisper breaking. A storm of sensations ignited her body's hunger. His thighs brushed against hers, his rigid length against her spine.

'Shhh—' His hand slid beneath the fabric, caressing the heavy fullness of her breast. 'Don't be afraid.'

'I'm not,' she lied. Not afraid of his touch, only of her crumbling will-power.

'I've been wanting to touch you all day.' He cut off any further arguments by lifting her chin to kiss him. As his tongue met hers, his skilled hands moved over the fabric of her nightgown, tantalising her. He touched her stomach, caressing her down to her hips. Emily stiffened, keeping her legs shut.

Tell him to stop, her mind pleaded.

But his warm mouth was melting away her uncertainty, making her want him. If she offered herself up, it would be wonderful, like before. Could she separate her body from her conscience and accept him? Could she take comfort from his touch without it meaning anything?

No. It would hurt too much when he left her. She broke away. 'Stephen, I—'

'I'm only going to give you pleasure,' he whispered, and her cheeks heated at the things he promised.

Beneath the covers, his hand eased up the hem of her nightgown until he touched her bare thigh. His hand moved up to the slit between her legs. A moan escaped her as his wicked fingers slid past her curls and inside her. Flames of desire licked at her skin, making her burn for him.

Sweet Lord above, he knew just how to dissolve her resistance. Her skin rose up beneath his touch, her nipples puckering.

'I want to make you my wife,' he whispered roughly, stroking her until she arched her back. She hungered for him, her hands moving across his firm skin. 'I want to move deep inside you, feeling you around me.'

His words aroused her, while a shuddering sensation built up, a rising tide of need. Though his intimate touch embarrassed her, she was beyond thinking clearly. Every one of her senses was alive.

She had to stop him, to keep this from happening. But she couldn't seem to gather her thoughts together. He increased the tempo, his thumb exerting firm pressure against her tight bud.

His mouth covered her nipple, his hands arousing her. Another finger thrust inside her, mimicking the rhythm of lovemaking. Deeper he plunged, his thumb riding her, until she strained, her back arching. A violent release ripped through her as wave after wave of ecstasy flooded her skin. She couldn't move, couldn't form a single word.

'It was like this before,' she whispered. She hadn't forgotten a single moment of their wedding night, and the way he'd made her feel beautiful.

What if he left her again? She couldn't stop the tears spilling on to her cheeks. *He doesn't love you.*

When he saw her tears, he stopped immediately. 'Did I hurt you?'

She shook her head, biting her lip to keep from sobbing. No, he hadn't hurt her. Not physically. But she should have known better than to share a bed with him.

'This was a mistake,' she whispered.

For a long moment, he stared at the ceiling, not

speaking a single word. Then, at last, he rolled over and turned his back to her.

Emily curled her hands into a fist, wishing she'd never let him back into her heart.

Chapter Thirteen

*When a dinner is spoiled, it does no good to cry
about it. There are worse things in life than
burned meat and undercooked potatoes.*
            —Emily Barrow's *Cook Book*

Upon their arrival at the house, Farnsworth
mumbled apologies. 'My lord, the other servants
arrived only a few hours ago. I am so terribly sorry.
I fear your rooms may not be ready yet.'

'Then prepare them now. Put my wife's belongings with mine.'

Emily bristled at his order. Her face burned at the
thought of their stolen night at the inn and her
refusal to lie with him. 'I would prefer to sleep in
my own bedchamber.'

Stephen's gaze fixed upon hers in a direct challenge. But he voiced his command to Farnsworth.
'Obey my orders.'

Emily's posture stiffened. So, he was angry. Nevertheless, she didn't regret her decision. Too much was unsettled between them. There would be time to argue about this later.

Victoria awoke and started whining, her fists rubbing her eyes. Royce said nothing, hanging back behind her skirts. 'Farnsworth, please prepare the children's rooms first,' Emily instructed. Both children had reached the point of exhaustion.

'Are you hungry?' she asked Royce. They had eaten supper at a village hours ago, and the boy shook his head.

'Then let's get the two of you off to bed. You'll feel better in the morning.'

Royce's face grew worried, and he stopped to tug at Farnsworth's sleeve. 'Did my father come for me while I was gone?'

The butler blinked. 'I beg your pardon?' He sent Emily and Stephen a questioning look. She shook her head, sending him a silent warning.

'Royce, it's late. We've discussed this before.'

'He wouldn't leave us here without coming to get us. I know he wouldn't.'

She didn't know what to say. Though she had told him that Daniel was never coming back, her nephew denied it.

Stephen took the boy's hand in his. 'It is time for bed, Royce.'

The boy fought him, kicking Stephen in the shins. 'You cannot tell me what to do. You're not my father!'

'Your father is dead,' Stephen said softly. Emily winced at his direct tone, but there was nothing to be done. 'And you dishonour his memory with your temper tantrum.'

The boy let out an infuriated roar, pounding his fists upon the Earl's shoulder.

'Let go of me! I don't want to go to bed.'

Stephen ignored him. To Emily, he directed, 'I shall look after him. See to the baby.'

She wanted desperately to interfere. Would he give the boy a whipping for his tantrum? The determined expression on Stephen's face suggested that he would brook no further arguments.

The infant wailed louder, and Emily was forced to give Victoria over to Anna to feed her.

When it abruptly fell silent upstairs, Emily worried that the Earl had done something drastic.

'Your aunt is not here to rescue you, so you might as well be silent,' Stephen told Royce. 'If you continue to disobey me, you will receive a sound thrashing.'

He had never actually beaten an errant child before and had no real wish to do so. But as he'd hoped, the threat worked. Royce stopped struggling, staring at Stephen with fascination.

He wasn't staring out of fear, but out of curiosity. 'What is that?'

In the midst of Royce fighting him off, he'd clawed at Stephen's shirt, loosening the collar. Likely the boy had glimpsed the tattoo.

Stephen turned around to reveal the full design. 'Have you seen this before?'

Royce bobbed his head. 'Father had one.'

Interesting. Though he was no closer to learning the meaning of the design, he wondered whether Carstairs or Hollingford had been responsible for the stolen shipment profits.

'Do you know what it means?'

The boy shook his head. 'I asked Father to let me have one, but he said not until I was older.'

'Your father was right.'

'I *am* older,' Royce argued.

'Not old enough.'

Royce scowled, even as he climbed into bed. 'I still don't like you.'

'I still don't like you either. Go to sleep.'

'Are you my uncle now?' Royce asked. 'I don't want you to be.'

Stephen hadn't thought of it, but he supposed he was. 'To my great misfortune, I am your uncle now.'

'If you die, you won't be my uncle any more,' Royce offered.

'Planning to do me in, are you?'

Royce pondered this a moment before saying, 'Not until I'm older.'

'How very reassuring. I shall sleep better at night, knowing it. Be sure to let me know the date on which you plan to kill me, won't you?'

A devilish smile creased Royce's mouth as he closed his eyes.

Stephen shook his head at the boy's active imagination and pulled the door shut behind him. Down the hall, he heard Victoria shrieking loudly enough to shatter glass.

He ignored it and entered his room. Farnsworth had delivered the baggage to his room. But his wife's belongings were nowhere to be seen.

Why did Emily insist on being so stubborn? After opening the door to her original chamber, he found the battered valise. Upon a quick inspection of its contents, he saw that it contained only the black dresses she owned and the lavender tarlatan gown. She'd brought none of the day dresses, nor the jewels he'd given.

Almost as if she didn't want any part of him.

Last night, he'd made her cry. He'd been completely unprepared for the tears, after he'd been caught up with the intent of seducing her. Though she'd claimed that he hadn't hurt her, he knew differently.

He'd hurt her when he couldn't remember their

wedding, or their first night as husband and wife. And the night at his family's ball, when he'd refused to acknowledge her.

Stephen discarded his travelling clothes and changed into a silk dressing robe. Pouring himself a glass of sherry from the decanter, he relaxed in a chair. Victoria was still crying, from the sound of it.

He propped up his feet, wondering if it were even possible to gain Emily's affections. He'd expected the gifts of dresses and jewels to make her happy, but she'd left them behind. He realised that he knew almost nothing about her. Only the book of cooking recipes had made her smile.

The sound of Victoria's incessant screaming kept interrupting his thoughts.

Time passed on and there was no sign of Emily. The baby's cries would die down, only to rise up again within minutes. Stephen didn't know what was going on, but if it meant he had to take charge of matters, so be it.

Victoria sobbed, her face puckered with fury. Emily tried to rock her, but the motion only made the infant cry harder. Looking at the baby, Emily wished she knew what was wrong. She had never felt so helpless.

She walked the length of the nursery, holding

Victoria to her shoulder and bouncing her in a rhythm. Victoria's cries diminished at the new position, and her arms clenched around Emily's neck.

She walked the distance six more times before the baby's cries subsided into hiccups. When Victoria drifted into sleep, Emily tiptoed to the crib. She prayed that Victoria would finally surrender to her exhaustion.

The moment she laid her down, the baby shrieked and screamed louder. Emily lifted her up again, shushing the child as tears ran down her own face. How had she ever thought she could do this? How could she believe she would make a good mother when she could not even put a baby to sleep?

The door opened and Stephen stepped inside. 'What is going on? Why won't she stop crying?'

'I don't know. She's already been fed. Perhaps it's the unfamiliar room. She might be frightened.'

'Don't be foolish. The child can't be old enough for such nonsense. Put her to bed and after she cries a bit, she'll sleep.'

'This isn't the same thing at all,' Emily protested. 'I've tried that already.' Victoria's screams escalated, and Emily shushed her, bouncing while she paced.

'Give her back to Anna.' Stephen glared at the baby, as though a harsh look would make the child stop crying. 'She needs to sleep.'

'Don't you think I know that?' But her own weariness from the journey had crept over her, making it harder to remain calm. 'Anna has already tried, but she won't stop crying.'

Stephen held out his arms and took Victoria. The baby wriggled in his grasp, arching her back and howling. 'Here, now,' he said gently. 'What seems to be the matter?' He patted her on the shoulder, but it did nothing to soothe the infant.

Emily itched to take the baby back from him, but she dared not. He wanted to help, and she owed him the chance to try.

Just as before, Stephen settled Victoria into a rhythm of walking, holding her close and rubbing her tiny shoulders. His deep voice murmured words of comfort to the baby.

'Go to our room,' Stephen instructed. 'I'll be there as soon as she's asleep.'

'But what if she doesn't? What if—'

'You're tired. I'll look after her until she falls asleep.' He settled Victoria against his chest, and the baby wept with fatigue. His eyes gleamed. 'You could always await me naked in bed.'

She didn't respond to his teasing. Desperately, she wanted to accept his help, but she hated the thought of leaving. 'Are you certain you want to stay with her?'

'Go.' He kept up his pattern of walking, and

Emily left them alone. The crying slowed, and Victoria emitted whimpering noises.

Emily closed the door and waited with her ear pressed up to the wood for several minutes. The crying didn't stop, but she felt a rhythmic vibration on the floor from Stephen pacing. Though he had told her to go back to the room, she couldn't until she knew Victoria was asleep. She sank down against the door, her body weight resting against the wood.

As time drifted on, she hugged her knees to her chest, exhaustion weighing down on her shoulders like a heavy woolen blanket. Minutes drifted into hours, and at last she fell asleep when Victoria's crying faded into silence.

'Lady Whitmore?' a male voice asked. Emily opened her eyes and saw Farnsworth standing before her. Her back ached, and she had no idea what time it was. But somehow it was morning. Farnsworth carried a tray with a teapot and at the sight Emily longed to snatch it from him. Nothing seemed more inviting than a hot cup of tea.

'I shall take the tray to the Earl,' she volunteered, rising to her feet. Her neck felt as though someone had hammered it repeatedly with a mallet, but she accepted the tray.

Farnsworth waited, and Emily nodded toward the room. 'Open the door for me, if you please.'

He did, and after he closed it behind her, Emily gaped at the scene she beheld. Stephen lay stretched out, his feet propped up while he sat in a stuffed wingback chair. Upon his chest, Victoria snored, her body draped across his.

He must have walked the floor for hours, comforting the baby. She couldn't begin to tell him how much it meant to her.

She set the tray down, tiptoeing so as not to wake them. His dark hair fell over his eyes while a strong arm held the baby securely in place. Victoria gripped his silk dressing robe in her fists.

The sight of them held her transfixed. She longed to tell him how grateful she was for helping with the children. Last night he had handled both Royce's tantrum and Victoria's crying.

She reached out to him and brushed the wayward strand of hair from his forehead. His straight nose and gentle mouth lured her closer. Before she could stop her impulse, she leaned down and pressed her mouth to his.

Stephen woke at the touch of her lips. For a moment, he appeared confused about where he was. Then he straightened, careful so as not to wake Victoria.

'How did you get the baby to fall asleep?' she asked.

'I put a warm cloth beneath her left ear.' He

pointed to a discarded blanket. 'She kept tugging at it last night, and the heat seemed to ease her pain. You might wish to have Dr Parsons examine her today, however.'

'I'll send for him.' She poured him a cup of tea and set it on the table, taking Victoria from his arms. The baby moaned, tucking her head beneath Emily's chin. Gently, Emily set her down in the crib. Thankfully, the child did not awaken.

Stephen took a sip of tea. 'Somehow I doubt you waited for me in bed last night.'

She shrugged. 'I slept outside the door.'

'And I suppose you were wearing clothes, too.'

'I didn't want to shock Farnsworth.'

'Don't wear them tonight,' he said, his voice deep and resonant.

'Stephen, I don't think—'

'I made you cry,' he interrupted. 'I'm sorry for that. But not for touching you.' His voice took on a deeper timbre, making her flush. 'You didn't kiss me properly before.'

'It was only meant to thank you,' she said. 'I didn't intend to bother you.'

'I want you to bother me.' He leaned forward, resting his wrists upon his open knees.

'What is it you want, Stephen? You haven't even decided whether or not to keep me as your wife.'

'And what if I do?'

'I don't know if I believe that. Even if there wasn't a threat on your life, we've become so different.'

Stephen rose and took a step forward. Then another. 'We weren't so different years ago.'

He lifted her chin until she could not turn away. His hands cupped her face, his eyes weary. Beneath the shadows of fatigue, she saw a man who had stayed up all night for a child he barely knew.

'Let us try, Emily.'

She lost herself in those eyes, in his compassion. When his mouth met hers, she met his kiss without holding herself back. Heat and feverish sensation spiralled through her, awakening her with desire. His mouth moved over her lips, not forcing her, but letting her know the fullness of his own need.

It was happening again. She was falling under his sensual spell, letting herself believe in the fairy tale.

She pulled back, her pulse trembling. His dark hair was unkempt while her lips were raw from the bristle of his unshaven face.

'Send for Anna and the doctor.'

Her brain wouldn't work, couldn't understand what he wanted. 'Anna and the doctor?' she repeated.

'Anna can watch over the baby until the doctor can have a look at her. In the meantime, we've unfinished business between us.'

He laced his fingers with hers, pulling her towards him. Emily suspected his intent, but she shied away. 'What are you talking about?'

His hand moved down her spine, fingers curled below the dip of her waist. 'I'd rather show you what I mean.'

'It's too soon.' She hugged her waist, taking another step away. 'We barely know each other.'

'I shared your bed once before, didn't I? On our wedding night.'

'Yes, but you don't remember any of it.'

'I remembered everything last night. All is clear.'

'Liar.' She didn't believe a word of it. 'I think you would say anything to me, if it brought me back into your bed.'

He nodded solemnly. 'I would, yes.'

At his blunt honesty, a choked laugh escaped her. 'Not a good idea, Whitmore.'

'I could show you what a good idea it would be.' He moved her palms upon the muscles of his chest.

Emily shook her head. 'I need time first.'

'What do you mean?'

'I want a day without arguing or fighting.' She moved her hands to his shoulders, away from temptation. 'A chance to get reacquainted. I married you because of who you were growing up. I want to know who you are now.'

'I'm your husband.' He captured her lips again,

devouring her mouth until fire ignited upon her skin. She felt alive as sensations swelled within her. Her hands threaded through his hair while he taught her what it meant to burn for him.

She pulled herself back again. Her breathing was unsteady and she held on to him for balance. She was afraid that when he let her go, her knees might buckle.

'And I promise to tempt you as you've never been tempted before,' he said huskily.

His words made her long to cast her inhibitions away, to welcome him into her arms. But she was afraid to trust him, afraid that he'd betray her again.

'You can try,' she said at last, terrified of what she had just agreed to.

Chapter Fourteen

The devoted wife wishes, above all things, to please her husband. And the most devoted husband is better pleased with having good bread and butter upon his table than with the most learned dissertation in Latin...
—Emily Barrow's *Cook Book*

Emily held Victoria tightly in her arms while the baby grabbed fistfuls of her hair. Doctor Parsons offered a small bottle of tonic. 'Give this to her before she sleeps at night. It will ease her pain,' he said. 'Her ears are troubling her.'

Stephen had suspected as much, but if the physician's reassurances brought Emily comfort, so much the better. He was grateful Victoria would not endure another night like the last one. He hid a yawn, hoping to rest before tonight.

But first, he needed to make further progress on

the identity of his assailant. The only definitive link between himself, Carstairs and Hollingford was the tattoo.

When he entered the library, he rummaged through his desk for paper to make a list when he saw Royce hiding behind the curtains.

'You may as well come out. I can see you hiding there.'

Royce peered out from behind the heavy curtain. Stephen saw the boy holding a tattered book. When he drew nearer, Royce tried to hide it behind his back.

'What are you reading there?'

'Nothing.'

'May I have a look?'

He stretched out his hand, but Royce shook his head. 'It's mine.'

Stephen sat down beside the boy, crossing his legs. 'If it's so interesting, why don't you read it to me? Perhaps I'd enjoy it.' He tilted his head to the side to make out the title: *The Perfumed Garden.*

He bit back a laugh. He had to give the boy credit for pinching one of the more interesting books out of his library. As he recalled, he had tried out several of the lovemaking positions detailed in the book. Like as not, the boy could not read it. The entire manual was translated into French.

'Is it a good story?' he asked, pretending as though he didn't know what the book was about.

Royce frowned. 'It has nice pictures.'

I'm sure it does, Stephen thought wryly. Emily would have Royce's head on a pike if she knew what he was reading. Still, Royce wasn't the first lad to find such a book.

'I could use your help in a small matter, if you wouldn't mind.'

'I'm reading,' Royce said. 'I haven't the time just now.'

'Ah. Well, it's about the tattoo you said your father had.'

Royce's ears perked up in interest. He closed the book, as if trying to decide whether or not to give Stephen his attention.

'You see, I'd like to make a copy of the design to learn what it means. But it's on the back of my neck, and I cannot see it properly. Would you hold a mirror for me?'

'I'm busy,' Royce argued.

Stephen was never one to turn away a challenge. If it meant using his wits to convince the lad, so be it. He was counting on the child's natural curiosity.

First, he rang for Farnsworth and ordered two mirrors. Royce had not moved, but was now studying a pair of lovers engaged in a spread-eagle position. Stephen resisted the urge to comment.

When Farnsworth returned, he carried a covered silver platter, along with the mirror. 'My lord, Lady Whitmore sent this.' He set the platter upon the desk.

Now what was Emily up to? Stephen lifted the cover and found a china plate neatly covered with slices of pound cake. Atop the cake rested luscious strawberry halves, drenched in sweet cream.

He tasted the dessert, savouring its sweetness. Whether it was an apology or a bribe, he didn't know. Perhaps both. He did know that she enjoyed baking, and it had taken time and care to make this.

It tasted all the sweeter because of it.

He offered some to Royce, who used his bare fingers to soak a piece of cake in cream. 'Mmm…' the boy sighed. With strawberry streaks upon his lips, he wiped his hands upon his trousers and returned to his book.

After he'd finished the dessert, Stephen set the plate aside. He'd have to thank Emily for it later, and that was something he anticipated with pleasure.

He balanced the mirror against a stack of books on the side of his desk. Then he loosened his shirt, placing the mirror between his knees to see the design more clearly.

'I wonder if this tattoo has any meaning,' he mused out loud.

Royce merely licked his finger and turned the page.

'Of course, I'm certain your father never told you what it was. Such a thing would be quite a secret.'

Royce shifted in his seat, but said nothing.

Stephen traced the design, dipping his pen into the inkwell. The swirling black symbols resembled an ancient language. Quentin had thought it was Sanskrit.

'Did your father ever travel to the Orient?' Stephen asked.

'Yes.' Royce turned the book over, holding it up to the light. 'And I'm going to travel to India some day.'

'Why India?'

'Our butler was from India. Anant was his name. He used to tell me stories of battles between his people and ours. He once slit a man's belly with his sword.'

'Did he, now?'

'Some day, I shall learn how to slit a man's belly.'

'A worthy occupation, to be sure.' Stephen finished copying the tattoo and was surprised to see Royce had set the book aside.

'No, truly. I want to be a soldier.' The earnest tone in the boy's voice and the solemnity of his posture gave Stephen pause.

Royce came and stood beside him. 'You have that part wrong,' he said. Stephen handed him the pen, and Royce redrew the tattoo. 'There.'

'Thank you.' Even with Royce's correction, the design was nothing like anything he'd seen before. 'Do you know this symbol?'

'I don't know what it means, but Father had one on his arm.'

'When did he get it?'

Royce lifted his shoulders in a shrug. 'A year ago. When he went to India with Anant.'

'Where is Anant now?'

Royce shrugged. 'In the village, I think. Father made him leave when we had no money for servants.'

It was worth investigating. The man might be able to shed light on the meaning of the tattoo. Stephen set the design aside, intending to ask Emily to accompany him to the village later. 'So you want to be a soldier, do you?'

Royce bobbed his head. Stephen didn't mention that as Daniel's only heir, it was unlikely Royce would ever have such an opportunity. But the boy needed to learn how to govern his own lands, since he'd inherited his father's title of Baron.

'Then you'll have to learn how to ride a horse, won't you?'

A sudden shining hope dawned in Royce's eyes. 'We never—I mean, I never rode a horse before.' Royce took Stephen's hand in his. 'Can we go now?'

At the feeling of the small palm grasping his, a

tightness rose up in Stephen's chest. He wanted to be a different man than his father had been. Though Royce was not his flesh and blood, the boy was now his responsibility. He would be the one to teach Royce how to sit a horse, how to command the animal.

'Yes, we can go now.'

With the boy's hand tucked in his own, Stephen passed Emily on the way, offering her a look of what-could-I-do? while Royce babbled on.

'And I'm going to learn how to gallop and I'll go faster than anyone!'

His wife had a smudge of flour in her honey-gold hair, and never had any woman looked more delectable. He wanted to brush the flour aside, kissing her senseless.

'The cake was delicious.' He caught her hand and kissed the inside of her wrist.

'You said you liked strawberries. I was in the mood to bake a cake, so…' She shrugged, as though it were nothing.

But she had tried to please him, had created the dish with her own hands. She cared.

Deep topaz eyes met his, and, on impulse, he caught her by the nape and kissed her. Her lips parted in surprise, but she kissed him back. It was too short by half, but the softness of her touch, the scent of vanilla, inflamed him.

'Uncle Stephen, come *on*.' Royce pulled him away, and at last he relented.

'Later,' Emily whispered, after they had both left. She wanted so badly to believe he could be her helpmate and friend. But a part of her held back.

For three months she'd been alone. It had been the worst time of her existence. Stephen had disappeared, and she hadn't known if he was dead or alive. She'd woken up in the middle of the night, wondering if she'd only imagined the marriage.

And when he returned, he hadn't remembered her at all. Would he ever learn to love her? And if not, was it enough?

Farnsworth cleared his throat, interrupting her thoughts. 'There is a solicitor to see you. Mr Terence Robinson.' The butler handed Emily the man's card.

What was this all about? A wave of fear washed over her. She hadn't seen Mr Robinson since her brother's death, when they'd been unable to locate Daniel's will. They had assumed that the title and entailed property went to Royce.

Dread gathered in the pit of her stomach, gaining momentum. Was there something wrong?

She wiped her hands upon the apron. 'I must change my gown. Please serve him tea in the parlour while I prepare myself.' Then she added, 'Send for Lord Whitmore.'

The butler bowed, and when he had gone, Emily raced up the staircase, tearing off her apron. When she reached her room, she rummaged around, looking for something suitable to wear. There was nothing, save the lavender ball gown, which was completely inappropriate.

Oh, why hadn't she brought any of the new gowns Stephen had given her? She'd left them behind, afraid to wear them. Almost as if putting on the silks and satins would force her to become a true lady and a Countess. But it was too late to worry about that now.

There was no choice but to continue wearing the black serge dress. Quickly, she pinned up her hair, moaning in dismay at her appearance. Flour spots marred her hair and she tried to blot them out with water. She washed her face with scented soap, drying it with a towel. She prayed it would not take long for Farnsworth to find Stephen.

Her heart pounding, she took a deep breath. Each step toward the parlour felt like a step closer to an execution.

Emily opened the door, preparing for the worst. Mr Robinson sat upon the couch, a cup of tea in his hands. His dark wool jacket strained against the buttons, and he brushed the crumbs of a treacle biscuit from his buff-coloured trousers.

'Lady Whitmore.' Her brother's solicitor rose and inclined his head in greeting. 'Thank you for receiving me.' With a warm smile, he added, 'I am glad to hear that your husband has safely returned.'

'He has, yes.' She bade him sit down. 'What business brings you to Falkirk, Mr Robinson? Have you located Daniel's will?'

'I have.' He accepted a fresh cup of tea when she poured it. 'As you know, after your brother's untimely death, we spent several months searching for it.'

'Royce inherited the title and lands, didn't he?'

Mr Robinson nodded, and Emily was able to breathe again. 'Good. That's good, isn't it?'

The solicitor took a sip of tea, his eyes troubled. 'I'm afraid there's more. It came to our attention that your uncle Nigel was named legal guardian of the children, instead of you and your husband as we assumed.'

Her mind barely registered his words. Uncle Nigel? As an elderly widowed gentleman, Nigel had no use for young children. Why would Daniel have done such a thing?

'Nigel is still in India,' she informed Mr Robinson.

'He was. But he has recently returned to his estate here, upon hearing of your brother's death. His men contacted me, and, thanks to his efforts, we were able to locate the will. It seems your brother put it into his safekeeping.'

Emily's suspicions darkened. It seemed a bit convenient for Nigel to suddenly find the will. She barely remembered her uncle, from when she was a little girl. He'd been a stout man, always smiling. But they'd had little contact with him before he'd gone off to India, save the occasional letter.

'Why hasn't he come to see us, if he is back in England?'

'He has invited you and the children to come and visit. Here.' Mr Robinson handed her a folded envelope.

Emily read the contents of the letter, and when she'd finished, she clenched her hands into fists. 'He expects me to leave them behind.' It was a struggle to control her anger. 'The children belong in my care. I have taken the place of their mother for almost a year now.'

'True, yes. But according to the law, they are now under Mr Barrow's protection. Unless he agrees to name you as their guardian, you have no choice.' Mr Robinson reached for another treacle biscuit, offering her a sympathetic smile. 'I would suggest that you go and ask him to relinquish his rights. He may well agree—'

She cut him off. 'I will not give my brother's children to Nigel or to anyone else.' With a hard stare at the solicitor, Emily rose to her feet. 'Good day.'

'Forgive me, Lady Whitmore, but if you do not abide by the conditions of the will, Mr Barrow has the right to alert the authorities.' He shook his head. 'While I hope he would not do so, I beg of you not to impose such a hardship upon the children.'

'I will have a footman escort you to the door, sir,' Emily repeated.

The solicitor sighed. 'I am sorry to have upset you, Lady Whitmore. I shall send over a copy of the will for you to peruse at your leisure. And you may wish to answer your uncle's invitation.'

Her answer was to crumple up the letter and toss it onto the hearth. 'Good day, sir.'

Mr Robinson bowed and departed.

Emily clenched her skirts, willing herself to remain calm. She was not going to allow anyone to take Royce or Victoria. Will or no will, they belonged to her. Not her uncle, who hadn't even bothered to come and see her once in almost fifteen years.

At long last, Stephen and Royce arrived. Her nephew's hair was rumpled, his face glowing with excitement.

'I rode a horse!' Royce exclaimed breathlessly. 'He was a brown gelding, almost fifteen hands high. Lord Whitmore taught me how to canter him.' The joy in the boy's voice made her not want to spoil the moment.

'You wanted to see me?' Stephen asked.

'I'll tell you about it later,' Emily replied to Stephen. 'I would like to hear about your first ride.' Giving Royce her full attention, she forced a smile while he described his experiences.

Her eyes met Stephen's. There was amusement in his expression, almost fatherly in the way he listened to Royce's boyish excitement.

'He did well, though I imagine his backside will be sore in the morning.'

'I am fine,' Royce insisted. 'Can we ride more today?'

Stephen shook his head. 'Tomorrow.' With a glance down at the empty plate, he asked, 'Why don't you go into the kitchen and see if Cook has any more biscuits?'

After the boy had left, Stephen turned his attention to Emily. 'You look worried,' he said. 'Is everything all right?'

He reached out to rub the tension from her neck, and gooseflesh rose up on her skin. Emily could smell his skin, the light scent of shaving soap and the outdoors. It made her want to pull him closer.

She wanted so badly to pour out her troubles, to lay her head on his shoulder and let him relieve the burden of responsibility. 'My brother's solicitor,

Mr Terence Robinson, came to speak with us about Daniel's will.'

'What did he want?'

'The original will was finally found. Mr Robinson claims that Daniel did not name us as guardians of the children. He named my uncle guardian.'

Stephen's hands moved down to her waist. 'Have you seen the will?'

'Not yet. He says he'll send a copy to us.' She gripped his hands in hers. 'My uncle also invited us to visit and bring the children.'

'You're troubled about it. Why?'

'It seems too sudden. Why now? Why wouldn't Nigel have contacted me after Daniel's death?'

'It takes time for a letter to reach India, Emily.'

Stephen nipped at her lips, and Emily found it difficult to think clearly while he was touching her. He lowered his mouth to her neck, sending fierce shivers through her skin.

'Don't, please.' He was not taking her seriously. 'This is important to me.'

'Why are you afraid? Is there something the matter with your uncle?'

'No, there's nothing wrong with Nigel. But I can't understand why he would want custody of small children, at his age. Something feels wrong about this.'

'Royce and Victoria are under my protection.

You needn't fear.' Stephen took her hand, his thumb caressing her knuckles. 'I'll look into the matter. I'll go and talk to your uncle myself, if you wish.'

She forced herself to calm down. He'd given her his promise. It would have to be enough for now. 'Thank you.'

Stephen sat down and poured himself a cup of tea. 'Earlier today, Royce told me about your former butler Anant.'

'Anant Paltu. He worked for us a few years ago.'

'If Mr Paltu still lives in the village, I want to pay him a call tomorrow morning,' Stephen said.

'Why?'

'He may know something about the tattoo on my neck.' He loosened his collar, revealing it to her. 'Royce claimed that Mr Paltu accompanied your brother on a trip to India.'

She knew Daniel had got the marking in India, but had never questioned why or what it meant.

'It's not a coincidence that both of us have the tattoos,' Stephen said. 'My ship must have gone to India when I was away those three months.'

'What do you think the mark means?'

'I don't know. But I intend to find out.' He stifled a yawn, and then took her hand, pulling her forward. 'Come to bed.'

Her face turned scarlet. How could he think of

such a thing now? She kept her feet anchored in place, refusing to move. 'We discussed this. It's far too soon for me.'

A smug look overcame his face. 'That wasn't what I had in mind, dear wife.'

'Then what did you have in mind?'

'I'll show you.' He stood and beckoned for her to follow. He led her down a corridor and upstairs. At the door to their bedchamber, he waited. His shirt collar remained loose from where he'd revealed the tattoo. The sight of his skin made her remember what it was like to touch him.

She waited at the threshold, shaking her head. 'Why do I sense this is not a good idea?'

'You are entirely too suspicious,' he remarked. Once inside, he sat down and removed his coat, waistcoat and shoes. 'I am the one at your mercy, not the other way around. You might try to force yourself upon me.'

He laid back upon the pillow, his eyes mischievous. 'I am willing to risk it, however. You should remove your dress and those damned petticoats first.'

'No.' She wasn't fooled at all by him. Crossing her arms, she leaned against the doorframe. 'Whatever you have to say can be said without me disrobing.'

He sighed and caught her wrists. 'Trust me, Emily.'

'I don't trust you at all.' And yet, she let her hands fall to her sides, while he unbuttoned her dress. 'Why is it that every time I am alone with you, you keep trying to remove my clothing?'

'Because it's fun?' he suggested. Turning serious, he continued, 'You cannot sleep in that contraption.'

'Sleep?' The idea of sinking into a soft bed was as appealing as a dish of strawberry ice. 'But it's still the late afternoon. They'll be expecting us for supper. And what about the children?'

'Farnsworth will hold our supper for us. And I feel certain that he won't deny the children their food.' He helped her lift away the heavy petticoats and crinoline before unlacing her stays. Then he leaned back upon the vast bed, patting the pillow beside him.

Emily climbed into bed wearing only her chemise and drawers. He pulled her close. 'This is nice,' he said. His arms surrounded her, warm and strong. The spicy scent of his shaving soap made her want to snuggle into his neck. 'I slept little last night, between Victoria's crying and your snoring outside the door.'

'I do not snore.'

'Of course you do. And if you snore while I am napping, I'll be sure to kick you.' His hand moved below the curve of her breast, his mouth upon her cheek.

If he believed she could fall asleep like this, then the man had gone mad. She wanted to turn towards him, to run her hands inside his shirt and feel the ridges of his muscles. Perhaps if she counted sheep, she might be able to ignore the heat of his skin against hers.

'Do not take advantage of me while I sleep,' she warned, closing her eyes.

'Don't worry, Emily,' he said. His voice was like a swirl of cream upon chocolate. 'If I take advantage of you, you'll know it.'

Though his hands never moved, her nipple tightened into a hard bud.

One sheep. Two sheep. Sixteen sheep.

She grabbed a pillow and squeezed it hard. Her body craved him, but she refused to weaken.

Beside her, she heard his breathing grow deep and even. He held her close, her back pressed up against him.

It reminded her of the way he'd held her the first time he'd made love to her on their wedding night. Skin to skin, he'd treated her with such gentleness. Sadness pricked her eyelids, for he hadn't loved her then.

And she didn't know what he felt for her now.

Chapter Fifteen

When picking fresh blackberries for a tart, be sure that the berry is plump and easily plucked from the thorns. A berry that is not yet ripe will stubbornly cling to its vine and prove sour and unpalatable.

—Emily Barrow's *Cook Book*

They rode out the following afternoon. Stephen was accustomed to riding, his body naturally adapting to the horse's gait. Emily, in contrast, hung on to the reins with white knuckles. He suspected she hadn't ridden a horse in years, and her backside would be sore later. And yet he knew she'd die before complaining.

The village appeared upon the horizon, a pastoral scene of thatched cottages and wisps of smoke rising from the chimneys. A farmer driving a horse-drawn cart rumbled along the dirt road.

When they reached the centre of the village, wooden signs hung outside to mark the establishments. Stephen motioned for Emily to ride behind him as the streets grew narrower. They passed a tavern, a blacksmith's and a shoemaker's, before Emily called out for Stephen to halt.

He dismounted and put his arms around her waist to help her down. His hands lingered a moment, but she said nothing. Last night he had managed to sleep beside her without making love to her, though the effort had nearly been his undoing.

He was waiting for her to turn to him. He wanted her to desire him, to give their marriage a chance. But it had to be her choice.

She had blossomed here, comfortable as she'd never been in London. Perhaps she was right, and he should let her live at Falkirk.

Tethering their horses outside the shoemaker's, he walked alongside her until they reached an apothecary shop. The spicy aroma of cinnamon and cardamom filled his nostrils as they entered. The owner, a stout man with long hanging jowls, set down his mortar and pestle at the sight of Emily.

'Why, Lady Whitmore,' he greeted her, 'it is a surprise to see you.'

'Hello, Mr Barmouth,' she responded, offering

the man a bright smile. 'May I present my husband, the Earl of Whitmore?'

The apothecary gave a slight bow. 'My lord.'

Stephen greeted the man and added, 'I hope you may be able to assist me in a small matter. I am looking for a man called Anant Paltu. He used to work in my wife's household.'

'I am afraid Anant is not here at the moment,' Mr Barmouth apologised. With a quick glance toward the back room of the shop, he shrugged. 'I shall give him your message, however. Is there a place where he can find you?'

'I will be at the Baron's estate in the next hour,' Stephen offered. 'Or if he cannot meet me there, he may come to Falkirk.'

Emily's expression sharpened when he mentioned Daniel's house, but she thankfully said nothing. He hadn't told her of his intent to search the property.

Mr Barmouth promised to send the message on their behalf, and they departed. Once they were back outside, Emily accepted his assistance onto her horse. 'Why do you want to visit Daniel's estate? There is hardly anything left.'

'If your brother had any records relating to *The Lady Valiant*, they would be at his house.'

'Unless someone found them first.'

'Which is what I intend to find out.' He handed her the reins.

Emily took them and sighed. 'You're right. We'll go and see what we can find.'

'Not you.' He didn't know what to expect at the estate, and he refused to endanger her. 'I'll escort you back to Falkirk first.'

'You're not leaving me behind, Whitmore.' She spurred her horse into a gallop, wincing at the jostling horse.

With no choice, Stephen followed her. They passed the village and rode into the open countryside. Amidst the profusion of wildflowers, a modest manor house stood atop a hillside. Abandoned and broken, Stephen doubted if there was much left to it.

The horses travelled uphill until they reached the gates. Emily dismounted without waiting for Stephen and led the animal to the stables.

He didn't like the look of the place. Once, Hollingford had possessed an estate known for breeding the finest horses. Now all that remained was a crumbling manor and empty stalls.

The malodorous scent provoked a sudden memory. Visions poured through his mind, filling in the rifts of the past. He remembered travelling by coach to Scotland, Emily's face radiant with happiness.

He'd brought her back to Falkirk three days after the wedding. She had worn a simple blue dress, and it had snowed that morning. A thin layer of ice had caused him to stumble upon the threshold.

Vivid memories crashed into him, and bitterness filled his throat when he recalled her smile. 'You were in love with me, weren't you?'

Emily tethered her horse to one of the stalls and stopped to stare at him. 'What do you mean?'

'You married me because you loved me. You said it on the day we wed.'

'I don't know what I said.'

He remembered it as though he were standing beside her just yesterday. 'You said you'd dreamed of marrying me. That this was what you'd hoped for.'

She kept her gaze averted. 'I might have been caught up in the moment.'

He drew nearer, trapping her against a stall. 'I married you to avoid my father's interference. And to take you away from here.' He rested both hands upon her shoulders. 'You never knew that your brother sent me, did you?'

She shook her head.

'He asked me to come and ensure that you were all right. When I saw this place…' He shook his head. 'You didn't deserve to live like that.'

After a pause, she inclined her head. 'It no longer matters.'

But it did. He could see it in the way she

guarded her emotions. 'You thought I was in love with you. Would you have married me if you had known the truth?'

She shrugged. 'You said everything I wanted to hear. I had no one to blame but myself.'

'I hurt you when I left. I am sorry for it.'

A tremulous expression glimmered in her eyes, but she shielded the vulnerability. Though she might have dismissed it as unimportant, he knew better. He wanted to atone for it, to start again.

Without acknowledging the apology, she said, 'Let us go into the house.'

The manor boasted fourteen rooms, but Stephen could not remember a time when the house had held all its furnishings and paintings. The brick façade was covered in ivy, the vines smothering cracked windows. The panes were rotted, the wood crumbling in places. It was a home that evoked despair.

'Are you certain you wish to enter?' he asked.

She nodded. 'It wasn't always like this.'

Emily moved up the crumbling steps, running her hands along the entryway until she felt a loose brick. Wiggling it forward, she reached into the hollow and withdrew an iron key. She unlocked the door, and pushed it open. The smell of dust and decay permeated his senses.

Nothing of value remained. The walls were discoloured with light squares where paintings had once hung. As he walked toward the drawing room, he spied an old, battered Grecian couch peppered with moth holes. Spider webs glistened against the heavy green velvet curtains by the windows.

'Daniel sold the *étagère*,' Emily remarked. 'Just before we married. I used to love tracing my fingers on the wood. Mama had porcelain shepherdesses on display.'

'Were you happy here?' he asked.

She shook her head. 'They always argued over money, over which pieces to sell. After Papa died—'

A shudder pulsed through her. Her family's tragedy had been retold in countless drawing rooms. Rather than beg for help from a family member, her father had hanged himself. She buried her face in her hands, trying to gather her composure.

'Were you there when it happened?'

'I was the one who cut him down.'

Stephen was aghast. 'What of your brother? Where was he?'

Emily took a breath. 'Daniel had gone to play faro. He brought home money that night. It was one of the few times he won.'

Stephen placed an arm around her shoulders. He

wanted to grant her support, to let her know that he regretted what had happened. 'You should not have had to face such a tragedy alone.'

'I was not alone. Daniel's wife was with me. But she was pregnant and could not help.' A cynical expression formed. 'I should have found a way to stop it from happening.'

'It wasn't your fault. No one blames you.'

'No, but it is a convenient excuse for the ladies of the *ton* to keep me out of their drawing rooms. They know that this is what I came from, Stephen.' She gestured toward the dishevelled room. 'This is who I am.'

'No. It was a tragedy, not a judgement of your character.'

She didn't argue, as though it wasn't worth the effort. He could see the disbelief in her eyes. Silks and fancy gowns would not conquer her vulnerability. He didn't know if he could change that.

'Let us go into my brother's study,' she suggested. 'There might be some papers that could help you remember the night you were attacked.'

He followed her, stepping over a fallen table and broken glass. When they reached the study, ledgers lay everywhere, the room in shambles. Someone had searched thoroughly for something. Evidence, Stephen was certain. But what?

'He was here before us,' Emily guessed, trying

to push a heavy desk upright. 'The man who attacked me.'

Stephen assisted her and they picked up the fallen drawers. 'I agree. But he may have overlooked something.'

They spent the next hour sorting through the papers and righting furniture. Stephen knew that the family had lost everything, but seeing the reality was much worse than he'd imagined. Only months ago, Emily had lived here with her brother and the children. He didn't like to think of rats living here, much less his wife and family.

His family. The thought sobered him. He was responsible for their well-being and protection. Although Royce and Victoria were not of his blood, he was growing accustomed to them. And whether or not he retained guardianship, he made a personal vow never to let any of them suffer through this kind of existence again.

Stephen continued searching through the books when he spied a tin horse, just the size of the soldiers belonging to Royce. The horse was small enough to fit inside his palm, the brown paint nearly gone. Stephen tucked the toy inside his waistcoat pocket, planning to return it to Royce later.

'Look at this one,' Emily said, handing him a bound log. Stephen thumbed through the pages, stopping when he saw the name of one of his ships: *The Lady Valiant*. It was the same ship whose cargo profits had been stolen. But several pages of the log were missing.

'This was my ledger, not Daniel's. I wrote these entries.' He frowned, wondering how Emily's brother had come by the pages. 'How do you think it ended up—' He stopped short when a dark-skinned Indian man entered, dressed in flowing robes of beige.

The man was not tall, but he moved with the grace of a tiger, swift and sure. A vision flashed through his mind. This man had raised a knife, delivering a vicious blow against someone…a shattering pain invaded Stephen's body…and later he recalled the scent of healing herbs pressed against his wounds.

'Mem Sahib,' he greeted Emily. A strange expression crossed the Indian's face when Stephen was about to introduce himself.

'It is good to see you, Anant.' Emily took the man's hands in her own. 'You look well.'

The Indian returned her smile, and he seemed like an older brother, protective of Emily. He bowed to Stephen, his eyes discerning. 'Sahib, I see you have recovered from your injuries.'

From the way the Indian noted the healing, Stephen ventured his prediction. 'You were there the night I was attacked.'

'I was.' Regret shadowed his face. 'To my sorrow, I arrived too late to save Lord Hollingford's life. But yours—' He broke off, his gaze flickering toward Emily before he shielded the thoughts.

'What happened to me after the attack?'

The Indian glanced at Emily again. 'While I fought your attackers, you escaped…elsewhere, Sahib.'

'Where?'

After a long moment of hesitation, the Indian admitted, 'It was a woman's house.'

Emily's face whitened. 'Your mistress.'

Though he wanted to deny it, Stephen couldn't. A vision flashed through his mind, of staggering through the streets, blood drenching his shirt. He'd gone to Patricia's home for sanctuary.

'Yes,' he admitted.

Emily's gaze turned away from him, as though she couldn't bear to look upon his face. Did she still believe he'd been unfaithful? He'd been bleeding, while men were hunting him. Infidelity was not even possible. His anger flared, for they'd been through this before.

But he could see the questions in his wife's mind, the suspicions rising. Although they'd begun rebuilding their marriage, a servant's words were already tearing it down. His resentment rose higher, and he forced back his temper. Later. He would talk to her later, and allay whatever mistrust she was feeling.

He redirected his interrogation back to Anant. 'Why were they trying to kill me? Were they Daniel's creditors?'

Anant shook his head slowly. 'They wanted the profits from your ship, *The Lady Valiant*.' A dark undercurrent cloaked the servant's words, almost as though he resented the loss. 'I overheard them arguing about it. They were trying to locate the missing funds and thought that Lord Hollingford knew where they were.'

Emily rubbed her arms and shivered. 'Daniel would never steal anything. Why would they suspect him?'

Anant bowed his head. 'I regret, my lady, that he had numerous debts.'

'What happened when he went to India with you last year?' Stephen questioned. 'Royce told me about a tattoo that Daniel received. Was it Sanskrit?'

Anant looked uncomfortable. 'It was Chinese, my lord. But I'm afraid that's all I know.'

Stephen didn't believe him. The marking most definitely had a darker meaning, one that the servant did not wish to disclose. He didn't question him further, but at least now he knew the language of the foreign emblems.

Anant turned to Emily, his expression softening. 'The children, Mem Sahib. Are they well?'

Emily forced a smile and nodded. 'They are at Falkirk, should you like to see them.'

The two talked quietly, Anant helping her to set the room back in order. As the sun grew lower, Stephen drew Emily to his side. 'Go and wait with the horses. Before we leave, I wish to speak with Anant alone.'

'There is nothing that cannot be said in my presence,' she argued.

'It does not concern you.'

Anger blistered in her eyes. 'All of it concerns me. If you plan to talk about my brother, I deserve to know what happened.' She clenched his arm. 'Or is this about your mistress?'

'We'll discuss that later.'

'Discuss what? That you went to her residence instead of your own family's? What am I to think?'

'I was bleeding, damn it. I wasn't about to ravish her. She saved my life.'

Her shoulders lowered in defeat, and he added, 'Wait at the stables, and I'll take you back.'

She obeyed, but from her demeanour, he sensed that this conversation was far from over.

When he was certain she'd gone, he returned to Anant. 'The Chinese tattoo. There is another man who wears the same marking.' He chose his words carefully, not wanting to reveal too much. 'Carstairs is his name.'

'Were I you, I should not trust him, my lord. The man betrayed Lord Hollingford to his enemies.'

Stephen recalled the Viscount confiding financial troubles. Could Carstairs have stolen the shipping profits and tried to behave as though Daniel were the thief? Or someone else?

'If I have more questions, will you be in the village?'

Anant nodded. 'I will answer whatever I can, Sahib.' His dark face softened. 'And if you would permit it, I should like to see Master Royce and young Victoria once more. I helped to care for them when Lord Hollingford was unable to do so.'

Stephen granted permission and thanked Anant once more for the information. The Indian bowed deeply, and moments later, he disappeared on foot towards the village.

The revelation troubled him deeply, for he had trusted Carstairs at one time. And yet, he was not prepared to accept Anant's assertions without proof. The events were more complex than he'd anticipated and would take time to unravel.

One matter was certain. He would protect Emily and the children above all else.

That night in their bedchamber, a fire burned low in the hearth. Her maid had turned back the covers of the bed, while Emily sat with her knees curled up to her chest, her cotton nightgown covering her from neck to ankle. When the door opened, she jerked her gaze and saw Stephen.

'What are you doing here?' She gripped the hem of her gown, for he looked furious. All through the ride back to Falkirk, he hadn't spoken to her. Now, he reminded her of a wolf, stalking his prey.

'You know why I'm here. We have an argument to finish.' Stephen removed his riding boots, then his coat. He turned away to unbutton his shirt, catching her attention. At the sight of his bare back, her cheeks heated. His muscles appeared sinewy with rough planes, like carved marble. Upon the back of his neck, she saw the Chinese tattoo.

The foreign marking gave him a dangerous edge, like a mercenary. Fear rippled through her, and she wondered what it meant.

He leaned against the chair, his corded muscles tight in the firelight. He stood so near, she smelled the faint trace of brandy on his breath. But there was no doubt he was sober.

'Oh.' She'd been so angry with him this afternoon, hardly able to talk to him. No, that wasn't right. She'd been jealous. Another woman had tended his wounds, putting him upon a ship so that his enemies wouldn't find him.

Though logic reminded her that he'd done nothing wrong, she wanted to claw the woman's eyes out for touching her husband. Even if it was innocent.

Stephen's hand curled around the back of her neck. 'You accused me of letting your brother die while I was with my mistress.'

She rose from the chair, putting her hands upon his warm flesh. 'I was angry at the thought of your infidelity, yes. And I did blame you for Daniel's death.' She lowered her gaze. 'That was before I knew the truth.'

'I never touched Patricia that night or any other night afterwards. I swear to you.'

Emily rested her forehead against his chest, and she believed him. His hands settled upon the crown of her head, his thumbs brushing her temples. 'Aren't you going to lash out at me? Threaten to poison my tea?'

'I thought about it. And you're right. It would be difficult to ravish a woman while you were half-bleeding to death.'

He touched her neck, his hands moving down her back. Gently, he pressed her body closer until she felt the hard length of him through his trousers. 'I'd rather ravish you.'

A tiny spiral of fear hovered, but she pushed it

aside. She wanted to be with him tonight, to pretend for a moment that the danger didn't exist. To claim him as her own, removing the memory of any other woman but herself.

His fingers moved against her spine, gathering the fabric of her nightgown until it rose to her knees. He reached beneath the delicate linen, his palms cupping her bare bottom. At his touch, Emily closed her eyes.

'Did I undress you like this on our wedding night?'

'I…undressed myself. I was in your bed waiting for you.' Just remembering it made her nipples pucker against the cool fabric. As his hands caressed her *derrière*, warm heat blossomed between her thighs. He drew her against him, his manhood rock hard against the thin barrier of clothing.

He kissed her, his mouth conjuring up the past as though their wedding night were only a day ago. She wrapped her arms around his neck, holding him close.

'Help me remember everything,' he whispered.

Emily raised her arms, and he lifted her nightgown away. She stood naked before him, his eyes turning hot.

He kissed her again, a demanding embrace that took her mouth fully captive. Emily surrendered to his mouth, meeting his passion with her own feelings.

She needed him so much, needed to know that she meant something to him, even if for only this night. The lonely months fell away, and she ached to join with him.

He lowered his mouth to her breast, his tongue swirling upon her tight nipple. Another rush of wetness dampened between her thighs.

With trembling hands, she unbuttoned his trousers, freeing his erection. Unable to resist, she took him in her fist, stroking the smoothness of the length, the rounded head.

The expression on his face was of a man caught unaware. His eyes were closed, and he sucked in a breath when she dragged her hand in a gentle friction along his length.

'I touched you like this, before. Do you remember?'

He shook his head, groaning when her thumb caressed the wetness coating the tip of him. His mouth crashed down upon hers, a wicked kiss that made her body shiver.

He trapped her wrists, guiding her backwards on to the bed. She laid down upon the soft sheets, needing him. He dipped his fingers into her depths, caressing her in a rhythm that made her grip the sheets.

'You are my wife,' he whispered. 'There is no one else.'

A hot fist of desire caught up inside her, and when he stroked her velvet depths, her breath shattered. Blowing a light wisp of air against her body, his mouth moved lower, lower still, while his hands invaded and withdrew.

His kiss edged up the inside of her thighs, tantalisingly close to her centre. 'I want to taste you.'

Before she could protest, his tongue licked her intimately, sliding partway inside her. She arched her back, shaking with unfulfilled need. 'Stephen—'

But she could no longer speak when his tongue worked against her, pushing her closer to the edge. Her hands gripped his hair, her legs wide open until the madness swept over her, rocking her hips with waves of pleasure.

She felt the tip of his length hovering at her entrance. Then he slid partway into her folds, using his body to tease her. Her breath spasmed as he entered and withdrew, letting her moisture coat his length.

The look of fierce concentration on his face made her aware of his own aching needs.

'Come to me,' she pleaded.

There was a moment's hesitation, before he sank inside her completely. He held her bottom, easing himself back and then filling her again. The rhythm of his penetration caught hold until her body moved against his.

She had been so innocent, so unknowing on their wedding night, and yet he'd made love to her until her body was sore the next morning. Sweet heaven above, how she'd missed him.

Stephen forced her legs to wrap around his waist, deepening the strokes. He kissed her breasts, sucking her nipples hard as he buried himself inside her.

She was shaking, her body welcoming him deep within. He pounded his full length inside, seemingly growing harder. A rush of hot moisture flooded over her, and she bit back a scream, her tight well squeezing him with aftershocks. She saw his own release come seconds later, his hips flexing until he groaned aloud.

He lay atop her, his warm body covering her completely. Emily couldn't stop from trembling.

'Did I hurt you?' he whispered.

'No.' But she offered no elaboration. She couldn't bring herself to confess how much she'd missed him.

He withdrew from inside her, rolling her back against him. He pressed a kiss upon her bare shoulder. 'I need to return to London.'

'Why?'

'I want to speak with Carstairs again, about the tattoo and the shipment.' He slid his palm over the soft skin of her body. 'And I want you and the children to remain here.'

She didn't like the thought of him going off to fight an unseen enemy while she remained alone with the children. Thoughts of the solicitor's visit preyed upon her mind, and she rolled over to face him. 'What about my Uncle Nigel?'

'What about him?'

'What if he tries to take the children from me while you are gone? Mr Robinson said I had to bring them to his estate.'

'We will decide what to do when we see the will. And as I said, I'll go and speak to him. Perhaps I can convince him to wait.'

'And what if I have to give them up?' She couldn't even bear the thought.

His arms tightened around her. 'Then we must obey the law.'

She drew back and turned to face him, unable to believe what he'd just said. 'You'll just hand them over without fighting for them?'

His expression remained stoic. 'Do you honestly believe I would give the children into a stranger's care?'

'I don't know.' Emily sat up, folding her arms around her waist. A brittle pain laced across her heart as she reached for her fallen nightgown.

'You don't believe I'll protect them.' His visage darkened with resentment.

'I'm afraid.' Raw images seared into her

memory, of her laughing brother now gone, a cold corpse buried in the ground. 'I don't want anyone to be hurt.' Not the children. And especially not her husband. But the words wouldn't come forth.

'Trust in me,' he demanded. 'The children are safer here than in London. You know it as well as I.'

'No, I don't know it. I was attacked here,' she argued. 'We should stay together.'

Stephen set his hands upon her shoulders, pulling her back into his embrace. 'They want me dead, Emily. Not the children.'

She couldn't allow herself to think about him facing danger in London. Flipping back the coverlet, she reached for her wrapper, but he stopped her.

'Let me look into the matter. I'll do what I can to make sure the children stay with us.'

'I won't give them up,' she insisted, her eyes brimming up. 'They're my children. Not my uncle's.'

'You may not have a choice.'

Did he truly mean that? He didn't understand. Though she had not given birth to them, Royce and Victoria were the only family she had left. A storm of emotions tangled within her heart. 'I don't care what the law says.'

'I do.'

His words shocked her speechless. Would he truly

follow the law, rather than keep their family together? The iron set to his jaw suggested he would.

And she could not remain with a man who would not defend those she loved.

Chapter Sixteen

If too much salt is added to a dish, drop in a raw, peeled potato to absorb it. To restore rancid lard, cut up a green apple and fry it in the liquid. Sometimes that which has gone bad, may be renewed...
— Emily Barrow's *Cook Book*

The mid-morning sun cut a blade of light through the drapes. In the solitude of his study, Stephen occupied himself with household ledgers. Emily had ordered him to leave her bedchamber last night, which added to his foul mood. She was behaving like an overwrought female, refusing to see reason. He had become the enemy again, and it irritated him. After the night they'd spent together, he'd thought they were past this.

If the will did indeed grant guardianship of the children to Nigel Barrow, then the law protected those rights. Nevertheless, he would not give them over to a stranger's care without verifying the truth. He knew, better than she, what kind of a threat they faced.

A knock sounded upon the door, and Stephen rose. Perhaps the woman had come to her senses and meant to apologise. Instead of his wife, Farnsworth stood at the entrance. 'Forgive me, my lord. These were sent to you by the solicitor, Mr Robinson.' The butler handed him a sheaf of papers.

'Thank you, Farnsworth.'

After the butler left, Stephen studied the sealed document. He found it strange that papers could wreak such havoc in their lives. He withdrew a pair of spectacles from inside his pocket. Resting them on the bridge of his nose, he opened the will. Though he did not know for certain whether the document was legal, it did appear in order. Nigel Barrow was indeed named the guardian of Royce and Victoria, as Emily had feared.

Stephen read the will twice more, but could find nothing out of the ordinary. With no other recourse, he penned a note to his own solicitor. The only way to argue the law was with an expert. In the meantime, he would obey the dictates, but only with the greatest of caution.

Emily's uneasiness, that the will had been found

only upon Nigel's return, resonated with him as well. It was possible that the document was a forgery.

Nigel had invited them to stay, with the intention of leaving the children behind. It might be best to visit the man. Only then would he know whether or not Nigel was trustworthy.

No time like the present, he decided. And though his wife would be furious, he wanted to see for himself what sort of man her uncle was.

The journey lasted a day and a half. To his surprise, Nigel's estate was magnificent, far surpassing his expectations. His coach circled around the gravel entrance, and he noted the impeccable gardens and manicured lawns.

Although Emily's uncle did not possess a title, his wealth rivalled any Viscount or Baron. Falkirk would have fit into a single wing. It led him to question how Nigel Barrow could have led such a life of luxury while allowing his other family members to suffer in poverty. Unless Barrow had sent money and Hollingford had squandered it, which was possible.

After Stephen disembarked from his carriage, a footman opened the front door and accepted his card. He was led into a drawing room decorated with rose-and-blue wallpaper. Mahogany tables and French Louis XV gilded chairs adorned the space, while a piano was set against one wall.

Before long, a plump gentleman with snowy white whiskers entered, smiling brightly. He leaned heavily upon a walking stick. 'You must be the Earl of Whitmore.'

Stephen inclined his head, and the gentleman gestured for him to sit down. 'I am Nigel Barrow. Delighted to meet you, I must say. When I heard that you'd come, I had hoped my niece and the children would be with you.'

'On another visit, perhaps.' Stephen accepted a cup of tea, declining cream or sugar. Nigel seemed to be overly fond of sweet tea, for he measured out three heaping teaspoons of sugar.

'Well, then, what brings you here? I assume this is about the will.' Before Stephen could reply, Nigel continued. 'Terribly sorry to hear about my nephew. He always seemed to be pouring money into unfortunate investments. I regret that I could not be there to help him.'

'He was in India a year ago, I understand. Did you see him?'

Nigel nodded. 'Of course, of course. He told me about some of his losses, and I loaned him funds.' Shaking his head, he added, 'I should have sent them directly to Emily, it seems.'

Nigel sipped his tea, then added another

spoonful of sugar. 'I sent Daniel hundreds of pounds over the years, but I fear Emily saw none of the benefit. I was gratified to hear that she married you, by the by. She's had too much hardship in her life.'

Though the man's regret appeared genuine, Stephen wasn't entirely convinced that all was what it seemed to be. 'How did you hear about our marriage?'

'Daniel wrote to me about it several months ago. He seemed to think his fortunes would change, now that Emily was settled.' With a light shrug, Nigel set his tea cup down.

'About the children,' Stephen began. 'Emily was quite upset to hear that her brother named you their guardian. She has been like a mother to them, all this time.'

Nigel smiled warmly. 'I am sure she has given them the best of care. But you see, at the time Daniel made out his will, she was unmarried with no prospects. We thought it best that I oversee Royce's inheritance, should anything happen to Daniel. And, unfortunately, his life was cut far too short.' He shook his head sadly.

'Why did it take you so long to return to England?' Stephen asked. 'And, for that matter, Emily says you never once visited her or the children.'

Nigel rested his wrists upon his knees. 'There

has been unrest with the Sikh Army, I'm afraid. My own estates in India were threatened, and I've been preoccupied with them.' He brightened. 'But now that everything has been put to rights, I can atone for my mistakes.

'I'll confess,' he continued, 'I have the selfish desire to spoil Daniel's children, since my wife and I were never blessed with our own.'

Rising to his feet, he leaned heavily on the cane. 'Come, now. I should like for you to see their rooms. I fear, I went a bit mad with shopping. I couldn't decide what toys they would like, so I bought them all.'

As he led Stephen upstairs, the man had to stop at the landing to catch his breath. His wrinkled face gave an apologetic smile. 'Forgive me, Whitmore. The effects of being old, I'm afraid.' He leaned upon his cane and the banister, pausing a moment. His eyes glistened with intensity. 'I'll always regret that I couldn't help my nephew Daniel. I blame myself for it.'

With a heavy sigh, he added, 'But I look forward to seeing his children. And, as you can see, I have the funds to ensure their comforts.' He continued up the stairs, leading Stephen to a nursery that was brimming with toys and dolls of every kind. It contained everything a child could want.

And yet, Stephen hesitated about bringing them here. Perhaps it was because he'd grown to care about Royce and Victoria. He, too, was reluctant to see them go.

But they had to obey the will. There was no alternative.

'Will you bring Royce and Victoria here?' Nigel asked. 'I fear travelling does not agree with me. And have Emily come, as well. I should welcome the chance to see her again.'

'She has her doubts about you,' Stephen admitted. As did he, though he couldn't see anything wrong with the older man.

'Then allow me to set her mind at ease. All of you may stay for as long as you wish.'

He supposed he would have to accept the invitation. And he had no doubt that if anything were wrong, Emily would discover it.

'I will let them know.'

Upon his return to Falkirk, Stephen decided to speak to Royce first. Of the two children, the boy would be the most angry at having to leave.

But before he could seek out the boy, Farnsworth awaited a chance to speak to him. Clearing his throat, the butler looked embarrassed.

'What is it?'

'Young Lord Hollingford gave us quite a bit of

trouble while you were gone, my lord. He climbed a tree and refused to come down.'

'And what did Lady Whitmore do?'

'She sent him to his room without supper. But I did promise the boy I would inform you of his actions.'

'Would you care to thrash him yourself, Farnsworth?'

Scarlet suffused the man's cheeks. 'I would not dare, my lord. But the lad could use more discipline.' His colour deepened to purple. 'It is not my place to offer opinions, however.'

'No, it is not.' Even if the man was right, Stephen disliked the butler's implication that Emily did not know how to discipline the children. 'But I shall speak with him.'

'Thank you, my lord.' The butler bowed, keeping his gaze towards the floor as he left.

Stephen went upstairs to his bedchamber and retrieved the tin horse he'd brought back from Hollingford's house, days ago. Then he knocked upon the door to Royce's room. The imaginary sounds of battle and cannon explosions sounded from the boy's mouth. He entered quietly, watching as Royce clashed two tin soldiers in a pretend skirmish.

'I understand you were climbing trees again,' he began.

Royce stopped the battle and grinned. 'Farnsworth couldn't reach me. He looked like a sausage, red and puffing while he called for me to come down.'

It wasn't hard to envision the butler protesting and shouting, but Stephen knew he had to be firm. 'You must respect your elders. If you had fallen, you could have broken a bone. Perhaps your neck.' He reached out and ruffled the boy's hair, settling his palm on Royce's nape.

Stephen reached inside his waistcoat and pulled out the toy horse. 'Does this belong to you?'

Royce's eyes widened, and a broad smile spread across his face. 'It's Horse! I thought I'd lost him.'

Stephen held the toy out of reach. 'You owe Farnsworth an apology for your actions. And this day, you will follow him about his duties, helping him in whatever task he commands you to do. A good soldier must learn obedience.'

Though distaste lined the boy's mouth, Royce did not argue. Impulsively, the boy wrapped his arms around Stephen's waist and hugged him. 'Thank you, Uncle Stephen!'

The affectionate gesture caught him unawares. He had tried to hug his own father once, after William had died. The Marquess had boxed his ears, claiming he wanted to be left alone.

It angered him that his father could not grant him a kind word or an embrace. Awkwardly, Stephen patted the boy's shoulder.

'You're a good lad,' he said softly. 'And a brave one.' He hated having to impart the news that the boy would be leaving, even temporarily. A direct approach was the best way.

'Royce, have you ever met your Great-Uncle Nigel?'

Royce shook his head. 'He lives in India.'

'He used to live in India, but not any more. You'll be going to visit him tomorrow.'

'I don't want to.' Royce made a neighing sound and placed one of the tin soldiers atop the horse.

Stephen stopped himself from saying, *You have no choice*. Instead, he said, 'I wonder what sorts of adventures Nigel has had. Living in India, he must have seen many exciting things. He might even have one of those curved swords I've heard of.'

'Do you think he's ever slit a man's belly, like Anant?'

Stephen held back a smile. 'You could ask him and find out. It would only be a short visit. A few weeks, perhaps. Would that be all right?'

Royce pondered the idea. 'I want to stay here with you and Aunt Emily.'

'All of us can go together,' Stephen suggested.

'Victoria wishes to go and hear his stories. She's told me how eager she is.'

At that Royce shot him a suspicious look. 'Babies can't talk.'

'Oh, but she can. You simply have to learn their language.'

Royce wrinkled his nose. 'I don't believe you.' Then he suddenly waved at the door. Stephen turned and saw Emily holding Victoria in her arms. 'Look at what Uncle Stephen brought me!' he cried. 'He found Horse!'

His wife's face softened, but Stephen detected the cool anger beneath the veneer of serenity. 'I'm so glad.'

'And I might go and visit Great-Uncle Nigel. He's been to India, you know.'

At Royce's revelation, Emily's posture stiffened. She sent Stephen a look of fury before turning her back.

'I will see you at dinner this evening,' he told Royce.

'Thank you for Horse, Uncle Stephen,' Royce said again. His boyish face revealed pure happiness, and Stephen was glad he'd thought to bring the toy.

'You are most welcome.'

But although Royce was considering the possibility of visiting Nigel, Stephen sensed that his wife would be much harder to convince.

* * *

Emily remained silent all through dinner and when they were in their bedchamber.

'We've been invited to bring the children to your uncle,' he said. 'I met with him, and I think he would provide the children with a fine home and a good education.'

'You should have told me where you were going.' Emily struggled to remove her corset, fighting with the laces. Stephen came up behind her and loosened the stays. He did not touch her, suspecting that she would snap at him if he did.

'I wanted to investigate him myself,' he admitted.

'And what did you find?'

'Nothing. He has a large house and has purchased toys for the children. He seems eager to meet them.' Stephen stepped aside, trying not to get distracted while she removed the corset and pulled on a wrapper. The filmy fabric stretched across her breasts, making him want to take it off her again.

'I know my brother. He wouldn't have given the children to a stranger. Not after I married you.'

'Daniel made out his will before we married. And Nigel isn't a stranger; he's their great-uncle.' He came up behind her and laid his hands upon her shoulders. The silk was indeed as soft as it appeared.

'The will is legal, Emily. And if we wish to

petition for guardianship, we must follow the proper protocol. Defying the law will not help our cause.'

'But Nigel has never even seen the children.' She crossed her arms about her waist, turning to face him. 'He doesn't know them the way I do. Royce lost his mother when Victoria was born. Now he's lost his father, too. I'm all they have.'

'You are not all they have,' he said quietly. 'They have me, as well. I promised you I'd protect them.'

Why couldn't she see him as a part of their lives? It was as though she'd cut him off without a second thought. 'I think we should go together when we take the children.' He slid his arms around her waist, drawing her closer. 'If there is anything that bothers you, we'll leave.'

'You're not taking the children anywhere. They're staying here, where they belong.'

'Do you think to defy the law?' He kissed her shoulder, trying to soothe her bad temper. 'Come with me, Emily. Meet him for yourself.'

'No. As I've said, the children will not leave Falkirk. And neither will I.'

'You're being ridiculous. Hasn't it occurred to you that this may be a place where you'll be safe? The last time I left for London, you were attacked here. My enemies know where we are. It's only a matter of time before they find us.'

'I don't want to go,' she said quietly. 'Nigel never

did anything for us while we were struggling to keep the estate running. Why would he help us now?'

'He's old, Emily. He admitted that he wanted to make up for what happened years ago.'

'I don't like it. And I don't want you taking the children, either.'

'The will states—'

'Hang the will. If you try to take them, I'll find a way to stop you.'

'How? By sabotaging the carriage?' The flicker of interest in her eyes made him wish he hadn't made the sardonic remark.

'I will do whatever it takes.'

Emily couldn't breathe with the suffocating rage infusing her. If Stephen thought he was going to take the children from her, then he was sorely mistaken.

She paced the floors of her room, trying to think. What could she do? She dismissed the idea of tampering with the carriage, for that would only hurt the children.

In the looking glass, she caught a glimpse of herself. Her pale face appeared haunted and drawn. Blonde hair tumbled about her shoulders, desperately in need of attention. Raising her palms to her cheeks, she realised she would make any man run in horror. Simply dreadful.

After removing the pins, she began to brush her hair. She had to stop Stephen from leaving the house. Somehow, some way. If he couldn't leave, then he couldn't take the children.

Would seducing him change his mind? She knew a woman could control a man with her body. Emily glanced down at her own form, doubtful that she could do the same.

Yet, she didn't rule out the possibility. Her skin prickled at the thought.

She pulled on her wrapper and padded downstairs to the kitchen. The scullery maids were sleeping in a corner of the room, and Emily tried not to awaken them while she made herself a cup of tea. The scent of burning coal mingled with the faint aromas from the evening meal. The large wooden table held knife scars where the servants had sliced vegetables.

As she rubbed her cold feet near the stove, an idea formed. There wasn't much time. But it might work.

She opened a drawer and searched for the sharpest knife she could find. This wouldn't be easy. But then again, nothing worth doing was easy. She lifted the knife and headed upstairs to Stephen's bedchamber.

The next morning, Stephen did not wait for his valet to help him dress. He'd slept poorly that night, wishing he could coax Emily to go with him to Nigel's residence.

He pulled on a shirt and waistcoat, fumbling with the buttons in the darkness. When at last he was fully dressed, he reached for his riding boots and slid them on.

His foot went completely through the sole. The bottom of his boot hit the floor with a loud thunk. He cursed and forced his foot into the other boot. Like the first, the boot had no sole.

When he opened the wardrobe, he realised someone had butchered every pair of shoes he owned. And he knew just who that someone was.

He strode barefoot down the hallway to his wife's room. With a loud crash, he threw her door open.

'Good morning,' she muttered sleepily, yawning.

'Do not "Good morning" me,' he demanded. 'You ruined my best pair of riding boots!'

'Yes, I did. Now you won't be leaving the house.' She yawned and rolled over. 'Close the door. I'm going back to sleep.'

He obeyed, but only to keep the servants from hearing their argument. 'If you think such a childish trick will prevent me from leaving, you are wrong. I'll simply borrow shoes from Farnsworth.' He sat down on the bed and threw back the covers. He'd not allow her to sleep through this disagreement.

'You don't wear the same size.'

'I'll leave whenever I damn well please, boots or not.'

'Do you truly wish to leave?' she asked softly. He saw suddenly that her nightgown was of the sheerest silken fabric, completely revealing every curve. 'Or would you rather do as you please?'

His words caught in his mouth. 'You don't control me, Emily.'

'No?' Her hands stripped away his waistcoat and shirt until he sat bare-chested beside her. He didn't know what her intentions were, but so long as she was removing clothing, he did not particularly care.

'We're not finished arguing,' he informed her.

In response, she lowered the bodice of her night-gown and pressed her breasts against his skin. 'No. We're not finished. I can see how angry you are.'

Anger was the furthest thing from his mind at the moment. It took only moments to rid himself of the rest of his clothing. 'I'm furious.'

He pushed her onto her back, pulling her hips against him. She wore nothing beneath the night-gown, and his body reacted instantly.

Too fast. He needed to slow her down, to take control of the situation. He suspected she intended to seduce him. It was a blatant ploy to get her way. But he had more restraint than she knew.

He moved the tip of his manhood to hover at her slick entrance while his hand palmed her breast. She gasped, the nipple pebbling in his fingertips. Though she tried to bring him inside her, he kept her trapped in place. He moved his mouth against the soft curve above her ribs. Then with his thumb, he teased her womanhood.

A good wife was supposed to obey her husband in all things, heeding his judgement. She'd gone too far this time, destroying his best pair of boots. Most husbands would beat their wives, but he had a more pleasurable punishment in mind.

He slid a fraction of himself inside her.

'Stephen?' she whispered, her tone begging.

He withdrew, caressing her folds gently. Softly. Tormenting her in the darkest form of sexual pleasure. 'Was there something you wanted?'

'You,' she breathed.

He exhaled upon her bare skin, watching her breasts tighten with excitement. 'Do you want me to kiss you?'

Emily nodded, lifting her lips to his. Eager and urgent, she reached for him. He took possession of her, and she pressed her body close to his.

His mouth vanquished her lips, and Emily moaned in surrender. If this was his idea of punishment, she intended to be disobedient every day for the rest of their marriage. She had missed this.

Like a luscious slice of chocolate cake, he tempted her past all reason.

He ran his mouth over her neck, down to her collar-bone and shoulders. His warm tongue tasted her sensitive skin, drawing close to her breasts, but not granting her what she needed.

Her womanhood grew damp, and he startled her when he pushed her knees back to her chest. Spreading her apart, he moved on top of her and penetrated deeply. Shocked, she cried out at the wicked sensation.

He drew himself out, excruciatingly slow. Then he invaded her folds again. He pulled back, moving with such tormenting ecstasy that it bordered on pain.

She didn't know when she had surrendered to him, when she'd allowed him to command her. Somehow he had regained the upper hand.

The new position gave him complete mastery of her body, letting him slide against every inch of her until she thought she would go mad.

She shattered in his arms, the pleasure intensifying with each stroke. He kept up the driving force until she broke apart again, spiralling pleasure fisting deep within. Waves of need burst forth until at last he took his own release.

He wrapped the sheets around her, holding her close. She wept silent tears, for this was what she'd wanted all along. Her husband, loving her again.

But she had tried to use the sexual pleasure as a weapon, to keep him from sending the children away. Worse, he knew it.

Her body felt more weary than ever before. Safe in his arms, she closed her eyes. Only for a moment, she thought. She'd sleep for just a moment.

Later that morning, bright sunlight pierced through the bed curtains. Emily awoke, filled with dread at the empty sheets beside her. When she went to find Stephen and the children, they had already gone.

'I am relying on you to remain with the children and alert me if there is anything suspicious about Mr Nigel Barrow,' Stephen said to Anna, while the coach continued the journey toward Nigel's estate. Though nothing had struck him as unusual or wrong, he wanted to be certain that all was well. Servants were notorious for gossiping, and likely, if anything was amiss, Anna would hear about it.

He handed her a sovereign. 'I will stay here until Lady Whitmore arrives. Send word to me if anything goes wrong.' Only then could he assess the true character of Emily's uncle.

The wet nurse cradled the baby in her arms, her eyes wide. 'Of course, my lord.'

'After that, I will be in London. I trust that you can get word to me, if I am needed.'

She nodded, but looked worried.

'I will see to it that you are rewarded for your service,' he reassured her. 'An extra year's wages will be added to your pay.'

Anna's mouth opened in surprise. 'I promise I will take good care of them, my lord. But—' she patted Victoria on the back, her worry deepening '—are you certain Lady Whitmore will come?'

'She will be arriving shortly,' he told the wet nurse. He had no doubt that Emily was already on her way to Nigel's residence. And though she would hate him for this, he had to keep them safe. Nigel, if he was truly the man he seemed, could provide a haven.

The problem was, convincing his wife to stay here. Never had he met a woman like Emily, so determined and stubborn. He couldn't drive her from his mind. The way she threatened him, and the way she welcomed him into her arms… Like a seductress, she captivated him. Leaving her soft warmth was harder than he'd thought it would be.

He glanced down at the pair of cracked leather shoes he'd borrowed from a footman. Such foolishness.

By the next afternoon, they arrived at Nigel Barrow's estate. Robust and jolly, with a set of snowy whiskers, the man greeted them with enthusiasm.

'So glad you've come, Whitmore. And the children. Ah, you must be Royce.' Nigel bent down and smiled. 'The new Baron of Hollingford. You're the image of your father, I must say.'

Royce drew back, but Stephen put his hand on the boy's shoulder for reassurance. 'It's all right,' he said beneath his breath.

'I don't believe you were really in India.' Royce kicked at the carpet, his face sullen.

'That I was, my boy. I even rode an elephant while I was there.'

Royce reached out for Stephen's hand, not at all convinced.

Nigel sent Stephen a wink. 'And this must be young Victoria. Why, you are a pretty little thing.'

Victoria buried her face in Stephen's neck and wailed. Although Anna offered to take the baby, Stephen refused to hand her over just yet. He soothed the infant, rubbing her nape.

Stephen accompanied the children to their rooms, hoping that Royce would brighten with all the toys. Instead, the boy clenched one of his toy soldiers. 'I want you to stay,' he pleaded with Stephen.

'I shall. But as soon as your aunt arrives, I must return to London. It will only be for a short while.'

Victoria rubbed her eyes, whining to go to sleep, and Stephen exchanged glances with Anna. The nurse nodded in silent understanding.

Victoria unleashed a furious howl when Stephen handed her over to Anna, crying out, 'Da, da, da!' Though he was not her father, he'd wanted nothing more than to turn around and sweep the infant into his arms. Leaving her behind would be even more difficult than he'd thought.

But it was only temporary. As soon as he spoke with his solicitor, he would try to coax Nigel into giving back custody of the children. He leaned down and touched the boy's shoulder. 'It's late, Royce. Best get to bed.'

The boy glowered at Nigel before he took Anna's hand and let her take him into the bedroom.

'It will take time for them to know me,' Nigel said sadly. From the look of longing on his face, no doubt he'd been disappointed by the children's reaction.

'Indeed.' As Stephen followed a servant to his own room, he tried to dismiss the uneasiness creeping over him. This was for the best, he knew. Though he'd have preferred to bring Emily and the children together, she'd made her feelings quite clear. Only in this manner, could he ensure that she made the journey.

Stephen grimaced, wishing he'd thought to take the rest of his wardrobe with him. He didn't like to imagine the state of his shirts at the moment, given what Emily had done to his boots.

Chapter Seventeen

Above all things, do not attempt to impress your guests beyond what you can afford. There is nothing worse than to sow the seeds of unhappiness and disaster by setting a table conveying a wealth beyond that of its owner...
—Emily Barrow's *Cook Book*

Emily's body was numb, cold with fear as the coach pulled up to Nigel Barrow's residence. The estate sprawled across acres of green fields, a stone manor with turrets similar to a castle.

Her husband had known she would come after him. In fact, he'd had a coach waiting, along with her packed belongings and the two footmen. Though she had tried to catch up to them, her coach had been mired in the muddy roads, and they'd lost several hours on the journey.

Then, too, she'd had to spend the night at an inn

along the way. Even with her escorts, she'd hardly slept at all, worrying about someone following her.

Now, it had been a full day since she'd last seen Stephen and the children. She'd missed Royce and Victoria desperately, her heart sick with fear.

How could Stephen have left her behind? It infuriated her that he'd done it, and she intended to blister his ears once she saw him again. Right now, the very thought of her husband made her want to strangle him.

As the footman helped her disembark from the coach, she moved as if in a trance. Nigel lived like a king, but it made her even more nervous at the thought. Though he was wealthy, it did not mean he would treat the children well.

A middle-aged footman with red hair welcomed her, accepting her cloak and bonnet, before leading her into the parlour. 'Mr Barrow hoped you would come, Lady Whitmore,' he said. 'I am Roberts, and if there is anything I can do to ensure your comforts, you need only give the orders. I've arranged for refreshments, and I shall inform Mr Barrow of your arrival.'

Emily did not sit, but studied the room. Oil paintings of landscapes hung at intervals, along with portraits she recognised. She saw her mother and father, and a deep loss cut through her. She had been only fourteen years old when her mother had died of consumption. And Father had—

She winced at the memory, not wanting to relive his death.

'Emily?'

She turned and saw Nigel. A stout gentleman, with long white whiskers and a balding pate, he gave her a warm smile. 'I am delighted you have come. I hope you will stay for a while?'

She did not answer the question. She had come with the intention of taking Royce and Victoria back to Falkirk. Without prelude, she demanded, 'Where are the children?'

'They are playing upstairs in the nursery. Would you care to see them? I promise you, I have not sent them to a work house or enslaved them.' His eyes gleamed with amusement.

'Yes, I want to see them.'

'Come, then.' Nigel offered her his arm, and she took it with reluctance. He leaned heavily upon a walking stick, and from his slow, steady movement, she realised Stephen was right. Nigel's age revealed a weakness she'd not expected, and she saw the pain he tried to hide as he moved up the stairs.

'What about Lord Whitmore?' She tried to keep her voice nonchalant, but nerves broke through. 'Is he here?'

Nigel tilted his head, stopping to catch his breath. 'He is out riding, I believe. He told me you would arrive soon.' He led her down the west wing, and gestured toward one of the doors. 'The nursery is here.'

He was about to open it, but Emily stopped him. 'A moment, please.' Nigel inclined his head, and she gently eased the door open. Inside, she saw Royce playing with his tin soldiers. The soldiers were lined up around a wooden castle, complete with catapults and wooden carts. He clashed the soldiers together in a mock battle.

Victoria was grasping the edge of a toy chest, holding fast while taking steps around it. She reached out to accept a biscuit from Anna.

As soon as she saw Emily, Victoria's face lit up. 'Mum-mum-mum,' she chortled. Then she crawled towards Emily, determined to reach her aunt with all haste.

Emily scooped the baby up, cuddling her close. She hadn't known it was possible to miss the children this much. It was evident they were well treated.

Then Royce spied her. 'Aunt Emily! There you are.' He flew into her arms, squeezing her tight.

'Are you enjoying your visit?' she asked while Victoria clutched her hair and tried to stuff it into her mouth.

Royce shrugged, seemingly uninterested. 'There are a lot of toys.'

'I was just telling Royce that he should come with me tomorrow to help choose his own horse. He'll have to decide what colour he wants.' Nigel smiled indulgently.

The blatant bribery incensed her. How dare Nigel try to entice her nephew by offering a horse? But Royce seemed unaware of it, and he returned to his tin soldiers. His lack of excitement made her wary.

'Why don't we go and have a chat?' Nigel suggested. 'I'm certain you must have many questions for me.' He opened the door and gestured for Emily to accompany him.

She handed the baby back to Anna. Victoria let out a screech, but Emily dropped a kiss on the child's cheek, stroking her hair. To her nephew, she added, 'I will see you later, Royce.'

When they were alone, Emily commented, 'Do you feel it necessary to buy his affections? My nephew is more intelligent than that.'

Nigel's smile faded. 'Is it wrong to provide the boy with the things he wishes to have? You would do the same, were you in my position.' As before, it took him some length of time to descend the stairs, but at last they reached the parlour.

'Why should I believe you want to provide Royce

and Victoria with toys and luxuries when you never lifted a finger to help the rest of our family?'

'Now that is not true at all. As I told Whitmore, I sent money to your father and your brother every year. It might not have been a fortune, but certainly it was enough to feed and clothe your family.'

'You sent nothing,' Emily replied, angry at his lies. 'You abandoned us and went to India.'

His face paled. 'Is that what your brother told you?' He looked visibly shaken. 'I knew he gambled some of it away, but all of it? You truly thought I never cared?' An expression of pity moved over his face. 'No wonder you must hate me so.'

He led her inside the parlour and sank down upon a pale blue wingback chair, signalling towards a parlour maid, who brought a tray of tea and refreshments. 'Emily, would you pour, please? I'm afraid my hands aren't as strong as they used to be.'

She did, noticing that his face was worn and haggard. Deep lines creased his mouth as he added sugar to the tea cup. Nigel took a sip, his hands trembling. He cleared his throat. 'I still cannot believe that Daniel withheld everything from you. It doesn't seem possible.'

He set the cup upon the saucer. 'I do not know what happened to the money, but I must explain matters to you. In particular, about the children. First, did your brother ever mention Royce's inheritance?'

Emily thought of Daniel's desperate attempts to bring in more money. 'I don't think there was anything left for Royce, except the entailed lands.'

Nigel's concern doubled. 'A few years ago, Daniel contacted me about a shipping investment he wanted to make. He borrowed money from me. The ship turned wonderful profits, enough to support your family in a fine manner. Then, from what I heard, he gambled the fortune away at the tables.'

Emily did not deny it, but she had difficulty believing Daniel would risk their future. 'He did gamble, but often he brought home money to us.'

Nigel's face sobered. 'He gambled a great deal more than that, Emily. Which brings me to the children. I saw what was happening to your family, and I made an agreement with Hollingford last year. I would loan him money on another shipping venture, but with one condition.' He sipped the tea, adding even more sugar to the cup.

'You must understand, he was gambling away young Royce's future. I could not let it happen. And so, I asked him to grant me guardianship of Royce, should anything happen to him. Hollingford changed his will accordingly. We took the profits and set the funds aside for Royce's inheritance.' Nigel held his cup out and Emily refilled it.

'I am sure you believed I had something to gain by becoming the children's guardian,' Nigel said. 'But in all honesty, I was merely trying to protect Daniel's son. Royce is my great-nephew, after all, and the new Baron of Hollingford.'

Emily set down her own cup, a sudden fear rising up. She eyed Nigel, but he seemed to anticipate her worries.

Nigel smiled. 'I can tell what you are thinking, but in all honesty, my dear, I never had any interest in your brother's title. As you can see, money has never been a problem for me. I make my living buying and selling property.' He leaned forward. 'But I am concerned for Royce. And for the family, now that I can see what has happened to you.'

A sad smile creased his face. 'I presume that Daniel never told you where he'd hidden the money for Royce's inheritance.'

Emily shook her head. 'I knew nothing of it.'

He drained the cup and offered a slight smile. 'Well, I am certain the funds will turn up. In the meantime, I've been wanting to congratulate you on your recent marriage.'

Emily would not let him distract her from the

subject of the children. 'Why did you want guardianship of the children?' she asked. 'You have nothing to gain by it.'

His eyes softened, the lines growing deeper as he smiled. 'I feel as though your brother has given me the chance to be a father. I want to experience that joy. Is there no greater gain than to watch a child grow up?'

His countenance transformed into a wistful smile. 'I can understand your reluctance to let them go. Royce is such a mischievous young imp and Victoria a pure delight.'

If Nigel were lying, it did not seem so. His interest in the children appeared sincere, and there could be no doubt that he had offered them the greatest of comforts.

'If you wish to stay with us while your husband travels to London,' Nigel suggested, 'it may ease your mind. Whitmore mentioned that he has business to attend there.'

Emily thought of the bitter argument between herself and Stephen. Perhaps it would not be so bad if she stayed with the children. At least then, she would know they were safe from harm.

'I have only a few of my belongings with me,' she admitted. 'I came with all haste.'

'Would you allow me to gift you with some new clothes?' Nigel asked.

'No, really, I—'

'Allow me to put it this way,' Nigel said. 'You were meant to grow up with lovely dresses and the best foods to eat. It was not your fault that your brother made other choices. This would be my way of making up for that.'

'I still—'

'No, I shall see the matter done. No arguments.' He rang a bell and when the servant appeared, Nigel made all the necessary arrangements. It was rather like being battered by a jovial thunderstorm.

He leaned forward and smiled at her. There was no trace of guile, no falsehood in his eagerness. 'Now I would love to hear the story of your marriage. Tell me everything.'

Nigel poured her another cup of tea, and Emily held it in her palms. She couldn't believe she was drinking tea with the man who wanted to take the children from her. But she explained the story of their elopement, and Nigel beamed to hear it.

'Excellent. I am delighted to hear that you've made such a splendid match with a powerful man,' Nigel said. 'And he's very organised and business-minded, from what I've heard.'

Emily thought of Stephen's immaculate library, his neat handwriting documenting every estate expense in a numbered log, in ordered columns. Then, too, he had been detail-oriented when he'd made love to her, kissing every inch of her body. She ordered herself not to think of it.

'I am certain you'll want to go and speak with him,' Nigel remarked. 'It warms my heart to see your tender feelings.'

Missing him was not exactly what she felt at the moment. Confusion mingled with anger, perhaps. 'We are married, nothing more.'

'But you must enjoy your new position as a Countess. Surely it is far better than you dreamed.'

She expelled a harsh laugh. 'I am no Countess at all.'

'Do you feel unworthy of the status?' Nigel suggested.

'What do you mean?'

He shrugged. 'It is not surprising. You never received the upbringing of a lady. Why would you feel comfortable married to an Earl? The responsibilities of a Countess are many.'

'Are you trying to insult me?'

He shook his head, his features suddenly piercing. 'I was offering to help you. I think our visit could be put to good use. With new gowns and the appropriate training, I think you would do quite well.'

Emily thought of the last ball and shuddered. 'No, thank you.'

'Still afraid, are you? I thought you had more courage than that.'

'I have more sense than that. They are cruel to outsiders.'

'And who has been cruel to you? The Marquess of Rothburne?'

'How do you know about the Marquess?'

Nigel only smiled. 'Your father-in-law is rather intimidating, isn't he? But you needn't worry about him. You have my full support.'

She pondered his offer. 'No, I don't want to face him again.'

Nigel's face turned compassionate. 'Have you thought of what Victoria will think?'

'Victoria?' She gaped at him. 'She is still a baby.'

'And when she grows older, do you want her to remember you as the Countess who stood up to the Marquess and gained a position of respect? Or do you want her to see you as a coward who remained in hiding?'

She could almost imagine Stephen's voice: *Stop snivelling*. She was tired of people telling her what to do, how to behave. 'What right have you to counsel me?'

'I've upset you. Forgive me,' Nigel said. 'I truly have only your best interests at heart.' He stood and moved towards the door. 'I shall leave you alone to do as you see fit. In the meantime, my servants will prepare a room for you. You may stay as long as you desire.'

After he had left, Emily paced across the parlour. His words bothered her more than she wanted to admit.

She crossed the room and watched the children, who had gone to play outside. She was envious of their freedom and their innocence. They would have all the opportunities she had not received. She would stay and guard them herself. And she would try not to think of her husband.

A soft knocking interrupted her thoughts. Emily turned and saw Stephen standing there. He wore riding clothes, impeccably shaped to his body. His dark hair looked as though the wind had mussed it, and she gripped her hands together to keep from straightening a wayward strand.

'You were supposed to arrive yesterday,' he said by way of greeting, removing his hat.

'Why did you bring the children?' she demanded. 'I told you before, I'm not giving them up.'

'I don't expect you to. But you can pretend to be upholding the will while I speak to my solicitor in London. I want you to stay here, with Nigel, so that you're protected.'

'How do I know it's safe?'

'It's the best I can do. I won't leave you back at Falkirk.' He glanced at the door and lowered his voice. 'And I know that you or Anna will send word to me, if anything appears wrong.'

'I suppose Nigel has been a saint.'

Stephen lifted his shoulders. 'He's bought them everything they desire. He seems eager to play the doting uncle.'

That much, she'd seen for herself. 'I still don't like this. You're risking too much, by going to London alone.'

'I'd rather go alone than risk anything happening to you.' He moved forward, taking her into his arms. Emily lowered her forehead to his shoulder.

'You're not invincible, Stephen.' There had been two attempts upon his life already, and there was bound to be another. Her worry magnified at the thought.

'I need to end this. I won't live my life always looking over my shoulder. Someone wants me dead, and I need to know why.' He kissed her lightly. 'I believe you'll be safe here. And if anything happens to make you distrust Nigel, I know you'll notify me immediately.'

'Don't get yourself killed,' she warned. If any man laid a finger upon her husband, he would live to regret it.

Chapter Eighteen

Good, sharp knives are essential to any kitchen. Tend all blades carefully, for they are the greatest weapons in a woman's arsenal for a good meal.

—Emily Barrow's *Cook Book*

'Why is he still alive?'

The hired assassin lowered his gaze. He chose his words carefully, fearing the consequences for his failure. 'It has been more difficult to kill Lord Whitmore than I anticipated.'

'The man gave a ball in full view of everyone in London. He has not hidden from us. You could have taken care of him at any moment.'

'He was in public, not alone. And the woman and children were with him on other occasions. You did not wish for them to be harmed, I believe?' The assassin enjoyed seeing the look of irritation.

'What of the evidence? Have the ledgers been destroyed?'

'There was nothing to be found.'

'Imbecile. Whitmore always keeps records. Did you believe he would leave them for anyone to find?'

'He did not have time to hide anything.'

'I will not take that chance. Search everywhere until you find them. I'll not risk having my reputation destroyed because of him.'

'As you wish.' The assassin relaxed, since it did not appear there would be repercussions for his initial failure. 'He is alone and unprotected now. It will be an easy matter to kill him.'

'Good. I want him dead. Fail me again and you will suffer for it.'

Emily had endured enough pins to feel like a hedgehog's cousin. In the past few days, Nigel had sent a dressmaker to fit her for morning gowns, evening dresses, riding habits and enough clothes to outfit her according to her rank of Countess.

She had loved every moment of it. But her favourite gown was one sent by her husband. Made of ivory tulle, trimmed with cream Limerick lace and pink roses, it was the dress a princess might have worn. Stephen had included matching gloves, fans and leather slippers that fit her perfectly.

She recalled the first pair of dancing slippers

he'd purchased. Though they were truly horrid instruments of torture, she remembered dancing barefoot with him on the night of the first ball. And the way he'd kissed her. She shivered, touching her fingertips to her mouth.

Being without Stephen bothered her more than she'd thought it would. She'd had nightmares about him dying, reliving the moments of when he'd been missing. She couldn't bear it if something happened to him.

She remembered his touch, the handsome cast of his face, the way his eyes would devour her.

She missed him.

Oh, she was weak. She had even ordered him several new pairs of leather boots and shoes to atone for her earlier tantrum. As if that would make it all right again.

During the day, she distracted herself with cooking. Nigel's staff members were polite and allowed her full rein in the kitchen. And they enjoyed the fruits of her labours, since she shared the desserts with any servant who wandered into the kitchen. The cook, Mrs Graham, even taught her a few techniques for making delicious sauces.

She also spent hours upon lessons. Nigel had hired dancing masters and tutors, true to his word. Emily absorbed every bit of information, determined not to be defeated by her earlier failures.

She would win the battle against the ghosts of her past.

Living with her uncle was like living with Father Christmas. He had bought not one pony, but two— a black one for Royce and a white one for Victoria.

Emily had protested that Victoria would not need it, since she had only just begun taking her first steps. With her arms outstretched for balance and her chubby legs bowed, Victoria seemed determined to master walking within a few weeks. But Nigel did not want Royce to receive gifts that Victoria did not also have.

Though she felt uncomfortable about his generosity, Nigel ignored her protests and bought whatever he wished. His wealth appeared endless, and despite what he'd said, she couldn't quite let go of her resentment about her family's years of struggling.

Maybe Daniel and her father had spent all the money. Maybe it had been lost at the gaming tables. But the fact remained: regardless of what Nigel had sent, she'd not seen a penny of his support.

That night, she buried her face in the coverlet, warming her feet with the hot brick placed by the maid. She was restless, and she reached out towards the empty side of the bed.

Her heart thudded when the door to her room

creaked open. Emily swallowed hard. 'Anna?' she whispered. There came no reply. She shrank beneath the coverlet, her hand closing upon the flannel-wrapped brick. Blood pounded in her veins at the idea of an intruder entering her bedchamber. By God, she wasn't going to cower beneath the covers while someone tried to slit her throat.

As soon as the person drew near enough, Emily sprang into motion, cracking the brick across the intruder's head. At the contact, a man yelped.

Cursing with pain, he slid to the floor. 'I should have known you'd do something like that.'

The familiar voice of her husband transformed her fear into dismay. 'Stephen?' Horrified, she turned up the lamp light. He clutched his head, blood seeping from his temple.

'I suppose this is a quicker way to die than from poison. But you didn't strike me hard enough.'

'What are you doing in my bedchamber?' She found a handkerchief and pressed it to his head.

'Visiting you. I see you haven't forgiven me for going off to London.' He groaned when she increased the pressure to stop the bleeding. 'Nigel seems to be taking good care of you.'

'He is,' she admitted. 'But I don't like staying behind while you go off to get yourself killed.'

'You nearly killed me just now.'

'It's a good thing my aim did not strike true.'

He leaned closer, resting his head against her breasts while she held the cloth to his temple. 'You could have used your nightgown to stop the bleeding.'

She understood that his intention was to get her naked. 'Were you trying to seduce me in bed?'

'That was my general hope, yes. I seem to have blundered.'

'You should have announced your presence.'

'But that would have ruined the surprise.'

'It might have saved your head.' Her hand moved to touch his temple. The bleeding had stopped, but a vicious swelling rose up.

'How are the children?' he asked.

'Well enough. Nigel is spoiling them, but Royce keeps asking when you're coming back. I think he misses you.'

She ran her palm over his cheek. 'Nigel wants to bring us to London. He spoke of re-introducing me into society.' She hadn't yet made up her mind on whether to go. Her uncle kept insisting that she face her fears.

'No. I want you to remain here, out of harm's way.'

She didn't argue. 'You seem to have brought yourself into harm's way.' Lightly she touched the wound again, and he hissed. 'I am sorry for this.'

'You could kiss me to atone for it.'

As if a single kiss would heal all between them. She had longed to see him again so much, in spite of everything. Now that he was here, her will-power crumbled into dust.

Before she could think, he met her lips, tracing them with his tongue. Threads of desire spun a silken web of need through her skin.

Was it truly that horrible if she let him make love to her? Did that make her weak? Of course it did.

'What about the will?' she whispered. 'You went to investigate it. Can we overturn the custody of the children?'

'Why can you not close your sweet mouth for ten minutes until I've finished ruining you?' His hands moved beneath her nightgown, cupping her warm breasts. She shivered. Ten minutes was not such a bad thing. And when his mouth lowered to torment her nipple, she lost the memory of everything she'd meant to ask him.

He hauled her to her feet before she could change her mind and lowered her upon her stomach on the bed. Parting her legs, he slid a finger inside her. Emily gasped, her body fully ready for him. He used his hands to caress her intimately, his fingers sliding deep within her wetness.

'I thought about you each day since I left,' he murmured.

And I thought of you, she wanted to say. But she

could not speak at all when his hard length invaded her softness. The position made her completely vulnerable to him, powerless to move as he drove inside her.

He trapped her hands, filling her with every inch of himself. The fierce rhythm kept her breathless, her body shuddering with the roughness of his lovemaking. With their hands interlaced, he penetrated, his weight pressing her into the bed. Faster he moved, driving himself deep within until Emily cried out at the sensations that poured through her. A rising ecstasy fragmented her body until she grasped the sheets, her core milking his length.

After he met his own release, he kept moving gently within her. At last, he lay atop her, his body still joined with hers.

I love him, she realised. *And he's going to leave me again.*

'Don't go back to London,' she whispered.

'I have to.' Slowly he withdrew from her, then turned her over. 'But I'll stay for this night.'

'I'd rather go with you, than be left behind again. Surely if I travel with Nigel, we'll be safe. The man has enough money to hire an army.'

'And I'd spend every second worrying about you.' Stephen shook his head. 'No. You'll stay here. I'm going to meet with Lord Carstairs in a few days. Find out what he knows.'

'Another reason why I should come. I don't want Lily Hereford laying her pretty gloved fingers upon my husband.'

He chuckled and caressed her hair. 'In a ballroom fight, I have no doubt you would be the winner, my dear.'

She didn't smile. He didn't know how hard she'd been working, trying to learn all about becoming a Countess. Did he think she would embarrass him in public?

She didn't ask about the will again, not really wanting to know the answer. For now, she wanted him to hold her until morning. Eyes dry, her heart filled with apprehension. It was hard to sleep, just thinking of Stephen in danger.

In the morning, she awoke to an empty space beside her. She touched the sheets, feeling the warmth where his body had lain all night. Lowering her cheek, she closed her eyes as if to imagine him there once more.

And when at last she opened her wardrobe to choose her morning gown, every single pair of her shoes was gone.

'You wanted to see me, Whitmore?' Carstairs rose from his chair in the parlour where the footman had bade him wait.

'I did, yes. Please make yourself comfortable.' Stephen gestured toward the chair again. He offered a smile in greeting, though he was wary of the Viscount. He'd asked Carstairs to meet him at Rothburne House, rather than his own residence. It was unlikely that Carstairs would attempt an attack in so public a venue, if he had been involved with Hollingford's death or the attempt upon his own life.

'Have you learned more about the stolen profits from *The Lady Valiant*?' Carstairs enquired.

'Not yet.'

A tea service awaited the two men on a side table, the cups already poured. His mother's cat Alexander rubbed against his leg as Stephen seated himself. A low purr emerged from the feline's throat. The creature would eat anything, it seemed, and already it was begging for food.

He addressed the Viscount. 'The last time I saw you, you revealed the tattoo on your arm,' he began. 'May I see it again?'

Carstairs frowned, but rolled up his sleeve. 'Bad times, weren't they, Whitmore? Hollingford and I were lucky to escape Calcutta with our lives.'

'You were in India with him?' Anant had spoken nothing of this.

'I was. Damned Chinese officials were inspecting the ships bound for Canton. They thought Hollingford and I were involved in opium shipments, if you can believe it.

'Between you and me...' Carstairs leaned forward, lowering his voice, 'I think Hollingford might have been smuggling it. He kept disappearing with that servant of his. Wouldn't say where they were going or why. With my blasted luck, I got caught and blamed with him.' He coughed, his face deepening in colour.

Stephen studied Carstairs's tattoo, noticing the puckered skin surrounding it. 'They branded you.'

'Yes. And I spent a good deal of money buying our lives. The penalty for opium smuggling is execution.'

A prickle of uneasiness rose up on the back of his neck.

'What about you?' Carstairs asked. 'How did you receive your marking?'

Stephen didn't want to admit that he had no memory of the tattoo. Obviously it had been done to him while he'd been on board the ship. He hedged, saying, 'Like you, I was merely in the wrong place at the wrong time.'

Carstairs grunted. 'Unlucky, that's what.' He took a sip of tea and offered Stephen the plate of biscuits. 'Could use a bit of luck right now. Wish I knew what happened to the shipment profits.'

Stephen took one, but did not eat it. 'Have you received any more threatening notes?'

'Yes. Last week.' Carstairs poured himself more tea. 'I borrowed money to pay the bastard that first time. But I can't afford another payment. He wants the money by tomorrow.'

Stephen passed him the plate of biscuits, but Carstairs refused, patting his stomach. 'I'm afraid I can't. Too much of a good thing, you know.'

'Who do you think is demanding the money?'

'One of the investors, I presume. Someone who thinks I know where the stolen funds are.'

'And you think Hollingford took the money?'

'I know he did. Who else could it have been? We both know how much he lost at the gaming tables. The man was desperate. He would have done anything to redeem his debts.'

The cat had begun purring more insistently, bumping at Stephen's fingers. He allowed the feline to have the biscuit, his appetite gone. The cat licked at the powdered sugar, nudged it once and abandoned it.

Carstairs leaned in. 'If you find that list of investors, I want to know about it.'

Stephen inclined his head, though he had no intention of disclosing any information. 'I'll advise you if I discover anything.' He rose, and escorted his guest to the door. 'Good afternoon, Carstairs.'

The Viscount departed, and Stephen was still convinced that he'd played a role in the lost shipment. Carstairs kept trying to place blame upon Hollingford, and though Stephen could not fault it, his suspicions grew.

He returned to the parlour, sitting down before the hearth. He steepled his fingers, trying to think. What had he missed? Closing his eyes, he struggled to piece together the images of that night.

The memories remained locked away, despite his attempts to uncover them. He suspected he would not learn more until he had found the list of investors. Someone had stolen the profits from *The Lady Valiant*.

Someone who needed money.

Silence permeated the room, and Stephen was about to leave when he noticed the motionless body of the cat. His spine grew rigid when he realised it was dead.

Beside the cat lay the abandoned biscuit.

Chapter Nineteen

Combine 4 oz butter, 4 oz cream, 12 oz sugar, 2 teaspoonfuls ginger, and 1 scant teaspoonful bicarbonate of soda. Mix enough flour to make a stiff dough. Roll thick or thin, as desired and bake in a hot oven.

Recipe for sugar gingerbread from Emily Barrow's *Cook Book*

The familiar grey skies of London greeted Emily as she disembarked from the coach. Nigel had insisted that she come with him on his trip to town. Although Stephen would be angry, she didn't want to remain alone at Nigel's residence.

Her uncle took her hand, assisting her down. 'Chin up, my dear. Remember, you are the daughter of a Baron and the wife of an Earl. There is no need to look as though you wish to flee into the streets.'

His warm smile encouraged her, so Emily straightened and followed him into his London residence. The town house was every bit as grand as the country estate with white window-sills against a dark brick façade.

They had brought the children with them, for she would not even consider leaving them behind. Royce had whined and moped, at first, but brightened when she mentioned seeing Stephen again.

The servants welcomed her, and her bedchamber was decorated in shades of delicate cream and blue. A thick, luxurious carpet covered the floors, and she warmed herself by the fire. Though she tried to rest from her journey by reading the book of cooking recipes Stephen had given her, she could not prevent herself from pacing.

The very thought of seeing Stephen again filled her with trepidation. He wasn't going to be pleased with her. And if she dared set foot in society, as Nigel wished her to do, he'd be furious.

Was it only because of the danger? Or was he ashamed of her? The self-doubts plagued her, multiplying with each hour.

In the past few weeks, Nigel had tried to build up her confidence. He'd practised dancing with her, despite the painful gout that plagued his knee. He'd shared long talks with her in the evening, encouraging her and listening when she confessed her fears.

She had come to see him as a lonely man who wanted to fill his days with the children. But she still didn't want to give them up, regardless of what Daniel's will stated.

Nigel had been especially indignant when he'd learned of Lord Rothburne's refusal to recognise her as Stephen's wife. He vowed to force the Marquess into accepting her.

Tomorrow night, he planned to escort her to Lady Thistlewaite's ball. He had it on good authority that Stephen would attend. The aching emptiness in her stomach tightened with anticipation, for she longed to see him. And yet, the thought of facing Lady Thistlewaite made her consider developing a sudden case of hives.

How would the Earl react when she arrived? Stephen did not want her here; he had made that quite clear. Neither did the Marquess. When she arrived at the ball, it would be without their knowledge.

She was strongly tempted to pay a call upon her husband, to warn him of her intent. Oh, he would be angry all right. But it would be worse if he learned of her arrival at the ball. Better to let him know sooner, rather than later.

She donned her cloak and bonnet, just about to leave when Nigel stopped her. 'Why, Emily. Is something the matter?'

'No.' She glanced at the door. 'I was planning to pay a call.'

'Not alone, I hope.'

'Of course not. I was going to take a footman as an escort.'

Her uncle relaxed. 'Very well. But you will, of course, take the carriage. I've no wish for harm to befall you on the streets when we've only just become reacquainted.' He summoned a servant. 'Have my landau and driver brought to the front. Lady Whitmore wishes to pay a few calls.' Nigel bowed gallantly. 'There is no need to walk.'

'It isn't so very far,' she protested.

'Perhaps not, but you are a Countess, and you must present yourself as such. I look forward to introducing you to society tomorrow evening.' His blue eyes grew thoughtful. 'It should have been done years ago. I am sorry once again that your circumstances were not different. But enough about the past.'

Nigel cleared his throat and predicted, 'You will enchant them all.' Offering her a wink, he added, 'I may not possess a title, but I do have connections.'

'Thank you, Uncle.' Impulsively, she gave him a hug. He smelled of tobacco and tea.

Nigel patted her on the back. 'Enjoy your outing then.'

'I shall.' The words bolstered her courage

somewhat. Then it occurred to her that she might soften Stephen up, were she to bring him the pairs of shoes and boots she'd ordered. After instructing the footman to bring them, she boarded the carriage.

Her journey through the streets was very different from the last time. Nigel's open carriage, painted black with gold trim, made her quite conspicuous. The din of horses, carriages and merchants enveloped her in a swirling haze of motion. She smelled the acrid city air and the familiar odour of horses.

While they travelled down Oxford Street, Emily gripped the edges of her cloak. Though she wore a perfectly respectable morning gown with a rose overskirt and cream underdress, she couldn't help but think of Lady Thistlewaite's criticism. Despite Nigel's instruction, it was hard to push past her hurt feelings.

Before long, the landau approached Rothburne House. Emily hadn't intended to call upon Stephen's parents, but as the carriage passed by, she saw Lady Rothburne leaving the house.

'Stop the carriage,' she ordered the driver.

This is not a good idea, her common sense chided. *Stephen's mother will want nothing to do with you.*

But she had to face Lady Rothburne, soon enough. It might not be that bad if she remembered her manners.

Behave like a Countess, she coaxed her wayward courage.

'My lady?' the footman asked, waiting for her to make a decision.

Emily took his hand and disembarked from the carriage. Forcing a bright smile, she greeted Stephen's mother. 'Good day, Lady Rothburne.'

The Marchioness pretended as if she hadn't heard her. She walked past Emily without speaking, giving her the cut direct. Unwilling to be ignored, Emily stopped her. 'Lady Rothburne, I—'

Lady Rothburne's face grew weary. 'Do not try to see my son. My husband has forbidden you to set foot in our house, and it is better if you leave.'

'He's here?' She'd expected him to be at his town house residence.

The Marchioness accepted help from a footman in boarding her own carriage. 'Yes, he's here.' She smoothed her skirts and offered a sympathetic look. 'Let him go, Emily. It is best for all of us. Stephen should never have married you, even if you were friends long ago.'

'I am the daughter of a Baron,' Emily said firmly. 'Not the offspring of a chimney sweep.'

'You know nothing of our lives. You'll never understand.'

'You are right. I don't understand why you try

to manipulate Stephen this way. He made his choice.'

'He made his choice to leave you and return home,' Lady Rothburne said, her words striking like a barb in Emily's heart. 'As far as London society is concerned, you trapped him into marriage, and he wants nothing to do with you. If you try to claim differently, you will be branded as a liar. No one will take your word against ours. You should remain in the countryside where you belong.'

The Marchioness closed the door to the carriage, leaving her behind. Emily felt as though she'd taken a blow to her stomach. What had happened to turn Lady Rothburne against her?

You don't belong here. They won't ever accept you.

Did Stephen feel the same way? She thought of the last time she'd seen him, when he'd sneaked inside her room. Her body warmed at the memory of the way he'd made love to her.

No. She couldn't believe that his actions were a lie. He had to feel something for her. And Marquess or not, she wasn't about to let go of her husband without a fight.

Emily strode up the stone steps to Rothburne House, the packages of shoes in her arms. Rapping sharply on the door, she waited.

Phillips nearly closed the door in her face when he saw who it was. Emily trapped her hand in the door frame. 'I am here to see my husband, the Earl. He will be most displeased if I am denied entrance.'

'I have orders from Lord Rothburne—'

'Is the Marquess receiving calls at the moment?' She cut him off, not caring what his orders were.

The footman hesitated. 'That is not your concern.'

'In that case, I assume he's not here.' Without waiting for permission, Emily forced her way across the threshold. 'You risk your position if you deny me the right to see my husband.'

'I'll lose my position if the Marquess finds out,' Phillips muttered, but he didn't stop her. 'You may await the Earl in the drawing room.'

He led her to a room decorated in shades of sea green and lilac. Gleaming white crown moulding framed the window, and a rich burgundy Grecian sofa rested in front of it. Porcelain figurines stood here and there, while a row of china plates adorned the fireplace mantel.

Emily handed him the packages meant for Stephen. 'See to it that Lord Whitmore receives these.'

Phillips bowed and took the parcels away. Afterwards, she sat, folding her hands in her lap. She tried to don a calm presence of mind. With each passing minute, she longed to pace the room. Where was Stephen? Would he refuse to see her?

The sound of movement drew her attention. Anger punctuated the Earl's stride, fury lined in every muscle of his frame. Callous grey eyes incinerated her with the full force of his wrath.

'You were supposed to remain in the country,' he said in a tight voice. He was holding back his temper, and she knew that she had best tread lightly.

'I am glad to see you, too.' She rose from the sofa and noted that he made no move to embrace or greet her.

The Earl turned his back on her, staring out the window. Tension ridged his spine, his knuckles resting upon the windowpane. 'You put yourself in danger by coming here.'

'Myself in danger? You were the one who came here alone to confront your enemies.' She walked to stand beside him. The scent of his shaving soap evoked the memory of his naked body atop her own. She closed her eyes, unable to stop herself from thinking of it. He kept his distance, and she wondered what it would take to break apart the wall between them.

'Did Nigel escort you here?'

'Yes. And the children. My uncle intends to introduce me into society properly.'

His temper erupted. 'I cannot recall when I've

heard a more ridiculous idea. Does he intend to parade you in front of my attacker?'

She bridled at his accusation. 'Should I have remained at Nigel's home, alone, while he came to London? He brought most of his household with him. It was safer to accompany him.'

'You don't understand what you're dealing with, Emily.' Stephen advanced upon her, closing the distance. Dragging her to her feet, he grasped her nape. 'Show some sense. Twice, someone has tried to kill me, and yet you behave as though you are immune to peril.'

'You're behaving the same way.' She covered his hands, only inches away from his mouth. Without letting him speak, she leaned forward and kissed him.

His lips touched hers with such gentleness, she wanted to weep. Dear God, if anything happened to him, she'd never forgive herself.

His grey eyes grew troubled. 'I want you to return to Nigel's estate. Wait for me there.'

She shook her head. 'I won't stand back and let you die.'

'I have no intention of dying.'

'Neither did Daniel. But intentions cannot stop a bullet.'

His palm caressed her nape, his fingers threading into her hair. The familiar touch, the sudden transformation of anger into desire, made her shiver. His thumb grazed a path towards her ear.

He embraced her tightly, and though he spoke nothing of his own feelings, no words were needed. His nose brushed against her temple, his mouth against her cheek.

'I investigated the will, as you asked. And Nigel is indeed the guardian of Victoria and Royce,' Stephen said. 'I could argue the matter in court, if you want me to pursue it further. But I doubt if we'd win.'

'I want them back,' she admitted. 'But he has taken good care of the children. And of me.'

He stepped back, his gaze passing over her rose gown. 'You look lovely.'

She blushed. 'I have a different gown for tomorrow evening. Uncle Nigel plans to escort me to Lady Thistlewaite's ball.'

'No.' The edge in his voice held a warning. 'You're not going.'

Her anger flared up, but he continued, 'I don't want you hurt, Emily. Not by the man who wants me dead. And not by the society matrons who would cut you down.'

Before she could protest, he stole another kiss. Temptation beckoned her to lose herself with him once more. Without thinking, she reached up to touch his dark brown hair, letting her arms settle around his neck.

'The matrons would not cut me down if you acknowledged me as your wife.'

'I can't do that. Not until this is over.'

Although she knew he meant only to keep her out of danger, his words bruised her heart. As if she weren't good enough for him. Though she knew it was foolish, she could not stop herself from thinking it.

'How long?' she asked.

'I don't know.'

The wall rose up between them again, only this time, she felt angry. She deserved to stand at her husband's side, more so than any débutante. 'I'm not leaving London.'

'You are playing a dangerous game, Emily.' His hand captured her wrist in an unmistakable warning.

She knew it. But blind obedience had gained her nothing. It was time to seize control and fight for what she wanted. Her heart constricted in her chest as she leaned close. His spicy scent drew her in, reminding her of the nights they'd spent in each other's arms.

'I am not going to run away this time.' She rose on her tiptoes, letting her palms splay against his chest. 'I won't be your wife in private, if you won't let me be your wife in public.' Her arms wrapped around his waist, her hips pressing close to his.

Desire flashed in his eyes, but he didn't move.

'You have a choice to make.' Emily drew back. 'At Lady Thistlewaite's ball, tomorrow night.'

The gauntlet had been thrown; the next move was his.

His day was rapidly getting worse, Stephen thought acidly. First, there had been the attempt on his life. Second, his wife had arrived in London without his permission. He hadn't told anyone about the poisoned cat, not even the servants. He didn't know who to trust any more.

After disposing of the cat's body in the garden, Stephen was more than convinced of Carstairs's guilt. He had offered refreshments, and the Viscount had declined. Carstairs had also been in the parlour waiting for him, long enough to add poison to the food.

But again, why? Why did anyone want him dead? Were they afraid he'd remember something?

It was enough to drive him mad.

He kept one of the biscuits and strode down to the kitchen. The clatter of pots and pans mingled with the servants' gossip. The noise came to an abrupt halt when he entered.

He held up the biscuit to the cook, Mrs Raines. 'Did you prepare these today?'

The stout, red-cheeked woman frowned. 'Yes,

my lord. But there was no powdered sugar upon them.'

Her confusion appeared genuine, and Stephen pressed further. 'Who brought the tea tray up?'

'I did, my lord. But I can't say as I know about that sugar. That would make the biscuits far too sweet, and I would never do such a thing. You aren't one to like your biscuits overly sweet, and—'

'That will do, Mrs Raines.' He could see her panic escalating.

'I'm so sorry if you didn't like them, my lord. I won't prepare them again.'

He lifted a hand. 'Did you bring the tea service after the Viscount arrived?'

She stopped. 'No, my lord. I left it there before-hand, since I wanted to be sure it was waiting for your guest.'

'Did you pour the tea?'

'Of course, not, my lord. It would grow cold, otherwise.'

His heart nearly stopped. The cups of tea had already been poured upon his arrival. Was the tea poisoned as well? But then, Carstairs had consumed a full cup. He relaxed a little. Likely he would have felt the effects by now, if that were true.

'Thank you, Mrs Raines.'

He departed the kitchen, his thoughts turning back to his wife. He wanted to throttle Emily for coming to London. The only thing worse than having his own life in danger was watching her face the same threats. He couldn't allow it.

If he had to tie her to a chair, Lady Whitmore would not attend the ball.

That afternoon, Stephen boarded his carriage, intending to discover the meaning of the tattoo on his neck. He'd instructed his driver to take him deeper into London, toward the Chinese merchant shops. He had armed himself with a revolver as a precaution.

He was so caught up in his thoughts regarding the tattoo, that he nearly missed seeing an Indian man, striding down the street. Anant Paltu.

Now what was he doing here?

Stephen tensed and narrowed his gaze upon the man. Though Anant walked with a quiet deference, he didn't believe for a moment that the man was here by coincidence.

'Follow him,' Stephen ordered the coachman.

Anant had been here, the night Daniel was killed. He was convinced of it, and as they moved further into London, the overpowering smells evoked images of that night. Smoke and the exotic tang of spices ripped through his mind, sending him back.

Cold. It had been so cold that February night, his

breath sending clouds into the frosty air. He'd tracked Hollingford, tracing the man's path back toward the Thames. Toward the ships.

Four men were arguing with Hollingford, and one pulled him back, confining his arms. His lungs burning, Stephen had raced forward to free the man. A long blade had flashed in the moonlight, and he'd stared in horror as Hollingford fell to the muddy streets.

Too late to save him.

A noise had sounded behind him and Stephen had turned, just as a knife cut him across his ribs, blinding him with pain.

The vision abruptly ended. His breathing was shaky, and his palms were damp.

'My lord?'

He gripped the edge of his seat and forced himself to inhale a full breath. 'Yes?'

'My lord, I'm afraid he's gone,' the coachman apologised. 'He went toward those shops over there.'

Damn. He hadn't expected to lose himself in the memory, but it had come upon him so suddenly, he'd lost track of his quarry.

'Await me here,' he ordered.

Though every instinct warned him not to pursue Anant, he sensed that the answers were close now. He would not let fear dictate his moves.

Stephen felt for the revolver within his coat. 'If

I don't return in ten minutes, I'll need your help.' Though he didn't know where Anant had gone, he intended to question the shopkeepers.

The heavy scent of incense assailed him when Stephen entered the merchant's shop. An oak table displayed bolts of colourful silk and bags of tea leaves. A woman lowered her head in respect before whispering to an elderly man. The man wore a grey beard so long, it nearly reached his middle. With pale skin and almond-shaped eyes, the merchant greeted him. 'My lord.'

Stephen did not waste time in responding, but instead held out a small pouch containing ten shillings. 'I'll add twenty more pounds to this, if you answer my questions truthfully.'

The shopkeeper bowed again. 'What can I do for you, my lord?'

'I am seeking a man called Anant Paltu.'

The shopkeeper exchanged glances with the woman. 'I have heard of him. Is there something I could help you with, my lord?'

'I saw him only moments ago, in the streets. I want to find him.'

'If you want my advice, stay away from him, my lord. He is an opium eater. Very dangerous.'

The mention of opium made him recall the tattoo on his neck. He loosened his collar to reveal the marking. 'Can you tell me what this means?

It was done to me while I was on board a ship. I'm told it is Chinese.'

The shopkeeper's expression turned curious. 'It is the brand of a criminal, my lord.' He sent a hesitant glance towards the woman, who kept her gaze averted.

'What does it mean?'

'It is for opium smuggling. If you are caught a second time, you will be executed.'

A strange sense of finality struck him. Now that he knew the tattoo was the same as the one given to Carstairs and Hollingford, it made him understand why the stolen shipment had even more value. The profits had involved smuggled opium.

But was Carstairs responsible? He'd admitted that he'd travelled to India with Daniel, but he'd claimed his own innocence, foisting the blame upon Emily's brother and Anant.

Stephen paid the shopkeeper and departed. As he returned to his carriage, he turned the events over in his mind. And he couldn't help but think that his time was running out.

Chapter Twenty

Combine 8 oz of black treacle with 1 table-spoonful of ginger. Dissolve 1 teaspoonful bicarbonate of soda into 2 tablespoons of warm water or milk. Add 4 oz of softened butter and enough flour to make a soft dough (about 2 and a half cups). Roll out one-third of an inch thick and cut into small rounds. Bake in a hot oven until firm to the touch. Dust with icing sugar while still hot.

Recipe for soft treacle biscuits from Emily
Barrow's *Cook Book*

Emily hadn't expected to see Stephen so soon. She heard his voice in the hall and saw him handing his gloves and hat to Nigel's footman. Tension knotted his face, but he relaxed when he saw her.

'What is it?' she asked. Had he changed his mind

about acknowledging her? Was he planning to bring her home with him? From the unsettled expression on his face, that didn't seem likely.

He took her hand in his. 'I'll tell you in private. Is your uncle here?'

'He had business with some associates this evening. He promised to return later tonight.'

'He left you alone?'

'We have a houseful of servants.'

Stephen shook his head. 'I'd rather know for myself that you're safe. I'll stay with you while he's gone.'

She led him into the drawing room, her apprehension rising when he closed the door. 'There was another attempt on my life.' He told her about the poisoned biscuits, and her insides turned to ice.

'I can't believe it. Who do you think would have done such a thing?' She took his hands, as if to reassure herself that he was all right.

'It may be Carstairs. He needs money, so he said.' He went to stand by the window. 'Or there's another possibility, one I can't eliminate. Earlier today, I saw your former butler walking in the streets.'

'Anant?' She frowned, turning the information over in her mind. 'Why would he be in London?'

'I suspect he was hired to kill me. Perhaps he

was the one who attacked you in the gardens at Falkirk, as well.'

Emily shook her head in denial. 'I don't believe that. He worked for our family for years. He has no reason to harm either of us.'

'He was there the night your brother died. And I do think he's connected with the attacks.' He closed the curtains, returning to her side.

'I hope not.' Even so, doubt threaded through her mind, the fear that he could be right.

Stephen loosened his cravat, revealing the tattoo. 'I also learned more about this marking. It was done to me in India, and it is Chinese, like your brother's.'

He sat down, letting her examine the back of his neck. 'What does it mean?' Her hands traced the foreign characters, swirling symbols etched in his bare flesh.

'It accuses me of opium smuggling. And a death penalty, if I am caught a second time.'

Emily shivered, not wanting to think of such a thing. 'But you're not a smuggler.'

'No. But the ship I was on might have contained such a cargo. I can't be sure.'

'But…such a journey. All the way to India.' Her mind ran wild with visions of him taken prisoner, of foreigners calling for his death.

'Don't worry. I've no intention of going back, for

any reason.' His voice caught her deep within, like a physical caress. 'Everything I want is right here.'

He stood, pulling her against him in a dark kiss. His mouth coaxed hers into a battle of lips and tongue, forcing her to yield against him. She clung to him, falling deeply under his seductive spell.

When he pulled away, he whispered. 'Thank you for the boots. And the shoes.' He brushed another kiss along her jaw. 'Phillips gave me the package you brought.'

His hand moved down her neck to the strand of pearls resting against her bosom. He fingered the strand, teasing the beads against her nipple as he'd done before. 'I like these on you. I'd like them better if they were all you wore.'

She shivered, fighting off the temptation. Although she ached to do exactly as he said, she'd made a vow not to let him touch her until he acknowledged her as his wife. And already she was breaking that promise.

'Stephen, I want you to stop.'

'Why?'

'Because you're treating me like your mistress, not your wife.'

'You could be both,' he teased.

She didn't answer his smile. Couldn't he see how much it hurt, being forced to hide from society? It brought back the terrible memories of his parents' ball, where she'd been so humiliated. After all these weeks, she'd worked hard, hoping not to embarrass him in a ballroom. She wanted to show him that she could be a Countess.

Dropping a kiss upon her head, Stephen added, 'This will all be over, soon enough.'

'When?' She bristled at his nonchalance. Did he think Lady Thistlewaite's ball was merely a social engagement? To her, it was much more—it was a second chance to prove herself.

'I'm tired of hiding away, as if you're ashamed of me,' she insisted. 'The gossips will think you're planning a divorce.'

'That's a foolish thought.'

'Is it? We're living apart.' She lowered her forehead to his shoulder, fighting back angry tears. 'I don't even know if you'll ever let me become your Countess. You keep trying to brush me aside.'

He gripped her tightly. 'I won't risk your safety.'

She took a breath, straightening a stray lock of hair. 'And if there was no danger? Would you escort me to the ball, and admit that I am your wife?'

He hesitated. 'If that is what you want. But you didn't appear to enjoy the last one.'

Tears heated her lids, but she would not let herself cry. It was the answer she'd feared he would say. 'If none of this had happened, you'd never have brought me to London. I'd be at Falkirk, even now, the wife you never wanted.'

He cupped her cheek. 'It's not that I don't want you beside me, Emily. But I won't watch someone hurt you or the children. My enemies are far too close now. You will not go out in public, and that is final.'

Her anger rose up, so painful her eyes burned with the unshed tears. 'If your enemies are too close, then why did you come here tonight? You've led them right to us.'

He said nothing, as though she'd struck him. She wanted to take back the angry words, to say she hadn't meant them. But it was too late.

Without another word, he bowed and left.

The tears broke forth, and she clenched her waist, sobbing quietly. So many excuses. So many reasons not to let her be with him.

Right now, she didn't know if he would ever acknowledge her as the woman he wanted.

Stephen returned to Rothburne House the next morning, his eyes blurring with exhaustion. He'd kept an all-night vigil in Nigel's study, leaving only when he'd heard Emily's uncle returning. Damn her for not trusting in him. When all of this was over…

It was difficult to even imagine the future, he'd lived with the danger for so long. Someone had murdered Hollingford, and Stephen no longer believed it was because of the man's debts or stolen money.

Daniel had known something. Likely he had discovered the opium smuggling, but all records of the cargo and stolen profits had been eradicated.

Somewhere, there existed a list of investors. And among them was the man he sought, a man who didn't want his involvement revealed.

Stephen sipped at a cup of strong tea, and only glanced up when his father entered the drawing room. James did not look well, his hair shot with grey, heavy lines drawing down the corners of his mouth.

'Your mother told me *that woman* has returned to London,' his father remarked.

'My wife, you mean.'

James cleared his throat, adding, 'Her uncle intends to escort her to Lady Thistlewaite's soirée tonight. I thought I should warn you of the gossip.'

Stephen rose and went to stand by the fire, staring at the coals glowing on the hearth. He hoped that Emily would abide by his orders and remain at Nigel's home where she would be protected.

'Thank you for your concern. But I have other, more pressing things on my mind than what a flock of gossiping matrons are discussing.' He stoked the flames, watching the sparks rise up. 'I suppose you should know that your own residence is no longer safe. I was nearly poisoned yesterday.'

His father stiffened. 'What do you mean?'

Stephen explained about the cat and the biscuits. He added, 'I believe that whoever keeps trying to kill me is the same person responsible for stealing the profits from *The Lady Valiant*.'

'Have you any suspicions?'

Stephen replaced the poker and shrugged. 'A few. But no proof.'

'Quentin might be able to help.'

Stephen looked up sharply. 'Quentin was involved in this?'

'He lost a great deal of money in the shipment. My money.' The Marquess grimaced, muttering about his brother's irresponsible ways. Stephen no longer heard the words. Quentin had mentioned financial problems, even teasing about Stephen's death. Had there been a darker meaning beneath it? He simply couldn't believe it.

'Where is he now?'

'I'm not certain. I thought he said he was going to pay a call upon Lord Carstairs.' The Marquess cleared his throat. 'I am hoping he'll develop an interest in Miss Hereford. Perhaps we might bring her into the family yet, since you insist upon keeping that creature as your wife.'

But Stephen was no longer thinking of Miss Hereford. Though he didn't want to imagine his brother had any part in this, he could not take the chance. 'I'm going to find Quentin.'

His father crossed the room and set a hand upon his shoulder. It was the first time in many years that he'd shown any sign of emotion. 'Be careful.'

Stephen gripped his father's hand. 'I will.'

When he arrived at Lord Carstairs's residence an hour later, Stephen pushed his way inside.

'My lord, Lord Carstairs did not wish to be disturbed,' the footman protested. 'He was not feeling well this day.'

'I am looking for my brother Quentin.' He strode past the man, forcing the servant to quicken his steps.

'I never saw him here, my lord. And I assure you, this is not a good time to intrude upon Lord Carstairs.'

The footman positioned himself in front of the study, his black waistcoat stretched across a large stomach that threatened to pop off the buttons.

'Perhaps not.' But had he eaten the poisoned biscuits, Carstairs's constitution would have been even worse. 'I must see the Viscount.'

Stephen forced his way past, which was no easy task considering the man's girth. Eventually, rank won over. The footman would not dare to defy an Earl.

He tried the door, but found it locked. Knocking sharply, he demanded, 'Carstairs, open the door.'

Silence.

He banged louder, to no avail. 'Have you a key?' he asked the footman.

The servant puffed out his indignation and his grizzled whiskers twitched. 'My lord, if the master does not wish to be disturbed, then it is my duty—'

'Hang your duty. A man tried to kill your master yesterday. Now are you going to find that key, or must I break the door down?'

The footman hesitated before another dark glare from Stephen sent him fleeing.

'What's all this about?' a female voice asked. Lady Carstairs peered over the staircase. Her dark gleaming locks hung in a state of disarray, her maid standing behind her with a brush.

Stephen inclined his head. 'Forgive me, Lady Carstairs, but I must have words with your husband. How long has he been in the study, might I ask?' He knocked on the door a third time.

'Since this morning. He did not wish to be disturbed.'

The butler returned with the key, and Stephen jammed it into the lock, twisting the metal. He shoved open the door.

The study had been ransacked. Papers lay everywhere, books overturned.

And in the middle of it lay the Viscount's body. Dead.

'My dear, why aren't you ready?' Nigel opened the library door where Emily sat reading. 'Tonight is your grand début. And aren't you planning to show Lady Thistlewaite that she was wrong about you?'

'My husband doesn't think I should attend. He says it's too dangerous.'

'Dangerous? Whatever is he talking about?'

She confided the attempts on Stephen's life. 'I haven't told you much about it, because I didn't want you to worry.'

'Does he suspect anyone?'

She nodded. 'I'm certain that it's only a matter of time before he remembers everything. And I'm afraid of something happening to him.'

Nigel met her gaze. 'Yes, I suppose it is only a matter of time before it all comes back to him.' Then abruptly, his seriousness left, and he offered a broad smile. 'But honestly, the only thing Whitmore should be afraid of is of some handsome dandy trying to steal you out from under his nose.'

She braved a smile. 'I wish that were the only thing.'

'Come now. Do you really think that anything would happen, while you're out dancing? You're safer there than anywhere else. And I am not about to let you continue your reputation as a wallflower.' He touched her chin. 'Go on, then. Have your maid prepare you, and meet me downstairs. Our carriage is waiting.'

She could see that Nigel wouldn't take no for an answer. He shooed her upstairs, promising he wouldn't leave until she returned.

Stephen wasn't going to like this. But Nigel was right—what could possibly happen in the middle of a ballroom, amidst hundreds of people?

Emily inhaled sharply, gripping the bedpost as Beatrice cinched her corset. Layers of crinoline and petticoats came next, and last the ivory ball gown Stephen had given her. Her husband had spared no expense, down to the soft leather dancing slippers that fit perfectly. The bittersweet memory of Stephen's first gift of shoes invaded, reminding her of the time they had danced in the garden.

'My lady, these arrived for you.' Beatrice held out a long velvet box.

Emily opened the box to reveal a glittering strand of diamonds. To her surprise, she saw they were from Nigel.

Although they were only meant as a gift, they were far too extravagant. Just the thought of wearing them made her feel cold inside. Like a woman on display instead of herself. Instead, she donned the strand of pearls Stephen had given her.

Emily finished preparing for the ball and went to check on the children. Inside his bedchamber, Royce's arms sprawled over the edge of the bed, his other arm wrapped around a pillow. In the adjoining chamber, Victoria rested in her crib. Her hands were drawn up beneath her chin while her backside pointed skywards. Emily could not resist smiling as she kissed the infant's downy head.

Inside the nursery, Royce had left toys strewn around the room. Unable to help herself, Emily started to tidy the mess. Though her crinoline and corset confined her movement, she picked up a jack-in-the-box and set it upon a shelf.

A row of books was about to topple, and Emily straightened the stack. Her gaze narrowed upon one of the volumes. It was one of the last gifts Daniel had given his son, a book of fairy tales. The book had belonged to her grandfather many years ago. Emily traced the broken leather binding and then picked it up for old time's sake.

Flipping through the collection of stories, she recognised the Brothers Grimm, Hans Christian Anderson and other beloved authors. Then her fingers came upon a familiar, well-loved page. It was the story of 'The Steadfast Tin Soldier', Royce's favourite. Emily smiled as she skimmed the first pages about the tin soldier's adventures in a rain gutter. Before she reached the end of the tale, the story changed abruptly. In place of the original tale, neatly glued into the binding, were pages of notes.

Her heart skidded to a stop. These were the hidden records, the ones Stephen had been looking for. Emily studied them, wondering what was so important about the meticulous columns of figures. As she reached the bottom of the page, she recognised names of at least a dozen ships, along with profits and losses. At the very end of the last page were the names of investors involved with *The Lady Valiant*.

One name startled her, but she dismissed any suspicion of ill doing. She tore out the pages from the book, tucking them into her bodice. Tonight she would show them to Stephen, and perhaps he could shed light upon their meaning.

There was little point in trying to question a hysterical Lady Carstairs. While she wept and clung to her daughter Lily, Stephen had searched through the mess of papers, looking for something that would lead him to the true assassin. This time, a dagger in the back had caused Carstairs's death.

Stephen knew he ought to feel something about the murder, but a numbing chill had frozen his mind to reality. He found it easier to dwell upon theories and lists than the fact that he had escaped death yet again. He shouldn't be alive now.

What did his enemies want? It had to be information, knowledge they believed he and Carstairs possessed. They had ransacked Hollingford's house and now Carstairs's study. They had not searched his father's residence, however. A mixed sense of relief flooded him when he realised his constant change in residence had likely protected the inhabitants.

Stephen sifted through another stack of papers, and he discovered a record of men who owed Carstairs money. Though it was simply a list, he had not come across Freddie Reynolds's name before. Annoyance pervaded him when he thought of the man who had tried to court his wife with flowers and awful poetry. Even when they were growing up, he'd never trusted the fop.

Then annoyance shifted into suspicion. The threads interwove into a pattern that seemed a little too convenient. Reynolds had continued to court her affections, even after Emily had told him of their marriage.

Did Reynolds have anything to do with the murders? Though his cowardly nature suggested an aversion to violence, Stephen could not afford to miss a potential clue. It made him wonder how many others he'd missed.

With a glance at his timepiece, he saw that it was growing far later than he'd imagined. The authorities had arrived, and after answering a few questions, Stephen excused himself to attend Lady Thistlewaite's ball.

Freddie Reynolds might be there. And if he was, Stephen intended to find out what he knew.

Chapter Twenty-One

A light dusting of confectioner's sugar provides a lovely sweetness to any cake or biscuit. A lady's good manners will do the same when she is entertaining guests.
—Emily Barrow's *Cook Book*

Lady Thistlewaite did not conceal her distaste when Emily arrived upon Uncle Nigel's arm. The matron wore an emerald gown with sixteen flounces while her abundant bosom thrust the front of the gown forward. Her lips pursed into a thin line as though she wanted to prevent Emily from entering the ballroom.

'Lady Thistlewaite, I was delighted to receive your invitation.' Nigel kissed her wrist and offered her a charming smile. 'You remember my niece Emily, of course.'

'Of course.' Lady Thistlewaite's gaze flicked across Emily's gown.

Emily wore the ivory-flounced tulle gown, trimmed with pink roses and Limerick lace. About her shoulders rested an embroidered India shawl with a long silk fringe. Her kid gloves had over thirty buttons to hold them snugly against her skin, and the pearl necklace hung against her neck.

'Lady Thistlewaite, thank you for your hospitality,' Emily said, nodding politely.

'Well, I am surprised to see you again, Miss Barrow. I mean, Lady Whitmore,' she corrected. 'Forgive me, but since I haven't seen you at your husband's side yet, it is easy to forget you are married to him.'

Don't let her provoke you, Emily warned herself.

'I am certain that will be remedied, soon enough.' Emily pasted on a bright smile, albeit a false one. 'Has my husband arrived yet?'

'I fear he has not.'

Emily's composure faltered. Just the thought of seeing Stephen again knitted her insides into knots. She tried to prepare herself for his rejection, for his undeniable wrath. But she was tired of feeling unworthy, angry at being looked down upon.

'I am sure he will arrive soon,' she said. *And Lord help me, when he does.*

Nigel patted Emily's arm. 'I, for one, am glad of his absence. It allows me to walk around in the company of an exceptionally beautiful lady. Until the Earl steals her away, that is.'

Nigel's compliment eased her, and as he led her inside, he whispered, 'Do not forget, Emily. You are a Countess.'

His reminder helped to clear her thoughts. The past was gone; she could not change it. But she had power now, power she had denied herself. It was time to take her place as Lady Whitmore.

Behind her fan, she touched the bodice of her gown, to ensure the papers were still there. She was certain that this was the evidence Stephen needed. If only she could understand the meaning behind the numbers.

The answers must be there. Daniel would never have hidden them were they not of critical importance. She felt on the verge of discovery, but with the excitement came a natural fear.

Her uncle arrived just then to rescue her. 'My dear, would you care to dance? I believe my knee might be able to stand a turn about the floor, if you are willing.'

'No, thank you.' Emily patted his arm. 'But you might find another young lady.'

'None so lovely as you,' Nigel argued. 'Come, now. You'll hurt my feelings.'

Before she could turn him down, he led her on to the floor. 'I've never quite grown accustomed to this scandalous dance, but I am told waltzing has come into fashion.' He captured her cold hands in his warm gnarled palms, offering a smile. 'Don't worry, child. You are a fine dancer.'

Emily's eyes burned at his kindness. Never once had her father escorted her to a ball, nor her brother. But Nigel had done this for her.

It was easier to follow his lead, after the dancing lessons he'd paid for. Nigel moved slowly, guiding her in the patterns of the waltz. In time, she relaxed, though she was still aware of the eyes upon her. Lady Thistlewaite, in particular, looked as though she had swallowed a lemon.

'The entire room is dying to know what Whitmore will do when he arrives,' Nigel said. 'I'll spread a few rumours about your elopement, to help you out.'

'I wish you wouldn't,' she admitted. She wanted to meet Stephen on her own terms, and no doubt he would be furious with her for coming here.

'He is quite late, I must say,' Nigel commented. 'I wonder why? I do hope nothing has gone amiss.'

Emily stumbled at the thought of Stephen coming to harm. Her uncle caught her, easing her into the next step. As she continued to dance, it was as if she moved in a daze. Fear clenched her gut, and she found it difficult to breathe. Fear clenched her gut; with everyone's eyes upon her, she needed a moment alone.

'Uncle, will you please excuse me?'

Nigel's gaze turned worried, but Emily reassured him that everything was all right. She left him, moving towards the ladies' retiring room. Thankfully, no one was there. She sat before a looking glass, staring at her pale face. Nothing had happened to Stephen, she tried to reassure herself. He would be here soon enough.

Fingers of foreboding settled across her shoulders, needling her with thoughts of *what if*. 'He will come tonight,' she told herself. 'I know he will.'

But as time slipped onwards, and the murmurs of society turned to gloating whispers, her fear transformed into dread.

In the cool darkness of night, the figure slipped into the shadow of Nigel Barrow's house. With a thin knife, he manoeuvred the locks, moving upstairs to where the children slept.

He stopped in the older boy's room first. The firelight cast shadows across the child huddling beneath the covers. Royce slept fitfully, and as the man drew near, the boy's eyes flew open.

'Shh…' The man raised a finger to his lips. 'I have come to take you to your father.'

Royce sat up, his fists gripping the coverlet. 'My father is dead.'

'That is what they told you. But he sent me to

come and take you to him.' The man held out a hand. 'You trust me, don't you?'

The boy nodded.

'Then let us go before anyone sees us.'

'What about Aunt Emily and Uncle Stephen?'

'Do not worry about them. They will come to you in the morning.'

The boy moved the covers aside, struggling to put on his shoes.

'You must be silent when we leave. Do not speak a word and stay out of sight in the coach.' The man handed him a blanket. 'Take this.'

'What about Victoria?' the boy protested. 'I can't leave my sister.'

'She will come with us.' The man held out his coat, and Royce fastened the buttons. With a longing glance towards his bed, at last he relented.

'Do you promise I'll see my father soon?' he whispered.

The man's face remained impassive. 'I promise you will see him very soon.'

As he closed the door behind the boy, his hand touched the curved knife blade hidden beneath his coat.

Stephen arrived at the Thistlewaite residence just past the hour of midnight. He had spent time at White's, investigating Freddie Reynolds's debts. It seemed that Reynolds and Emily's brother had done more than their share of gambling. Reynolds needed money—by any means possible.

When Stephen saw his wife's face amid the ballroom crowd, a slow fury built within him. The throng parted in half, and he moved straight towards her.

She wore pearls around a lovely neck he wanted to wring. The ivory tulle clung to the curves he had run his hands over just the other night. A sensuous strand of hair had fallen from the elaborate arrangement, and her lips held the slightest tint of red. Her beauty took his breath away.

Why could she not understand his need to keep her safe? Even now, the man who most likely had tried to murder him was standing only a short distance away. He glared at Freddie Reynolds, but the dandy pretended not to see.

When he reached Emily's side, he noted that her uncle was no longer with her. The idea of her being left alone appalled him.

'You're here,' she said, her shoulders relaxing with relief. 'I was worried about you.'

'Of course I am here,' he murmured. 'But you were supposed to remain at home.'

'When have I begun taking orders I do not agree with?' she returned, smiling sweetly.

He took her hand and tried to lead her towards

the refreshment table, but Emily refused to move. 'I am not going to walk with you. Not unless you acknowledge me. Already we are the centre of everyone's attention and gossip.'

Stubborn brat. He overpowered her, pulling her towards a private alcove. 'Come with me.'

'No.' She struggled, but he held her fast.

Before he could say another word, Freddie Reynolds appeared. 'Lady Whitmore, is everything all right?'

'Yes, of course.' Emily managed a smile upon her face, though Stephen noted her underlying anger.

Stephen had no intention of allowing the obsequious rodent near his wife. 'Stay away from her.'

Freddie did not back down, but stared back with determination. He was not as tall and had to tilt his head back a little.

'I believe you are my partner for the next set, Freddie,' Emily interjected, glancing at her dance card.

Stephen was about to drag her away from Reynolds when suddenly, a flock of matrons descended upon him.

'My dear Lord Whitmore, what a pleasure—'

'I've heard the most amazing tale about you and Miss Barrow—'

'Why on earth would the two of you elope?'

Their mouths fairly dripped with anticipation.

He, on the other hand, had better things to do than to answer their twittering questions.

'If you'll pardon me,' he said, giving them a hard look, 'I am going to have words with—'

The words hung upon his lips as he took a long look at Emily. God, she was beautiful. The ivory gown complemented her fair skin, contrasting against the dark golden hair. He'd never seen her like this before, cool and confident.

Like a Countess. And she belonged to him.

Emily stood a short distance away, pretending as if she didn't hear them. She expected him to feign indifference. And he had every reason to ignore her, in order to keep her safe.

But damn it all, she had been cut down too many times. And he couldn't let it happen again. Refusing to acknowledge her as his wife would not protect her. It would only slice another wound into their marriage.

'I need to have words with *my wife*.' He emphasised the last two words, making sure that everyone around them heard it.

Emily turned. Her lips parted, but she did not speak.

Lady Thistlewaite looked as though she might swoon. Another matron fanned her face furiously, but Stephen did not remain to listen to the agitated women.

He closed the distance, and raised her gloved hand to his lips. 'Shall we, Lady Whitmore?'

Sadly, she did not fall down at his feet with gratitude. Instead she looked as if she'd rather incinerate him.

'You could have done that with a bit more finesse,' she commented as she took his hand.

'I did just as you asked.'

Emily couldn't argue with that. Couples had lined up in a quadrille and she glanced towards Freddie. 'I really did promise him that dance.'

'If he touches you, I'll cut off his hand.'

'Don't be jealous. It's only a dance.' The quadrille was a square formation that involved switching partners, and it brought the three of them into close proximity.

Stephen sent Freddie a dark warning, but the poor man could not escape. When they switched partners, Emily sent Freddie a reassuring look. 'Don't worry about my husband.'

'I r-r-really don't think this was a good idea,' Freddie stammered, touching his palm to Emily's as they paired off in the quadrille.

She struggled to remember the steps of the dance. Now that she had a moment to speak with Freddie, she wondered why his name was mentioned in Stephen's accounts. 'I've been meaning to ask, did you ever invest in a shipment with my brother?'

Freddie's face grew shamefaced. 'To my regret. Please know that I hold the highest esteem for your late brother, but—'

Stephen cut him off, switching partners and taking Emily's hand. He dropped his voice into an angry whisper. 'Have you lost your wits? Reynolds was involved with the shipment.'

'I know,' Emily gritted out. 'I've been trying to get answers from him.' She changed palms and turned around. 'Stop behaving as though you are my puppet master.'

She was about to move in the other direction when Stephen caught her wrist. 'You should know that the Viscount Carstairs was murdered tonight.'

Murdered? Why would anyone wish to kill Carstairs? Her throat closed up, and stars blinked in her vision. It suddenly became more difficult to catch her breath.

They switched partners again, and Freddie took her hand. 'Your brother assured me that the investment was a wonderful opportunity,' he continued as he took her hand. 'I am still hoping that the missing funds turn up,' he added. 'But your Uncle Nigel has his doubts.'

At the mention of Nigel's name, Emily faltered. 'Nigel, you said?'

'Of course. It was his suggestion that I invest.'

'But he never—' Her words broke off, and

suddenly Nigel's earlier inquiries about Royce's inheritance made sense. He'd been looking for Daniel's records, to cover up his own involvement in the stolen money. Perhaps Royce's bedroom truly had been searched that night.

Stephen had overheard Freddie's remark and understood the implications immediately. They both continued the dance until the music ended, though Emily could hardly move.

'Nigel,' she breathed. 'I've been so stupid.' She'd been deceived by her uncle's silver tongue, believing what she'd wanted to believe.

'I'm going to find him.' Stephen left her side to search the ballroom.

Emily's head spun with the implications. Had Nigel arranged for Carstairs's murder? Had he tried to kill Stephen?

The evidence in her bodice seared her heart. For in the papers lay the truth. The man who had taken her father's place was the very man she never should have trusted. The floor seemed to sink beneath her feet as she slowly began to comprehend a fact far worse.

The children were at his house, even now.

Chapter Twenty-Two

Metals may corrode if tins are not properly cared for. A strong poison may be the result.
—Emily Barrow's Cook Book

'Lady Whitmore,' a steely voice interrupted. It was the Marquess. Merciful heaven, but she had no desire to cross swords with him now.

The Marquess stepped in front of her, a general poised for battle. Emily glanced around, hoping for a glimpse of Stephen, but he was nowhere to be seen. 'What is it you want?'

'You know what I want. And yet you keep insinuating yourself into places you don't belong.'

Years of denigration and unworthiness solidified into a wave of anger. Emily snapped her fan open, trying to cool her temper before she did something rash. *Calm down. He is nothing but an old curmudgeon.*

'Lord Rothburne, I have no wish to be your enemy. I married your son, and I've every right to be here.'

'You bring shame upon him.'

'No,' she said softly, no longer caring about those around her. 'You bring shame upon yourself. Perhaps it is you who should leave.'

The dance had ended, and her words echoed above the noise of the crowd. Lady Thistlewaite fainted across the lap of another matron, who desperately tried to revive her with smelling salts.

'You mean nothing to him,' the Marquess said, 'and you are a fool if you believe otherwise.'

'My wife is not a fool,' her husband responded. She saw Stephen coming towards her, and at the sight of him, she took comfort in his presence.

'Since you plan to make a spectacle of yourself, Father, let me make one thing quite clear. Anyone who humiliates my wife in public must answer to me.' Stephen took her hand in his and the magnitude of what he'd done struck her. He'd abandoned pride and duty, forcing the Marquess to accept her. She blinked back the tears, grateful for his interference.

'Now, if you will excuse me, I am escorting Lady Whitmore home.' He led her towards the door, lowering his voice. 'Nigel has already left. We must go now.'

She did not look back at the ballroom, but joined

Stephen as they hurried toward the carriage. Within minutes, they were inside.

Seated across from one another, she watched him, wondering what to say. At last she said, 'Thank you for defending me.'

He gave a nod, his attention focused outside. 'I don't know where Nigel has gone, but—'

She leaned forward and kissed him. She took him by surprise, and he did not react at first. Then he took her face in his hands, his thumb grazing her temple. 'That was far too short to be a kiss.'

Emily's pulse quickened as he drew closer. She could feel the hidden strength in his arms. Leaning in, he took her lips. Gently, he caressed her shoulders as his mouth captured hers. The carriage rumbled through the streets, and the rhythmic motion made it difficult to catch her breath. When at last he released her, her hands poised on his forearms.

'I'll find him, Emily,' he swore.

'The children,' she reminded him. 'We have to protect them.'

As the carriage moved closer to Nigel's town house, Stephen's apprehension heightened. If Nigel had somehow been involved in the deaths of Carstairs and Hollingford, he did not doubt the man would use the children as leverage.

'I meant to show you these earlier,' Emily said,

reaching inside her bodice. He raised an eyebrow as she handed him several torn pages. As soon as he saw them, he knew what they were: the missing list of investors.

'Where did you get these?'

'Daniel hid them inside Royce's fairy tale book,' she said. 'In the story of "The Steadfast Tin Soldier". I didn't see them until I picked it up.'

Though it was difficult to see in the moonlight, the columns of numbers triggered a flood of memories. Visions unfolded, strange illuminations that made little sense. He recalled removing the pages with a blade, giving them to Hollingford for safekeeping.

'What is it?'

'I made this list. Months ago.' He'd recorded every ship that had not earned a profit in the past four years, along with the names of their investors. 'They're the missing pages from the ledger we found at your brother's estate.'

Like a door opening, the memories returned. 'I noticed that several shipments appeared to have less cargo than they should. And when *The Lady Valiant*'s cargo was sold, all of the funds disappeared. I thought your brother was responsible, at first.'

Stephen folded up the paper. 'He swore he had nothing to do with the loss. Then he confided in me what had happened to him in India, when he was branded with the tattoo. He suspected the real thief was trying to frighten him. Or set him up to take the blame.' Stephen reached out and took her hands. 'He was more afraid for you and the children than he was for himself. He begged me to go after you, to ensure your safety. I promised him I would, and that's when I gave him the records for safekeeping.'

He kissed her fingers. 'I didn't intend to marry you, at first. And perhaps it was wrong of me to lead you on. But I wanted to rescue you, as well as escape my parents' scheming.'

Emily gripped his hand, sadness creasing her face. 'Do you remember what happened to my brother on the night he died? Why did you leave him behind?'

'I tried to save him, but I arrived too late. And there were more of them that night. If I had stayed, they would have killed me, too.'

'Did Nigel kill Daniel?'

Stephen relived the events, but did not recall Nigel among the attackers. Most of the men had worn hoods to obscure their faces and were not Nigel's size. 'No. These were hired men, but Anant was with them. He's the one who gave me this scar.' He touched the healed wound upon his rib. 'I have no doubt the stolen money went into Nigel's pockets.'

He placed the folded papers inside his coat. Piece by piece, the memories returned.

'Who took care of you while you were on board the ship?' Emily asked. 'You said your…mistress tended your wounds.'

Stephen didn't miss the pointed tone. 'She did. Rather than lead the men back to my family's house, Patricia put me aboard one of my ships. The crew tended me after that, I suppose.' He thought back, and remembered the ship bound for India. He'd endured weeks of endless rocking with the waves and the taint of a sickly sweet aroma. Opium, he now realised.

'When we arrived in India, the Chinese officials were waiting. They recognised the ship and confiscated it. They tattooed me, sending me back to England on another vessel that docked at Portsmouth. I was beaten upon arrival, as further punishment. Afterwards, I managed to drag myself to a hired coach. Falkirk was the closest estate.'

She looked stricken. 'I'm so sorry about the way I treated you. I was angry about Daniel and your mistress.' She stared outside at the night sky. 'And you didn't remember me.'

He could say nothing to take away her pain and fear. But he would atone for them, somehow. 'I remember now.'

* * *

When they arrived at Nigel's town house, Stephen lifted her down. Emily did not look at him, but kept her gaze focused on the residence.

She opened the door softly, but no footmen came to greet her. Inside, a strange silence seemed to hover. The servants were in their quarters with only the distant sounds of scullery maids cleaning the kitchen.

Emily rushed up the stairs, two at a time, while Stephen followed. The door to Anna's room was closed, but in his gut, he predicted what Emily would find in the children's bedchambers. As he'd feared, Victoria's crib was empty, along with Royce's bed.

Emily picked up Victoria's blanket, and the devastation upon her face struck him like a physical blow. 'He took them.' Her eyes shimmered with tears, her fingers clutching the soft wool.

Stephen knew there were no words to comfort her, but he said them just the same. 'I'll get them back.'

'What does he want?'

'I don't know.' Stephen studied the room and spied a folded paper with his name upon it. As he read the contents, he relayed the information to Emily. 'The children were taken to Nigel's country estate. I am to come alone, with all records of the shipment, if we want them back alive.'

Stephen handed her the note to read, but her face

clouded with doubt. 'If you go alone, he'll kill you,' she whispered.

'Nigel can't have gone far, Emily. I'll get to him before anything happens.'

She shook her head. 'Nigel didn't take them. Look.'

At the bottom of the page, a small marking of ink had escaped his notice, the initials A. P.

'Anant.' Emily emitted the name like a curse. 'He was with our family for so many years. I thought he was loyal to us.'

Stephen wanted to reassure her that everything would be all right, but the truth was, he didn't know. 'Stay here until my return.'

He cupped her chin, but she turned her face aside so his kiss brushed her cheek. 'You are not leaving me behind. The children are my responsibility.'

'They are *our* responsibility,' he corrected. 'And I am going to finish this.'

'And what of me? You expect me to wait at home while you go off again? The last time it happened, Daniel died, and you were injured, too.'

His own anger rose up, that she refused to trust him. He distanced himself from the emotions coiling inside of him. He would do what was necessary to protect his family. 'I won't return until I've brought them back to you.'

He did not try to kiss her again, knowing she

would refuse him. As he left her in the shadow of her uncle's house, he pushed all thoughts away until only the icy mindset of retribution remained.

Nigel Barrow had killed his last man. And Stephen would not stop until he had redeemed himself in the eyes of his wife.

Chapter Twenty-Three

Even the strongest cast-iron pots will crack if they are subjected to cold water when hot. The same may be said for a man's temper, which may be softened with calm words.
—Emily Barrow's *Cook Book*

'My lady, the Marquess is abed,' Phillips argued. 'He is not receiving calls at this hour of the morning.'

'I must see him. This is a matter of utmost importance.'

'As you already know, Lord Rothburne has forbidden you to enter his house.'

It was clear to Emily how a person could be moved to murder someone. At the moment, she had the urge to hang the footman by his starched cravat.

'This is not a social call,' she said firmly, trying to push her way past. 'This is about his son. Lord

Whitmore will die if you don't let me see the Marquess.'

Phillips shook his head. 'If you do not remove yourself from this house, I shall summon the constable.'

Before he could slam the door, the Marquess appeared behind him. 'Come to wreak more destruction upon the household, have you?'

Emily ignored his dry question. 'Stephen is in danger. He's gone after my niece and nephew.' Quickly, she explained the situation and waited for Lord Rothburne to respond.

'You spin a fine tale. But then, women such as yourself are good liars, so I hear.'

Emily closed her eyes. 'You and I will never be allies, I know. But that is of little consequence. He's gone alone, and I am not about to let him die.' She levelled a hard stare at him. 'If you do not wish to lose another son, then I'd suggest you help me.'

The Marquess said nothing, but turned his back on her. Phillips closed the front door, and Emily sagged against the frame, exhaustion aching from every pore. She had hoped that somehow the Marquess would believe her, that he would help his son.

How had she thought she could mend the breach between them? Such a foolish notion. Lord Rothburne cared about nothing, save duty.

The door opened slowly and she looked into the face of Stephen's younger brother Quentin. 'I'll go,' he offered. With a rueful grin he added, 'Eavesdropping. Sorry, I couldn't resist.'

In Quentin's face she saw an earnest desire to help. And yet, she grew wary. 'You invested money in *The Lady Valiant*, too,' she said, remembering the column of figures Stephen had deciphered.

A sheepish grin crossed Quentin's face. 'Unfortunately, I did. Lost every penny.'

'And did you know my uncle was an investor?'

He shook his head. 'I'm afraid not.'

'Uncle Nigel stole the cargo profits from *The Lady Valiant*. I'm sure of it. Now he's gone, and he kidnapped my niece and nephew.'

'I am sorry to hear it. But I would be glad to help.'

Though she didn't want to coerce Quentin into the danger, she desperately needed his assistance. 'Stephen went after them to Nigel's country estate…' Her voice faltered, but she hid her fear. 'I know Nigel won't release the children. He won't rest until Stephen is dead.' *And me*, she almost added. 'There is too much evidence against him.'

'How long ago was it?'

'His servant Anant kidnapped them hours ago. We'll never catch up.'

Quentin's gaze shifted as though he were turning

over an idea in his mind. 'There might be a way.' Before he could elaborate, the door opened again.

'Wait.' Lord Rothburne emerged. He wore a black cape, his silvery hair glinting against the darkness. In his hands, he held a set of pistols. 'We'll need these.'

Emily did not know what had changed his mind, but for the first time she saw a crack in his unyielding demeanour. It offered a small measure of hope. 'Thank you.'

A grim frown settled across his countenance. 'I will go on one condition,' he said to her.

'Name it.'

'After Quentin and I bring him back, you will retire to the countryside. Do not show your face in London again.'

Emily raised her chin to meet his arrogant gaze. 'No.'

When his expression turned baffled, she added, 'I am married to your son, and I will not leave him just to satisfy your overblown beliefs of what a lady should be.' She cleared her throat and folded her arms across her chest. 'I am also coming with you.'

The Marquess looked as though he were about to explode. 'You cannot think to possibly—'

Quentin put his hands up. 'Now, now. Do not be foolish, Lady Whitmore. You will stay here and wait for us to return.'

She shook her head. 'You are the foolish ones. You forget that I lived with Uncle Nigel for several weeks. I know his house better than you, and I can get inside without anyone knowing.'

'Stephen would have my head roasted on a platter if I allowed you to come,' Quentin argued.

'But he won't know, will he?' To cap it off, Emily continued, 'And if you leave me behind, I shall simply follow you. It is quite dangerous for a woman of my station to travel alone, even with a suitable companion.'

The Marquess's face transformed from crimson into purple. Emily moved forward and slipped her arm in his. With a firm pat upon his shoulder, she said, 'Shall we?'

Quentin offered her his other arm, coughing hastily to hide what might have been a laugh.

It took over two days to reach Nigel's estate. Stephen stopped only when nightfall made it impossible to go farther. As soon as enough light permeated the horizon, he continued on his journey. He'd switched horses twice, his mind focused on the task at hand. He wore a revolver at his side, a knife hidden inside his coat. Landscapes shifted into rolling meadows, sunsets merging until one day met the next.

Why had he not foreseen the danger? He blamed

himself for what had happened. Emily's devastation haunted him, her fingers curled around Victoria's blanket.

He remembered, too, the laughing smile of the baby who had drooled all over his waistcoat. Even when Victoria had sobbed herself to sleep in his arms, he couldn't forget what it had felt like to be a father.

And then there was Royce. The boy reminded him so much of himself—eager to please and yet shielding himself from hurt. It struck him that he must succeed in bringing them home. Emily was relying on him.

The thought encouraged him to increase the horse's gait. He envisaged Emily with her hands buried in bread dough, a smile meant for him. He wanted to make love to her until she cried out, arching her back and drawing him close. He wanted to wake up beside her.

He loved her. The knowledge filled him with an iron-clad resolution not to let her or their family down.

He drew his horse to a stop, the animal's sides heaving. In the distance he saw Nigel's country estate. Night descended over the landscape as he drew nearer, darkening the shadows until the glow of gaslights was all that illuminated the manor.

He could not go in alone; Nigel would kill him. He needed stealth, and at the moment, time was on his side. Nigel would not expect him for many days yet. No one else knew of his arrival.

If he moved too swiftly, he risked their lives. Stephen watched the house, turning over possible strategies in his mind. Without leverage against Nigel, the only means of rescuing the children was to overpower him.

He needed a diversion so he could move in for his own attack. It was critical to destroy Nigel's command of the situation.

He knew just what to do.

Why was it that men always insisted on leaving a woman behind? After surviving a horrid journey by train, riddled with soot and travelling at speeds no human should have to endure, the Marquess had ordered Emily to remain in the village.

Her patience had lasted little more than an hour. She needed to be there, to know what was happening. Already she had thought of a plan. She could stay hidden from the others and yet be inside the manor house.

After enquiring in the village over the course of the afternoon, she purchased clothing that would help her look like a servant. It hadn't been difficult to disguise her appearance, for she looked positively dreadful since Lady Thistlewaite's ball, days ago. Emily covered her hair in a mob cap, drawing it down low over her eyes. In her grey gown, no one would ever mistake her for a lady.

It took her most of the afternoon to walk to Nigel's estate. As she'd expected, men guarded the entrance.

One blocked her path, a stout man armed with a pair of pistols. 'And just where do you think you're going?'

She kept her face down. 'Beggin' pardon, sir. Mrs Graham asked me to come. I'm to be the new scullery maid.'

The men exchanged glances. The other guard shrugged and stepped forward. 'I'll take her and see if she's telling the truth.'

Emily bobbed a curtsy, 'Thank you, sir.' Her heart pounded with each step they took towards the house. Would the cook help her? She sent up a thousand pleas to heaven that Mrs Graham would not betray her.

The man led her to the servants' entrance in the back. Inside the kitchen, maids scurried about, peeling potatoes and stirring dishes. Mrs Graham directed the bustle of activity with the grace of a conductor.

'You, there, slice the bread. And, Mary, be sure to inspect the strawberries. There mustn't be a speck of white.'

The guard cleared his throat. 'This chit claims you've hired her as the new scullery maid.'

Emily straightened and stared hard at Mrs Graham. The other servants froze, eyeing one another. Emily gave a faint nod of encouragement, willing the cook to follow her lead.

Mrs Graham's eyes widened, but she did not argue. 'Why, yes. It's about time you arrived. You were supposed to be here this morning, girl.'

'Beg pardon, mum,' Emily murmured, bobbing another curtsy.

Mrs Graham took her by the shoulders and nodded to the guard. 'Thank you for bringing her. There's a meat pie on the table there, if you're hungry.' The guard's face relaxed, and he accepted the bribe before leaving.

Afterwards, Mrs Graham handed her a clean apron. Silence filled the kitchen as everyone stared. Emily donned the apron, tying it slowly. 'Please do not tell my uncle I am here.'

At their curious looks, she added, 'I cannot tell you everything now, but I give you my promise that you will be rewarded for your help.'

Emily cleared her throat. 'My nephew and niece— Royce and Victoria—are they upstairs with Anna?'

'They are here, my lady,' Mrs Graham answered, 'but the wet nurse is not. Mr Barrow hired another woman in the village to care for Victoria.'

'And my husband?'

Mrs Graham shook her head. 'I have not seen Lord Whitmore.'

The words dropped like a blade, slicing through her. Emily gripped the folds of her apron, masking her emotions. 'I am sure he will be along shortly,' she managed. 'In the meantime, I should like to remain among you. I—I can cook or clean or whatever you require of me.'

Mrs Graham must have sensed her agitation, for she took Emily's hand. 'I'll not say a word to the master, if that's what you want,' she offered. 'And neither will anyone else.' She sent a firm glare to the other servants. 'No one knows of your presence, save us.'

'Thank you.' Emily picked up a knife and a carrot. Her fingers shook as she struggled to peel it.

Stephen had sworn he would come for the children. He'd given his promise to save them. That night Emily had believed he would walk through the fires of hell. He cared for the children, perhaps loved them as she did.

But he wasn't here.

A numbing haze strangled her heart, until she had to set the knife down. Was Stephen already dead? The thought transfixed her imagination with horror. The vast feeling of emptiness consumed her, swallowing her up. To never see his face again or hear him tease her… It made her want to weep useless tears. She loved him, and the stupid man was not supposed to die.

Angrily, she pushed the tears aside, taking vengeance upon the helpless carrot with the knife. Weeping would not bring him back, nor would it help the children. At any moment, the Marquess and Quentin were planning an attack. She needed to be ready, should they require her assistance. Nigel would not get away with this.

She butchered another carrot, turning her attention to the stew next. A pity she had no arsenic, for at the moment, poisoning her uncle seemed like a fine solution.

Two days later, Stephen approached the manor, at last confident in his plans. It had taken more time than he'd intended to recruit the assistance he needed. His men stood ready, armed and hidden from view. Now nothing would stop him from seizing victory.

He walked towards the house, his hands raised in feigned surrender. Inside his coat he'd hidden a pepperbox pistol, fully loaded with six bullets. Two of Nigel's men guarded the gates.

'I have business with Nigel Barrow,' Stephen said. 'Tell him Lord Whitmore has arrived.'

Though he expected the men to draw their weapons, to his surprise, they lowered them. 'He is waiting for you,' one said. 'I'll escort you there.'

Stephen followed the man, not letting his gaze betray the presence of his companions. They knew to shadow him and would be ready at his signal.

A slight motion caught his attention. Stephen saw the glint of the other guard's revolver, and he spun, firing his weapon. The guard dropped forward and a second shot rang out from beside Stephen. A scarlet stain spread across the guard's heart, his eyes wide with surprise.

'They planned to murder you before you reached the house,' his friend Michael Thorpe remarked, emerging from the trees. 'Do you want us to accompany you?'

As a former schoolmate, Stephen trusted Michael to guard his back. Years of military service made it an easy matter for his friend to disappear from view.

Stephen nodded. 'Stay out of sight. Likely they heard the shots, and with any luck, they may believe I am dead.'

He moved towards the tall boxwood hedge surrounding the outer garden, working his way closer to the servants' entrance. The heavy scent of roses intensified as he reached the house gardens. Thankfully the hedges provided numerous hiding places.

He counted silently to thirty, waiting for the others to take their places. Outside, he saw a maid beating a large carpet, the dust billowing in the breeze. She stood between him and the entrance. He held his position, waiting patiently for her to return to the house.

She raised the paddle and gave a sound blow to the carpet, attacking it as though it were an enemy. After nearly five minutes of pounding the dust, she set her paddle down and glanced toward Stephen's hiding place.

Dear God in heaven. It was Emily, disguised as a maid.

Heedless of who might be watching, Stephen crept up behind her. Dragging her behind the hedge, he muffled her terrified shriek. 'What the hell do you think you are doing?'

Emily's face whitened, but she made no sound even when he released his palm from her mouth.

'I told you to stay in London where you'd be safe.' His grip upon her was so fierce, he wanted to throttle her. The very thought of her putting herself in danger was unacceptable. Did she think no one would recognise her?

'You're not dead,' she whispered, her hand moving to his face. 'I thought—'

'You thought I would try to rescue them alone?' He sighed in disgust. 'I am not an utter fool.'

He relaxed his grip upon her, suddenly aware that anyone could see them. 'Listen carefully. My men are going to surround the house and enter at my signal. You need to leave now and return to the village.'

She was shaking her head. 'Not yet. I—'

'He wants us dead, Emily. Both of us. We know too much about his business dealings for him to let us live.' He had to make her understand that Nigel was not a man to be reasoned with.

'Yes, I know that, but—'

'Then you should understand the necessity of staying out of harm's way. Why on God's earth you thought to come alone is the most idiotic—'

Emily's hand covered his mouth. 'If you will stop interrupting me, I have something important to tell you. Quentin and your father are here.'

If it were possible for his anger to get any worse, it did. 'You brought them into this?'

She stared at the grass as though it were the most fascinating vegetation alive. 'I wanted to help you. They accompanied me here and arrived a few moments ago. They are in the drawing room with Nigel, I believe.'

He closed his eyes, trying to calm the wrath inside him. 'They might die now, because of what you've done.'

He moved back into the shadow of the hedge. He

had already lost one brother; he didn't plan to lose Quentin, too. And though he and his father had their differences, it seemed he had little choice but to surrender to Nigel.

Emily's eyes glinted with unshed tears, and her mouth tightened. 'I asked them to come because I loved you. I didn't want you to die. I suppose I was an idiot to want to help you.' With that, she picked up her paddle and marched toward the house. As she passed the carpet, she gave a ferocious swing, sending another puff of dust into the air. Stephen watched her go, head held high.

Time stretched on, infinite moments passing while he deliberated what to do next. Though he wanted to blame Emily, he couldn't quite get his mind around what she had said earlier. She loved him? Had she really come this distance in an effort to save him?

He moved back away from the gardens, signalling to Michael. 'I am going after them.'

'I don't like the risk,' Michael responded. 'Nigel could kill you first.'

'If I don't return within the hour, move your men into place.'

Control settled over him once more. The task before him threatened the lives of everyone close to him. He had not been able to save Emily's brother before. Now he would save his family or die trying.

Chapter Twenty-Four

Recipe for smelling salts: sub-carbonate of ammonia, eight parts. Mix it with coarse powder into a bottle and add one part oil of lavender.
— Emily Barrow's *Cook Book*

'We've unexpected guests,' Mrs Graham informed the staff. 'His lordship, the Marquess of Rothburne, has come to call.' Her sharp eyes regarded Emily, but she did not ask why.

'We should prepare refreshments,' Emily murmured.

'See if we've any more strawberries,' Mrs Graham directed, 'and I shall make up a tray of biscuits.' To Emily she suggested, 'If you wish, why don't you prepare one of your tea cakes?'

While the girls hastened to prepare the food, Emily moved slowly. Her last conversation with Stephen made it difficult to concentrate. She began mixing the ingredients, but she kept hearing his angry words in her mind. He hadn't wanted or needed her help.

She cracked an egg into the bowl, wondering if she had made a mistake in coming here. Stephen was right. She should have remained in London.

Inside, she ached with fear for all of them. If anyone came to harm because of her, she could not bear it.

A flicker of an idea suddenly grew within her mind. There was a way she could help the situation. She stirred the cake batter rapidly, forming the details. Yes, it would work. It had to.

When she saw Mrs Graham setting up the tea tray, Emily stopped her. 'I will serve,' she offered.

'No.' Mrs Graham held up a hand. 'He would recognise you. You cannot go.' To another girl, she said, 'Claire, take the tray to our guests. Be sure you don't spill anything.'

'Not yet.' Emily stared hard into Mrs Graham's lined face. 'There is something I must do first.'

Stephen never made it to the entrance of the house. Strong arms took hold of him from behind. A black hood blinded him, and he fought against his attacker, cursing.

He jerked his head backward, smashing it against the assailant's face. A white-hot pain sliced his arm and he felt the warm wetness of his own blood. He'd given Michael strict orders not to interfere, not unless it meant his death.

The shock of the pain sent the rest of the memories flashing through him. Hollingford's body had lay bleeding in the streets, after they'd murdered him. Anant had attacked him, slicing with the blade.

Somehow, he'd managed to escape, striking back with his fists until he knocked Anant unconscious. He could almost feel the cold slickness of the cobblestones, smell the fetid odour of that night so many months before.

With a violent shove, Stephen ripped away the hood.

And stared into the face of Freddie Reynolds.

A sharp acrid smell brought him back into consciousness. Freddie must have knocked him senseless after he'd removed the hood. His head ached with a vicious throbbing, and Stephen struggled to open his eyes.

'Whitmore.' The jovial voice could only belong to Nigel Barrow. Stephen turned towards the sound and saw the smile of triumph lighting Nigel's face. 'I've been expecting you. Did you bring the records?'

'No. We both know you only used that as an excuse.'

Nigel shook his head. 'A pity, Whitmore. I might have changed my mind about killing you, had you brought them.'

His forearm throbbed with a vicious pain; no one had bandaged the knife wound. The parlour still had a feminine air with its touches of rose and blue. Nigel pointed to a wingback chair. 'Put him there.'

Stephen jerked his gaze and saw Freddie Reynolds standing behind him. Not a trace of remorse lay in the eyes of Emily's former suitor. Stephen fought against the ropes binding him, but Freddie dragged him into the chair.

'Where are my father and Quentin?' Stephen managed.

'Oh, they'll be along shortly,' Nigel said. 'I had Anant take care of them while Freddie brought you here.'

'Was Anant always working for you? Or was he ever loyal to Hollingford?'

Nigel shook his head in regret. 'He came to work for me last year, after I brought his family under my—' he paused to consider the right word '—protection, if you will. Anant saw that it was better to keep his loyalty to me, instead of Hollingford. In addition, I provided him with as much opium as he wished.'

Stephen did not betray a thread of his fear. 'There was no need to take my family captive.'

'Oh, they brought that upon themselves.' Nigel poured himself a cup of tea from the silver pot and added several spoonfuls of sugar. 'But they may be of use to me.'

'Emily believed you were a man of honour.' With a hard look towards Freddie, Stephen added, 'Both of you betrayed her.'

'Freddie has been working for me for several years now,' Nigel admitted. He grimaced at the tea and added more sugar. 'Killing is one of his greatest talents. Along with extortion, of course. He managed to get quite a bit of money out of Carstairs.' He lifted the cup to his lips and drank. 'Few would suspect it of him, which is what makes him quite good.'

Freddie rebuttoned the cuffs of his shirt, a slight smile playing upon his lips.

'You killed Emily's brother,' Stephen guessed. 'And Carstairs.'

'I did,' Freddie admitted. 'Hollingford owed me a great deal of money, and it was good to bestow justice.' The smile deepened, showing Freddie's pleasure in the deed.

Stephen struggled to loosen the ropes without drawing more attention. And yet, with each movement, the knots seemed to grow tighter. His skin had rubbed raw in a few places, but he kept working at his bonds.

The ropes did not budge, but right now he wished he could wrap them around Reynolds's neck. He wanted to suffocate the smile of satisfaction gleaming upon Freddie's face.

'Were you the one who attacked my wife in the garden?' Stephen gritted out.

'It was a hired man,' Nigel responded. 'I sent him to talk to my niece.'

'Threaten her, you mean.'

Nigel shrugged. 'Stronger means were necessary to gain what I needed. Emily knew where her brother kept his ledgers. I was afraid he'd kept records that might lead back to me.'

'You stole the shipping profits.'

'Of course I did. And if you hadn't turned up alive, no one would be the wiser.' He reclined upon the Grecian couch and sipped at the tea. 'Opium is quite a profitable export, really. A shame the Chinese keep interfering.'

'What is it you want, Nigel?'

The older man lifted his cup of tea. 'I should think that's obvious, Whitmore. I want to live my life in luxury. And no one needs to worry about how I got my money. Which is why, I'm afraid, there are several of you who will have to be silenced.'

He spoke as though killing did not bother him in the least. 'Where is my niece, by the by?' His tone held no trace of venom, only mild curiosity.

Stephen kept his expression neutral. 'She is safe in London, far away from you.'

'Oh, no, I rather doubt that. She is quite fond of Royce and Victoria, you know. And my informants tell me she was travelling with Rothburne and your brother.' Nigel sipped his tea. 'I do believe my men will find her soon.'

'Why did you want guardianship of the children?' Stephen asked. 'What use would you possibly have for them?'

'I rather like them, actually. And young Royce has been quite helpful, giving me information about his father. As the children's guardian, I could have full access to their father's records and accounts. Not to mention, Royce is a nice lad. I may let him live if you cooperate.'

'You would harm your own family?'

Nigel clucked his tongue. 'Now, now, Whitmore. We can't have the two of you telling everyone in London about my shipping habits, now can we?'

'You cannot kill everyone. Too many people know your secrets.'

'I suppose you may be right. We'll just have to find out, now, won't we?' Nigel gestured to Reynolds, sinking back against the couch. 'I'm not terribly fond of this house. A good fire would take care of the bodies, and no one would be the wiser.' He stifled a yawn and signalled to Freddie. 'Bring the Marquess and the younger brother to me.'

Stephen lunged towards Reynolds. He managed to knock the man off balance, but Freddie shoved him against the floor. The metallic taste of blood filled his mouth.

'I want to kill him now,' Freddie said, lifting a knife to Stephen's throat. His voice sounded dreamy, almost like a caress. 'And if he's dead, Emily will be mine.'

'For one so devoted to murder, you seem to be rather incompetent at finishing your work,' Stephen remarked.

Glass shattered and gunshots roared from the outside. Though Stephen could not see his companions, he used the distraction to wrench himself free of Freddie's grasp. The knife clattered to the floor, and Stephen threw himself towards it. With his hands bound behind his back, he struggled to grasp the weapon.

More gunshots erupted before an eerie silence fell across the room. Freddie lay in a pool of blood, his eyes open with surprise in the moment of death. Nigel appeared shaken, though he had fired several shots from his own pistol.

Anant emerged at the parlour entrance, holding the Marquess by one arm. 'The intruders are dead, my lord.' He bowed to Nigel, his black eyes vacuous. 'Our guards handled the problem. You may finish your task.'

'And the younger son?'

'Will be dead in moments. He attempted to join Whitmore's men and has a bullet wound.'

James Chesterfield seemed to have aged a full score of years. His face was waxen, his steps faltering as Anant forced him into the room.

'Lord Rothburne.' Nigel smiled and gestured toward a chair. 'So kind of you to join us.'

Stephen hid the knife behind his back, trying not to betray his motions as he eased the blade through the hemp. Nothing mattered unless he could free himself to save them. The ropes slipped, the threads fraying beneath the blade. Closer now…

'I possess a great deal of funds,' James said. 'We could reach an agreement.'

Nigel laughed. 'I have stolen more money from you and others through the years by my own wits. Your paltry funds matter little to me.'

'You cannot possibly believe to escape justice,' the Marquess insisted.

'I have lands in India and Africa,' Nigel said smoothly, mopping his brow with a handkerchief. He yawned again, his voice growing softer. 'And enough money to hide a multitude of sins.'

'No,' a voice said softly. 'Your work here is

finished.' Stephen turned and saw Emily standing. She entered the room, and Nigel aimed his gun at her.

Stephen's world lost its footing when he saw her standing before his enemy. His beautiful, stubborn wife had no business endangering herself.

He ripped through the remaining ropes, clenching the knife in his palm. Before he could reach Nigel, Anant attacked, throwing him to the ground. The weapon slipped out of his grasp, and Stephen cursed, rolling sideways. When he rose up to his feet, Anant now held the knife in his hands. The Indian struck with practised assurance, moving in a deadly circle.

Weaponless, Stephen had no choice but to wait for his enemy to attack. When the blade swung towards his head, he blocked the strike, grasping the man's forearm and wrist. Sweat beaded upon his forehead as he struggled to overpower the Indian.

'Stephen—' The words erupted from Emily's mouth in a terrified whisper.

With a burst of strength, he rotated Anant's arm, driving the blade down. The pair stumbled over Freddie's body and Anant twisted, falling to the ground. Stephen seized control of the weapon and rolled, driving the knife into Anant's chest.

He jerked at the sound of the revolver's hammer drawing back.

'Quite impressive,' Nigel said, waving the gun in a mock salute. 'But rather irrelevant, all things being equal.' He pressed the barrel to Emily's forehead. 'The only dilemma is which of you to kill first?'

'I was never a threat to you, Uncle,' Emily whispered. Her mouth trembled, and Stephen moved towards her.

'Take another step, and I'll pull the trigger, Whitmore.' Nigel's countenance appeared almost grey, his hands shaking. Stephen froze, not wanting the man to inadvertently harm Emily. Terror lanced him at the idea of her dying.

His friend Michael burst through the remains of the shattered window, holding his own gun. He was followed by two of Stephen's men. The three kept their weapons trained upon Nigel.

'Release her, Nigel,' Stephen said.

'I believe I shall kill her first,' Nigel said. 'My apologies, Emily.'

And he pulled the trigger.

Chapter Twenty-Five

Cooking is the knowledge of all herbs and spices, used to make that which is both healing and sweet.
—Emily Barrow's *Cook Book*

Miraculously, his wife remained standing. The empty click of the revolver stunned all of them. No more bullets remained in the chamber.

Nigel's eyes rolled backwards, and he collapsed to the floor. Emily's hands shook, her arms holding her waist as if to keep from screaming.

Stephen pulled her away from Nigel's body, holding her tightly against him. 'Are you all right?'

She nodded, and he pressed a kiss against her temple. Nigel lay upon the floor, unmoving. Yet there was no stain, no mark upon him.

The three men stared down at the fallen body,

unable to understand what had happened. Nigel had ceased to breathe.

'Perhaps his heart stopped beating,' the Marquess offered.

'Or perhaps he drank too much laudanum,' Emily returned.

Stephen eyed the tea cup upon Nigel's desk. 'You didn't—'

Her mouth creased in an awkward expression. 'I suppose I shouldn't have. I didn't know how much to add. I was hoping to drug him.'

'How much did you put in?' the Marquess asked.

'Two bottles. With a great deal of sugar to mask the flavour. He always did take too much sugar with his tea.'

His father coughed, but Stephen noted the look of admiration. The gruff demeanour appeared to have softened somewhat. 'Not a bad idea, I must say.' From James Chesterfield, the words were no less than a high compliment.

'Where is Quentin?' Stephen asked.

'He stayed to protect the children,' Michael interjected.

'How badly was he hurt?'

'One of our other men was shot, not Quentin,' his friend corrected. 'And he'll live, I should think.'

Stephen's hand caressed Emily's nape. In her ear, he whispered, 'I should have you horsewhipped for interfering. You could have been killed.'

'I'm not very good at obeying orders.' But even with the words, she buried her face in his chest.

He tasted the salt of her tears when he kissed her. Nothing felt better than to hold her in his arms again.

'I love you,' he whispered. 'And I'm going to make you a solemn promise.'

'You'll never leave me?'

Stephen shook his head. 'I swear I shall never drink a cup of tea prepared by your hand, unless you have drunk from it first.'

A startled laugh escaped her, but she nodded. Stephen turned to the Marquess. 'There is another matter. You have not treated my wife with the respect she is due.'

The Marquess looked pained at the observation.

'You will treat her as you would my sister Hannah, and Mother is to give Emily her full support. Is that clear?'

With great reluctance, Lord Rothburne acceded. 'I suppose she *is* a Baron's daughter and could be a suitable wife.'

A wailing noise cut through their conversation, followed by the sound of a boy running down the stairs. Stephen ordered Michael and the other men to conceal the bodies. He saw no need to frighten the children. After ripping down the heavy curtains, Nigel's body was hidden.

Quentin cleared his throat. 'Am I to be rescued now as well?' In his arms, he held Victoria.

'Da-da-da!' she sobbed, reaching for Stephen. He took the child into his arms, relieved to have her safe. Royce clung to Emily, who was smoothing his hair while he chattered nonsense about a horse.

They exchanged looks, and he saw the worry lines ease from her face at the sight of the children.

'Did you kill Great-Uncle Nigel?' Royce asked Stephen, tugging upon his waistcoat.

'No,' he answered in all honesty. 'But he was not a good man. He brought about his own demise, and he won't trouble you again.'

Stephen knelt down before the boy, and Royce gripped his neck tightly. 'I want to go home, Uncle Stephen.'

'We will, my boy.' With a quick rumple of Royce's hair, Stephen stood.

Emily took Royce by the hand and led him toward the Marquess. 'This is Lord Rothburne.'

Royce stared at the gruff Marquess, his mouth pursing into a frown. 'He hasn't got much hair, has he?'

'Royce!'

Stephen stifled a laugh at his wife's mortification. Pulling her into his arms, he rested his chin atop her head. 'I think it's time to go home.'

That night, when they were alone at the inn, Emily stood before her husband in her chemise. His eyes grew hungry, and she warmed beneath his admiration.

The darkness of the room cast an intimate spell. She came closer, touching the healed scar on his chest. Stephen bent down and kissed her, a melting kiss that pulled the pieces of her heart back together.

'I love you,' she whispered.

Shivers of desire and need overcame her, as he lowered his mouth to the soft part of her nape. 'I love you, too.'

'And you're very lucky, you know.'

'How am I lucky?' he asked as she lifted her chemise away. Skin to skin, she revelled in the hardened male body pressing against her softness.

She pulled him toward the bed, bringing him down on top of her. 'Let me show you.'

As Stephen pulled his wife into his arms, he thought that no man in the world could ever be as lucky as this.

Epilogue

The scent of burning cake filled the house. Emily sniffed the air. Was the house on fire? She raced down to the kitchen where she found Royce and Stephen, both staring at the stove.

Royce wore an apron tied around his waist while smoke wafted from the oven. He wrinkled his nose. 'I think it's done, Uncle Stephen.'

'Is it?'

Oh, dear Lord. Had Mrs Deepford lost her wits, allowing these two into the kitchen? Emily pushed past them and grabbed a towel. After removing the charred cake, she set her hands on her hips.

'It's very done.' She eyed her husband, who offered a sheepish grin. 'Burned around the edges, in fact. What were you trying to do?'

'Surprise you?' Stephen took Royce by the hand. 'We thought we'd bake you a birthday cake.'

Her birthday? She'd forgotten completely. With

another glance toward the guilty pair, her heart softened. 'Mrs Deepford could have baked one.'

She examined the cake. Though it was black around the edges, likely it was raw in the middle. They had stoked the fire too hot. 'You didn't have to go to all of this trouble.'

'It was baked with love.' Stephen came up behind her and wrapped his arms around her waist. He nipped at her ear, sending shivers through her.

'A great deal of love,' she managed, fighting a laugh. But when his mouth met hers in a soft kiss, she lost sight of everything else. When Stephen broke away, she realised Royce had gone.

'Smart lad,' Stephen commented. 'I'll have to reward him later.'

'He didn't have to leave.' Emily started to go after him when Stephen stopped her.

'He was obeying orders.' He reached into a small earthenware bowl and drew out a finger dripping with chocolate icing. 'Taste this and see if you like it.'

She licked the icing from his finger, letting her tongue slide over his skin. The look in his eyes turned dark and hungry.

'Did you make this?' she asked.

He stole a kiss, melting the sweetness against her mouth. 'Mrs Deepford did.'

The sweet chocolate tempted her, and she reached

into the bowl again. Stephen took her finger into his mouth, gently sucking the icing away. With a seductive glint in his eye, he spread more icing upon her lips and proceeded to kiss it off.

'We've been invited to Lady Thistlewaite's dinner party tonight,' Emily reminded him as he nuzzled her neck. The matron had grudgingly begun to include her on the invitation list, at Lady Rothburne's bequest.

'I curse the day my mother took you under her wing,' he murmured. 'I'd be overjoyed if I never had to attend another society event.'

Sometimes she felt the same way, but for now, she was enjoying herself. She had spent a fortune on new gowns that Stephen's mother insisted she should have.

'Let's stay home tonight.' He drew her against his body, fitting her against him.

Emily held him close, strongly contemplating it. 'Your family is expecting us. And I would like to attend.'

'You're trying to avoid our cake.' He cast a chagrined look toward the disastrous pastry.

'That, too.'

He caressed her hair and released a sigh. 'As it is your birthday, I will bow to your wishes. But you'll have to wait on your presents.'

His disappointment was so obvious, Emily

leaned up to kiss him. 'Not all of them.' She slid her hands beneath his coat, fumbling with his waistcoat and shirt, until her palms touched the bare skin of his back. 'Perhaps I'll unwrap one now.'

'Will you?' His voice deepened, even as he removed his coat.

Emily captured his cravat and wound her hand around it, using it to pull him forward. 'Unless you have an objection?'

Her husband remained decidedly silent.

* * * * *

HISTORICAL

Large Print

THE ROGUE'S DISGRACED LADY
Carole Mortimer

Lady Juliet Boyd has kept out of the public eye since the
suspicious death of her husband, until she meets the
scandalous Sebastian St Claire, who makes her feel things,
need things she's never experienced before. Juliet finds his
lovemaking irresistible. But does he really want her –
or just the truth behind her disgrace?

A MARRIAGEABLE MISS
Dorothy Elbury

When Miss Helena Wheatley's father falls ill, she is forced to
turn to one of her suitors to avoid an unwelcome marriage!
The Earl of Markfield honourably agrees to squire her
around Town until her father recovers. Then they are
caught alone together, and their temporary agreement
suddenly looks set to become a lot more permanent…

WICKED RAKE,
DEFIANT MISTRESS
Ann Lethbridge

When a mysterious woman holds him at gunpoint, Garrick
Le Clere, Marquess of Beauworth, knows he's finally met his
match! Alone, Lady Eleanor Hadley is without hope, until
the notorious rake offers a way out of her predicament…
Now Garrick has a new mistress, and she's not only a
virgin, but a Lady – with a dangerous secret!

 MILLS & BOON

HISTORICAL

Large Print

ONE UNASHAMED NIGHT
Sophia James

Lord Taris Wellingham lives alone, concealing his fading eyesight from Society. Plain Beatrice-Maude does not expect to attract any man, especially one as good-looking as her travelling companion. Forced by a snowstorm to spend the night together, these two lonely people unleash a passion that surprises them. How will their lives change with the coming of the new day?

THE CAPTAIN'S MYSTERIOUS LADY
Mary Nichols

Captain James Drymore has one purpose in life: revenge. But when he rescues a beautiful young lady, James allows himself to become distracted for the first time… As he slowly puts together the complex pieces of his mysterious lady's past, James realises he needs to let go of his own. Can he and Amy build a new future – together?

THE MAJOR AND THE PICKPOCKET
Lucy Ashford

Tassie bit her lip. Why hadn't he turned her over to the constables? She certainly wasn't going to try to run past him. She was tall, but this man towered over her – six foot of hardened muscle, strong booted legs set firmly apart. Major Marcus Forrester. All ready for action. And Tassie couldn't help but remember his kiss …

 MILLS & BOON

HISTORICAL

Large Print

THE RAKE AND THE HEIRESS
Marguerite Kaye

Any virtuous society lady knows to run from Mr Nicholas Lytton. But he's the one person who can unlock the mystery surrounding Lady Serena Stamppe's inheritance. Accepting Nicholas's offer of assistance, Serena soon discovers the forbidden thrills of liaising with a libertine – excitement, scandal…and a most pleasurable seduction!

WICKED CAPTAIN, WAYWARD WIFE
Sarah Mallory

When young widow Evelina Wylder comes face to face with her dashing captain husband – *very* much alive – she's shocked, overjoyed…and so furious she's keeping Nick firmly out of their marriage bed! Now the daring war hero faces his biggest challenge – proving to Eve that his first duty is to love and cherish her, forever!

THE PIRATE'S WILLING CAPTIVE
Anne Herries

Instinct told her that Captain Justin Sylvester was a man she could trust. Captive on the high seas, with nowhere to run, curiously Maribel Sanchez had never felt more free. Now she had to choose: return to rigid society and become an old man's unwilling wife or stay as Justin's more than *willing* mistress…

MILLS & BOON